The Cow Promise of Forever in Kansas

STAND-ALONE NOVEL

A Western Historical Romance Book

by

Sally M. Ross

Disclaimer & Copyright

Table of Contents

Letter from Sally M. Ross

"There are two kinds of people in the world those with guns and those that dig."

This iconic sentence from the *"Good the Bad and the Ugly"* was meant to change my life once and for all. I chose to be the one to hold the gun and, in my case…the pen!

I started writing as soon as I learned the alphabet. At first, it was some little fairytales, but I knew that this undimmed passion was my life's purpose.

I share the same love with my husband for the classic western movies, and we moved together to Texas to leave the dream on our little farm with Daisy, our lovely lab.

I'm a literary junkie reading everything that comes into my hands, with a bit of weakness on heartwarming romances and poetry.

If you choose to follow me on this journey, I can guarantee you characters that you would love to befriend, romances that will make your heart beat faster, and wholesome, genuine stories that will make you dream again!

Until next time,

Sally M. Ross

Prologue

Little Oak, Oklahoma

1879

Clara Eaves sat at the worn oak kitchen table, the glow from the oil lamp casting a warm, yellow light across the room. She looked at her son, Ben, his small face scrunched in concentration as he traced his pencil over the parchment. Ben was only six, his wisps of golden hair matching his father's, his blue eyes a mirror image of him, as well. The homework was taxing, but Clara was determined to see him educated.

Ben held his pencil tightly, carefully copying down the sentence that Clara had written for him to practice his penmanship. His handwriting was messy at best, but Ben was a fast learner. She was sure that he could improve it in no time. He had learned to read simple books when he was four, and he only struggled on bigger words he had never seen before.

Clara watched as he finished the sentence, noticing a mistake right away.

"Remember, darlin', the 'e' goes before 'i'," she instructed, pointing out the mistake in his spelling. Ben nodded, erasing the word 'believe' and rewriting it correctly.

She watched proudly as her son finished the sentence he was writing. When he was finished, Clara pointed to it and smiled.

"Very good, honey," she said. "Now, I want you to read it out loud to me."

Ben nodded, staring intently at the words. It took him a minute, and he sat reading to himself silently, his lips moving as he tried to work out the pronunciations of the words before he read them aloud.

"Tomorrow is the... holiday... festival, I believe," he said. His enunciation was slow and deliberate. But he was learning quickly, and Clara was proud.

"Very good, Ben," she said, ruffling his hair. "Why don't we take a break to have some cookies?"

The six-year-old boy's face lit up, and he nodded.

"You're the best, Ma," he said.

Clara gave him a gentle bop on the nose, gazing lovingly at her son.

"You are, my darlin'," she said.

She left Ben at the table, going over to the oak cabinets and pulling out the tray of sugar cookies she had made that morning. The sun was setting lazily lower in the sky, and she knew she would need to start supper soon. But Ben deserved a treat for doing so well on his schoolwork. She was sure that a couple of cookies wouldn't ruin his appetite.

She took a couple cookies off the plate, returning it to its cabinet. Then, she walked back to the table, handing them to her son with a smile.

"Just don't tell Pa," she said, winking.

Ben shook his head, biting eagerly into one of the cookies. Clara sat back in the chair next to him, flipping through the pages on the table. She decided that the next lesson would be arithmetic.

Her husband, Thomas, was really better with the subject than she was. But she had to admit that she was enjoying practicing with Ben. Besides, Thomas worked hard on their Oklahoma ranch every single day. She could never trouble him about helping their son with his schoolwork, even though she knew he would gladly help. Thomas loved his wife and son with his whole heart. And Clara and Ben loved him just as fiercely in return.

Suddenly, the kitchen door swung open with a loud creak, causing Clara to jump. A ranch hand, young John, was panting heavily, his face as pale as the moonlight streaming in through the window.

"Ma'am... there's been..." Tommy gasped, struggling for breath. "An accident."

Clara's heart stopped. She motioned him forward, patting Ben, who was now watching with wide, curious eyes gently on his arm.

"What do you mean?" she asked, startled by the sudden intrusion and confused about what could be so urgent that the ranch hand rushed to get her. "What accident? What's happened?" Something in her belly was tugging at her. But she couldn't pinpoint why. Her mind wouldn't let her understand right away.

John shifted uncomfortably, averting his gaze.

"It... it was out at the cattle run, ma'am," he said.

Clara glanced at the open door, noting that the young man was alone. She would have expected her husband to come with the young, distraught ranch hand. She bit her lip, looking at the ranch hand nervously. She rose to her feet, her chair screeching against the wooden floor.

"Where's Thomas?" she asked, her voice trembling.

John just shook his head, his eyes filled with fear.

Clara took another step toward the young man, reaching out toward him with a shaking hand.

"Where is Thomas?" she repeated. She already knew the answer. But she hoped against hope that she was wrong, that he was only tending to whomever had been injured in the accident.

Once again, the young man shook his head. When he looked at her again, there were tears in his eyes. He looked over at Ben, who had also left the table and joined his mother, holding on to her hand.

"Still layin' where he fell," John said finally.

Clara's stomach flipped, tying itself into knots. Thomas was the most skilled rancher she knew. Even better than her own father had been. In the seven years they had been married, he had never gotten so much as a splinter. What could have happened to cause an accident involving him, especially at the cattle run?

Without a second thought, Clara rushed out of the house, the cool night air stinging her hot face. She headed straight for the cattle run, her skirts bustling around her legs as she ran. Her vision blurred from the combination of tears and the cold air rushing into her eyes. But she found the cattle run without a problem, even in the weak light of the moon.

It didn't take her long to find her fallen husband. Three more ranch hands surrounded him, all of them shouting instructions to each other. She ran straight to them, nearly tripping as she reached them. The sight that greeted her was one she would never forget. Her husband was lying motionless on the ground, his body clearly broken. His eyes were closed, a bland expression on his face that belied the chaos around him.

Clara dropped to her knees beside him, her hands shaking as she reached out to touch him. "Thomas," she murmured, her voice choked with tears. "What happened?" She put her hands on his face, brushing his sweat-glued hair out of his closed eyes.

The men fell silent and looked at each other. She looked up at them, her eyes pleading with them to answer her. There was a long, painful moment of silence. She didn't realize that Ben, confusion etched on his innocent face, had followed her, until he grabbed her arm.

"Mama?" he asked, his voice sounding small and frightened.

Clara looked at him, trying to find a bravery she didn't at all feel.

"Ben, go back inside," she said with no conviction.

Ben shook his head, clinging more tightly to his mother.

"What's wrong with Pa?" he asked.

Clara was about to repeat her demand for her son. But the young ranch hand, John, stepped forward and took Ben's hand.

"Come on, Benny," he said, trying to keep his voice even. "I need your help feeding the horses."

Ben started to protest. But Clara nodded, nudging the boy toward the ranch hand.

"Go on, now," she said. "Stuff still needs doin'. We'll take care of your pa. You go finish up his chores."

Reluctantly, Ben nodded. He slowly followed John away from the group of men, looking back over his shoulder as he did so.

Once her son was safely out of earshot, Clara looked at the men again.

"What happened?" she asked again, her voice filled with desperation.

The oldest ranch hand, Jerry, rubbed the back of his neck.

"Not exactly sure, Mrs. Eaves," he said. "One minute, the cattle were herdin', pretty as you please. The next, they were stampin' and stompin' like something spooked the daylights outta them. Mr. Eaves went over to see what the matter was. Next thing we knew, there was a stampede, and he was... like this."

Clara looked around wildly, as if finding whatever had spooked the cattle would somehow make her husband all right again. She realized that, in all the time she had had her hands on his face, he hadn't moved. She sobbed, touching his battered neck with a trembling hand. She felt for a pulse, praying that she found one.

"He's still alive," she said, sobbing again with relief when she found a weak but very present pulse.

The men started murmuring to themselves, looking bewildered. But it didn't take Jerry long to start issuing orders.

"Barney," he barked, pointing to a ranch hand that resembled an older John. "Go get the wagon ready. Walter, you help me use those boards we brought to make a stretcher to slide under him."

The men nodded, getting straight to work. Clara had to move to give the men room to work around her husband. Her heart and mind raced as she watched them construct the makeshift stretcher from boards and cattle rope around her husband's broken body. How had this happened? How could things have gotten so out of control that Thomas couldn't keep the cattle from trampling him?

The other ranch hand pulled up with the wagon just as they finished pulling the rope taut on the stretcher. Clara watched with horror as they lifted her husband off the ground, and she saw the blood-stained ground beneath him. They loaded him hurriedly into the wagon, Clara climbing in behind him. As she settled in the floor of the wagon beside her husband, she saw Ben running up.

"Ma, I wanna go with you," he said.

Clara shook her head, exasperated and worried to death about her husband.

"You need to stay here with John," she said, watching as the flustered ranch hand trotted up to Ben.

Ben shook his head, scrambling to get into the back of the wagon.

"Pa is hurt, and I wanna be with him," he said, his voice thickening with tears.

Clara's heart broke. Thomas was Ben's father, and he had just as much right to worry about him as she did. And if going to the doctor with them would help him feel a little better, she couldn't deny him that.

"All right," she said. "But you stay right with me. No matter what."

Ben nodded, pulling himself up into the back of the wagon. He curled up beside his father at Clara's side, patting him gently on the shoulder.

"Pa?" he asked softly as the wagon pulled away from the ranch. "Can you hear me? You gotta be okay, Pa. You just gotta."

Clara's heart ached, and she put her arm around her son.

"We're gonna do the best we can, sweetheart," she said. "Everything will be all right."

But as the wagon rolled along, Clara wondered if that was true. Thomas was clearly terribly injured, and he hadn't even flinched when Clara or Ben touched him. A whirlwind of thoughts and emotions swept through Clara's mind, blending anxiety with a fierce determination to protect her family. She thought about the harsh reality of losing Thomas, the man she had loved since they were young, the man who had been her rock and the father to their precious son. A shiver ran down her spine as she imagined a world without him, a future where she would be left to shoulder the burdens alone.

How would she break the news to Ben if the worst were to happen? How could she explain that his hero, the man he idolized, might never come home with them? Clara's heart ached at the thought of the pain her son would endure, the void that would be left in his young life. She vowed to be there for Ben, to shield him from the harsh realities of the world for as long as she could, and to provide him with the love and support he would undoubtedly need.

Clara's mind raced, envisioning a multitude of scenarios that could unfold if Thomas were to pass away. She wondered if she would need to sell the ranch, the place they had built together, in order to survive. The idea tore at her soul, for the land held so many memories, so much of their shared history. But practicality demanded its consideration.

Would she have to seek help from neighbors and friends? Could she find a way to keep the ranch afloat, preserving the legacy they had worked so hard to create? Clara held her unconscious husband, his head cradled in her lap as they bumped along.

At the plain wood clinic, with the dull metal sign that read Dr. Sullivan, they were met by the physician. His face was a mask of professional concern as he looked Thomas over. Jerry quickly explained everything to the physician as they got the stretcher inside and back to an examination room.

Clara kept Ben in the waiting area, which was furnished with a couple of basic wooden chairs and a long bench, and a potbelly stove in the far corner, no doubt for warmth in the winter months. The secretary's desk was just as bland, with a round paperweight holding down a stack of files.

As Clara waited for Dr. Sullivan to examine Thomas, she sat beside Ben on the bench, wringing her hands nervously. Ben clung to her skirt, his small body trembling. Clara held him close, wishing that she could summon words of comfort for the child. But she knew that if she spoke, she would begin to cry, which would only upset the boy further. So, they sat in silence, listening to the rustling and low voices of Jerry and the doctor drifting out from the exam room.

Finally, the doctor came out to address Clara.

"I'm so sorry, Mrs. Eaves," he said softly, his voice barely audible over the sound of her pounding heart. "I did everything I could. But I'm afraid he was hurt too bad, and it was too late to help him."

Clara felt the ground sway beneath her. She fell into a chair, her mind reeling.

"No," she whispered, refusing to believe it. "He can't..."

But the truth was all over the doctor's face. Thomas was gone. The love of her life, her partner, her everything was gone. Her sobs filled the small room, the sound echoing through the emptiness that had suddenly surrounded her. Ben clung to her tighter, tears streaming down his own face. She held on to her son and the two of them cried. Her worst fears were confirmed. Now, she and Ben would have to find a way through life all alone. But how would they ever manage without Thomas?

Chapter One

Little Oak, Oklahoma

1880

A candle flickered as Clara stepped into the small, sparsely furnished home she shared with Ben and May Eaves, her mother-in-law, the warm spring breeze fluttering the makeshift curtains in the cracked living room windows.

The aroma of stale bread and spent candles hung in the air, a poignant reminder of their dwindling funds and the hardships they'd endured over the past year. The faded, threadbare rug rested pitifully between the tattered tan sofa and worn coffee table that was adorned with dingy old doilies. She closed the door quietly, noting the complete silence in the nighttime darkness that filled much of the little house.

Her days were spent behind the counter of the general store, and her nights scrubbing the floors of the local hotel. Her body ached with exhaustion, but she tried her best to keep her spirit from being broken.

After all, she had her son and mother-in-law to look after. They were the remnants of a life she had loved, a life she had lost, and the reason why she had to press on and do the best she could, even though she still missed Thomas every day. It had been a year since his death. But some days, it still felt as though it was just a single day.

Creeping into her son's bedroom, she found Ben curled up on his cot, moonlight cascading down on his cherubic face. A rush of affection flooded her as she brushed a lock of hair from his forehead, her heart heavy with the guilt of missed moments.

She was nearly always at work, trying to make enough money to make ends meet. The money she had when Thomas died had gone quickly, and she was almost out of money that she got from selling the ranch and their belongings. She had to work as much as she did just so they could have a little food each day. But it didn't make her feel any better that she was essentially neglecting her son. Especially when he had already lost his father.

Tiptoeing out of his room, she went back down the hall, following the glow of another candle. She found May waiting for her in the kitchen, her face etched with worry and fatigue as she sat at the cracked oak table.

Clara saw that there were fixings to make a small meal laid out on the cast iron stovetop, and there was a plate pulled from the pine cabinets and sitting on the short oak countertop between the sink and the ice box. The older woman gestured toward the rickety chair opposite her, and Clara sank into it, the weariness of her long day seeping into her bones.

"Let me fix you somethin' to eat, Clara," May said.

Clara shook her head, smiling gently. They had the same conversation every night when Clara came home from work. But Clara knew there was already very little food. She almost always went to bed without supper, so that May and Ben could have more to eat. She occasionally bought a piece of bread and cheese on credit at the general store, one of the places she worked. Her boss was kind, but he worked her hard. She didn't mind. She knew it was up to her to take care of her family.

"No, thank you, May," she said. "I'm not hungry."

May shook her head gently, giving Clara a look of sympathy and weariness.

"Clara," May began, her voice as worn as the floorboards under their feet, "this ain't no life for us, for Ben. You're working yourself to the bone and hardly eating, and for what? To barely scrape by?"

Clara nodded, her throat tight with the bitter reality of their situation. She knew it was hard, but she was doing what she could to provide for her family.

"I know, May," she said, looking down at her rough hands with broken, ill-maintained fingernails. "But it's what I gotta do. We won't survive unless I do this."

May shook her head slowly, her wrinkling white brow furrowing.

"Clara, I know these past months have been incredibly tough on you," she began gently. "I've watched you work yourself to exhaustion, trying to keep everything afloat. But I worry, my dear. I worry about Ben and the toll it's taking on him. He needs his mother to be home more. He's falling behind with his schooling, and even as his grandmother, I can't fill in a motherly role in his life."

Clara's shoulders slumped, her gaze fixed on the ground. She knew May was right but admitting it to herself was difficult. The guilt she felt at neglecting her son weighed heavily on her heart. It had ever since she had to start working the two jobs. She could see it in Ben's face every time she had to tell him that they couldn't have a picnic or play at the nearby lake. She never even had the time to pick berries for pies with him anymore.

"I know, May," Clara finally spoke, her voice tinged with regret. "I've been so focused on keeping us going, making sure we have enough to get by. But in doing so, I've been neglecting Ben. He deserves so much more than what I've been able to give him lately."

May reached out, placing a gentle hand on Clara's arm. "You're doing the best you can, my dear. I understand that. But Ben needs his mother, not just someone who provides for him. He needs your love, your presence. It's crucial for his well-being."

A tear welled up in Clara's eye as she nodded, a mix of gratitude and sadness washing over her. "I know, May," she said again. "And I feel terrible for it. Ben has lost his father, and now he's losing his mother to this constant work. He deserves better."

May's expression softened, her voice filled with compassion.

"You're not alone in this, Clara," she said. "We're family, and we'll find a way to support you. You don't have to bear the burden alone."

Clara looked up at May, her eyes searching for solace.

"I don't want to let Ben down, May," she said. "I want to be there for him, to be the mother he needs. But I fear I'm failing him."

May squeezed Clara's hand gently, her voice filled with reassurance.

"You're not failing, my dear," she said. "We all stumble, especially in times of hardship. What matters is that you recognize the need for change, and I believe you have. We'll figure this out together."

Clara took a deep breath, a glimmer of comfort igniting within her. May's words helped her to feel a bit better. But she still needed to make changes. She knew she couldn't continue on this path, neglecting her son and losing herself in the relentless demands of the finances. She had to find a balance, a way to be present for Ben while still managing the responsibilities that awaited her.

"Thank you, May," Clara said, her voice resolute. "I need your help, your guidance. I want to be the mother Ben deserves, and I want to honor Thomas's memory by nurturing our son."

May smiled warmly, her eyes brimming with love.

"You've always had my support, Clara," she said. "We'll find a way to make things right. Ben is lucky to have you as his mother, and together, we'll ensure he thrives."

Clara nodded, sighing. "I just don't know how I can make more time with Ben without shorting us of money we desperately need."

May's gaze was soft yet determined.

"I reckon it's time you thought about a marriage of convenience, Clara," she said.

The suggestion hung in the air, heavy and uncomfortable. Clara's mind raced with a thousand questions, a thousand doubts. What if the man was cruel, or had no care for Ben?

"May," Clara said, her voice barely a whisper, "what if I ended up with a man doesn't care for Ben? What if he's unkind?"

May's grip on Clara's hand tightened, the old woman's strength surprising.

"We'll make sure of it, Clara. We won't settle for a man who won't treat you and Ben right. But you need help, my dear. And Ben needs his mother."

Tears prickled at the corners of Clara's eyes, the weight of the world pressing down on her. She missed the days when

Ben would cling to her skirts, when they had time to laugh and play. She missed her son's childhood.

"I just want him to have a better life, May," Clara whispered, her voice choked with tears.

May nodded, her expression kinder and more doting than Clara had ever seen.

"And he will, my dear," May said, her voice filled with a determined resolve. "We'll see to it."

Clara looked into May's gray eyes, seeing a very comforting resolve in them. In the year since Thomas died, Clara had watched her mother-in-law's hair become drastically streaked with gray. Clara knew that she missed her son, just as much as Clara did. She felt terrible for the aging woman, but she could never allow herself to think too long about losing a son. She could never survive if something ever happened to Ben. Losing Thomas had nearly killed her. Losing Ben would finish the job.

She wanted to reject the idea of a marriage of convenience immediately. The possibility of getting a man who would be unkind to Ben once Clara had married him was great. And yet, May seemed confident in her words. Clara had to consider the possibility that she was only rejecting the idea of being a mail-order bride just because she didn't feel ready to move on from Thomas. It was true; she wasn't, and she didn't know if she ever would be. But she had to admit that having a husband would solve the problems of money and a home. Clara and Ben could have a more secure life, and they could stop draining May of all her resources. Clara also knew that Ben would eventually need a fatherly role model. She could work her fingers to the bone but she could never teach him how to be a man.

After a moment, Clara nodded, her decision made. She would look for a marriage of convenience, a way to provide for Ben, to reclaim the lost time with her son. For Clara knew, love may have brought her to this crossroads, but it would be practicality that guided their way forward.

"Thank you, May," Clara said, embracing the older woman. "Ben and I'd be lost without you."

May nodded, giving Clara another tired smile.

"Likewise, honey," she said. "But now, I'd rest much easier if I knew that you and Ben were taken care of proper, and that he had a father figure in his life."

Clara nodded once more.

"Me, too," she said.

May nodded, patting Clara's hand.

"Go get some rest, dear," she said. "I'll be doin' the same shortly, myself."

Clara nodded.

"I sure am exhausted," she said, rubbing her sore back as she stood. "Good night, May."

Her mother-in-law nodded, yawning behind her leathery hand.

"Good night, dear," she said.

With that, Clara made her way down the short hall of the small house, but she didn't go straight to her room. Instead, she stopped by Ben's room again, watching him sleep in the dim light from the half-moon shining in the window.

He was snoring lightly and murmuring in his sleep, just like Thomas used to do. Clara bit her lip, fighting back tears. Ben looked more like his father every day. And though Clara loved her son with her whole heart, it was painful for her to see the resemblances between Ben and Thomas. She would never let on, though. She could never let Ben think that it hurt her to look at him. Besides, it brought her a small bit of comfort that she still had a piece of Thomas.

Still, as she finally went to her room and laid her tired bones down in her stark, itchy bed, she couldn't help crying softly. A whole year later and she still couldn't adjust to lying in bed alone. And it still seemed terribly unfair to her that she, Ben, and May had lost Thomas in the first place.

She wiped her eyes and rolled over, turning her back to the empty space on the other side of her. And as she closed her eyes, she prayed for a night free of the nightmares that haunted her, of the day her husband died in her arms. *I miss you so much, honey,* she thought as sleep slowly took her. *Please, guide me on this next adventure in our lives.*

Chapter Two

Cattle Creek, Kansas

1880

Roger Banks descended the creaky wooden stairs of his homestead, his stomach growling like an untamed beast. The sun was still hiding beneath the sprawling plains, but the promise of another hard day's work awaited him. He sauntered into the pantry, hopeful for a morsel of anything to quell his hunger, but it was as empty as the last two mornings. With a sigh, he tossed the remnants of yesterday's dinner to Ollie, his faithful hound, who wagged his tail in gratitude.

"Mornin', Ollie boy," Roger said, stooping down to pet his four-year-old brown and white hound dog.

The dog finished his scraps, then turned to lick his master's hand. Roger smiled tiredly at the dog who had been his companion since he was a pup.

"Ready for another long, hard day, buddy?" Roger asked, rubbing the dog's head again.

Ollie wagged his tail and pranced on his front paws. Roger didn't know if the animal really enjoyed working, or if he just liked spending so much time with Roger every day. Either way, he was a big help, especially when it came to herding the cattle. He even often helped Roger dig fence post holes. And he was serious about protecting the ranch. Nothing could come up on the property without Ollie barking and alerting Roger to potential threats. Roger was as grateful for the dog as he was for his ranch hands.

Roger walked to the back door of the house, just on the other side of the small, bland kitchen. He patted his leg, and Ollie immediately joined him, panting happily.

"All right, dog," he said. "Let's get to it."

Ollie faithfully followed his master outside. Roger stretched, looking at the sky, which was just beginning to lighten just along the horizon. Ollie scratched his ear as he waited for Roger to step off the porch. Then, he ran ahead of Roger, doing his first patrol of the day as they made their way past the small, pathetic garden, the hog and chicken pens, and the horse corral.

With his stomach still protesting, he trudged out toward the stables. The morning air was crisp, carrying the scent of dew-kissed grass and awakening earth. Ollie stopped once to do his business, then he continued his patrol, sniffing the air and lifting his heavy ears to listen for any signs of intruders. Roger smiled and chuckled.

"Good boy, Ollie," he said. "Good boy."

When they reached the stables, Roger found that he wasn't the first to arrive.

"Morning, Roger," said Hiram Massey, his foreman. He was a seasoned cowpoke, as hard as a coffin nail and as reliable as a sundial. "Can't help but notice you're wearin' the same outfit as yesterday."

Roger ran a hand through his tousled hair, a rueful smile playing on his lips.

"Yeah, I've been scraping the bottom of the barrel lately, Hiram," he said, his gaze landing on the vast expanse of his inherited ranch. "Ever since I took over, I've been running on empty."

Hiram nodded, stooping to give Ollie, who ran over to greet him, a scratch.

"I hear ya," he said. "Maybe you ought to train Ollie here to cook ya some proper meals and wash your clothes."

Roger laughed.

"Ya know, if any animal could learn to do it, it would sure be Ollie," he said.

At hearing his name spoken so much, the dog began prancing between the two men. Hiram patted his haunches firmly once more before standing upright again.

"I believe it," he said with a soft chuckle. "That's the smartest dog I've ever seen."

Roger sighed, nodding.

"I'm afraid I'm just gonna have to get the lead out and do better with meals," he said. "When we got enough supplies, that is." He sighed, thinking about the rapidly-emptying cabinets and barn storage rooms. "Looks like we'll be needing to make a supply run soon, in fact. We're running low on essentials, and I reckon it's time we restocked."

Hiram nodded in understanding. He had been a steadfast presence on the ranch for decades, weathering both storms and triumphs alongside Roger's family.

"Yep," he said. "It's been a while since we last rode into town for supplies. I'll make sure the horses are ready for the trip whenever you're ready to send me."

Roger's gaze shifted toward the distant horizon, his mind momentarily lost in memories of happier times.

"I still can't believe it's been three years since they left us, Hiram," he murmured, his voice filled with a mixture of sadness and longing. "Every time I ride out, I can't help but feel their absence in every step the horses take."

Hiram placed a gentle hand on Roger's shoulder, offering comfort through their shared understanding.

"I know the pain runs deep, boss," he said. "But we've got to keep pressing on. Your wife and child would want you to find some happiness in this life. And maybe, just maybe, there's still a chance for you to find love again."

Roger's eyes met Hiram's, gratitude glimmering within their depths.

"I appreciate your words, Hiram," he said. "And I know we got a ranch to run, and duty to tend to. It's the only thing that keeps me going. I just miss 'em a lot, is all."

Hiram nodded, ever the practical man.

"Well, there's plenty of work to be done to keep you goin'," he said. "The fences near the south pasture need mending, and the cattle need to be checked. We've also got those stray coyotes causing a ruckus near the henhouse."

Roger sighed again, wiping his forehead, which was already breaking out with beads of sweat.

"Mercy," he said. "The coyotes are back again?"

Hiram nodded.

"I suspect that's what Ollie was tryin' to tell me yesterday," he said. "He went to the edge of the ranch and kept barking at the bush out that way. But every time I went to check, there wasn't nothin' there."

Roger pinched the bridge of his nose. The coyotes kept coming around, despite Ollie's presence, and trying to get to the chickens. The last time the chicken coop ended up needing repairs, two of the chickens escaped. Roger and Hiram searched for them for days. But the only sign Roger ever saw of them was a handful of feathers that clearly belonged to one of them. He had been certain that the coyotes had gotten them. Apparently, he had been right.

"Tarnation," he said. "Yeah, we gotta get the chickens secured, and check the rest of the animal pens before either of us go into town. Especially if the coyotes are hangin' around again. We can't afford to lose a single animal."

Hiram nodded.

"Sorry to have to give you such bad news, boss," he said. "But I figured you should know."

Roger nodded.

"Glad you did," he said. "I've been tryin' to get to the garden and get some more stuff planted, so I would have food, even if I hadn't had the time to butcher one of the animals."

Suddenly, Ollie perked up, pausing with one front paw in the air and his head tilted. Roger and Hiram instinctively fell silent, waiting to see what the dog would do. After a minute, he took off like his tail was on fire, racing across the ranch and through the paddock, until he was out of sight in mere seconds. Roger shook his head and chuckled. Hiram raised an eyebrow and smirked. Then, he glanced past Roger toward where the small, lacking garden grew.

"Looks like it ain't had any tendin' in ages," he said. "I've been meanin' to get one of the other hands to see to it. But we always got more work than we can handle, and it never gets done."

Roger nodded, feeling guilty. The men who worked for him were good men, and he knew he worked them too hard. He would have been glad to hire another hand or two, but the ranch was already struggling financially, and he couldn't afford it.

"Willa was great with the garden," he said. "She could get stuff to grow, even in the winter. I never had to worry about a thing where gardening was concerned."

Hiram chewed his tobacco thoughtfully, his eyes sizing up Roger with a discerning gaze.

"Ever considered a marriage of convenience, boss?" he asked.

Roger's eyes widened, taken aback. "Another wife?" he muttered, his voice barely a whisper. The memory of his late wife still lay heavy on his heart.

"Uh huh," Hiram said, spitting on the ground beneath him. "You gotta have some help around the house. You're gonna run yourself ragged. That won't help you make any money around here if you run yourself into the ground."

Roger made a face.

"I'll be all right," he said.

Both men knew that wasn't true. In the months since Roger inherited the ranch, he had discovered that running a ranch was much more work than he had expected. Back in Oklahoma, he had done much better for himself as a blacksmith by trade. He still felt largely lost most days on the ranch. Hiram was right; he was going to run himself into the ground. But what other choice did he have?

Hiram spit on the ground once more, looking at Roger intently.

"You really should think about takin' another wife," he said. "We both know you need the help. Maybe even more than you're lettin' on. And there's only so much these guys and me can do."

Roger nodded, his guilt from overworking his men returning. He knew that a woman would be a big help. Having someone to tend the garden and cook meals would go a long way for him. But before he could respond, a ranch hand came galloping up, interrupting their conversation.

"I saw a coyote out at the back edge of the property," he said. "Ollie scared him off, but I doubt that'll be the last of him."

Roger and Hiram exchanged glances, sighing in unison.

"We'll be right there," Roger said.

The work for the day was grueling, and it did well to keep Roger busy. As the wind whispered through the tall grass, Roger's thoughts turned to his conversation with Hiram earlier that morning. The two men had spent countless hours working side by side, their sweat mingling with the dust of the land, and he trusted his ranch hand and friend completely. However, Hiram had made a suggestion that tugged at the corners of Roger's weary heart.

Willa had been gone for three long years. Her infectious laughter, her gentle touch, and the love they shared seemed like a distant memory, fading with each passing day. They'd met in Cattle Creek, but Roger wanted to be a blacksmith. Together they had built a life in Oklahoma, a testament to their dreams and aspirations. But now, here, he was left to tend to his father's ranch and its vastness alone. Hiram's words echoed in Roger's mind, like the distant call of a lone wolf. He understood the logic behind it—practicality, even. The ranch demanded constant attention, and his days grew longer and harder without a partner by his side. He knew he could use a woman's touch, her gentle guidance, and the comfort of her presence.

But the thought of another woman sharing his life, of standing by his side where Willa had once stood, sent waves of guilt crashing over him. Willa had been his everything, his rock, his anchor in the storm. He missed her with a depth he couldn't put into words. Her absence was a void he feared could never be filled.

Roger leaned against the wooden fence, his fingers tracing the rough grain of the weathered wood. The sound of horses neighing in the distance provided a momentary distraction, but his mind remained fixed on Hiram's suggestion. Was he ready to move on? Could he find love again, even if it wasn't with Willa?

The decision weighed heavy on him, like an old saddle worn with time. He knew he couldn't avoid it forever, that life demanded he make a choice. But for now, as the sun sank beneath the horizon, casting a bittersweet glow over the land, Roger allowed himself to feel the warmth of Willa's memory. He took solace in the love they had shared and found comfort in the thought that, wherever she was, she would understand his hesitation. *No,* he thought resolutely. *I can't replace my Willa. Not ever.*

Later that night, however, Roger was forced to reconsider his decision. He found himself rudely awakened from his slumber by an incessant itching. At first, he thought Ollie might've brought in fleas, but the dog was well-trained and never set a paw on his bed. Flipping the coarse blanket aside, he discovered tiny red welts on his skin, a clear sign of bed bugs. He couldn't remember the last time he'd changed or washed the sheets.

Rubbing the sleep out of his eyes, he stumbled downstairs for a glass of water. The homestead was shrouded in the soft glow of moonlight, casting long, eerie shadows. As he passed by a window, he caught sight of his reflection. His face was pallid and gaunt, the rawboned look of a man neglecting his own needs for far too long. The sight sent a chill down his spine, stirring up a realization. He needed to start taking care of himself if he wanted to make the ranch a success. And he knew that there was probably only one way that was going to happen.

The following day, Roger approached Hiram.

"I've been thinkin' about what you said yesterday," he said. "About gettin' a mail-order bride. And maybe it's time I try."

Hiram looked him over, noticing his bed bug bites and chuckling.

"Looks like you had a rough night," he said.

Roger snorted.

"You could say that," he said. "Anyway, I was wonderin' if you could help me write an advertisement for a bride. My handwriting's as bad as chicken scratch."

Hiram laughed heartily.

"It sure is," he said. "Sure thing, boss. I'll help ya with that this evenin', once the day's work is done. How 'bout you come over tonight? I'll give you a proper meal, and you can help me figure out what you wanna say in the ad."

Roger smiled weakly at his ranch hand.

"That sounds good," he said.

And yet, as the men set off for their daily chores, Roger's mind spun wildly. Now that he had said it aloud, he wasn't sure he had made the right decision by agreeing to put out the advertisement. It might solve many of his problems to have a woman to help. But it would also give him another mouth to feed, and there would be another person's feelings to consider, when he was adjusted to living life alone. And then, there was Willa. He couldn't convince himself that she would approve of him marrying another woman just yet. Or maybe ever. Was he doing the right thing?

Chapter Three

Little Oak, Oklahoma

1880

The sun and moon had risen and set thirty times since Clara's last effort to find a suitor, and twice she had been met with rejection. She understood the reason, though it pained her heart. No man seemed to want a woman with a boy not of their blood. Young Ben, with his bright eyes and contagious laughter, was a joy to her but an unwanted responsibility to them. And after a month of trying to find a husband, she was close to giving up.

She was reluctant to just stop trying, however. Ben was counting on her to make things better for them, after all. After another long, sleepless night of indecision, Clara decided that she would try once more. She wrote a letter to one Mr. Roger Banks. Only this time, her letter read a little differently. And as she took it to the post office, she prayed for forgiveness for what she had chosen to say. Or rather, what she had chosen not to say.

May caught her in distress one morning. It was a rare day that Clara had off work, but she had woken early out of habit. She was pacing in the kitchen, chewing her lip. Since deciding that she would try to find a man to take on her and Ben, she hadn't considered the idea that she might not succeed. But now that it looked like she would, indeed, fail, she didn't know what to do. She looked at May as she entered the kitchen, knowing her face must look full of hopelessness. The older woman walked over to her, embracing her tightly before she spoke.

"Honey, what's wrong?" she asked. "You ain't thinkin' of goin' to work today anyway, are you?"

Clara sighed.

"The notion did come to mind," she said. "But I promised to take Ben down to the creek."

May smiled warmly. Clara noticed that her cheeks were looking gaunt and there were dark circles under her eyes. Clara's heart clenched, and she set about making breakfast for her mother-in-law.

"That's a wonderful idea," she said. "I know Ben'll enjoy that. Now, tell me what has you so fretful."

Clara had her back turned to her mother-in-law while she gathered the pans and food she would need to make the meal.

"It's just," she began, pausing. She didn't want to worry May, especially with her looking so tired and unwell. But she also couldn't lie to her mother-in-law. Exasperated, she sighed heavily. "What'll I do if I can't find a man to marry me? What'll *we* do?"

Behind her at the worn table, May was silent for a moment. Clara glanced over her shoulder and saw May giving her a puzzled look.

"What would make you think such a thing?" she asked. "You are a very lovely woman, Clara. And Ben is an angelic child. There ain't no way you couldn't find someone to marry you and take Ben as his own."

Clara chuckled dryly. "Then why have I been rejected by two men so far?"

May fell silent again as Clara turned back to the stove. She prepared to fry three eggs and ham slabs, wincing when she saw that they only had ten eggs and two large chunks from which to cut the ham left. *Maybe I should go to work today,*

35

after all, she thought. *I don't know if we'll have enough money for food if I don't.*

"Goodness," May said. "I didn't realize you'd been having such trouble. Have the men said why they aren't interested?"

Clara nodded. She couldn't bring herself to tell May about the last letter she had written. She knew that it was her only hope. But part of her hoped for a rejection from this man, as well. If only because of the fact that she had purposely not told him about Ben.

"Because they don't wanna take on another man's child," she said. "I s'pose I can't blame them. That's an awful big responsibility. But what will we do if no one accepts us?"

May rose, moving beside Clara to help her prepare the food. Clara started to insist that her mother-in-law sit down and let her do the cooking. But the older woman held up a gentle hand and shook her head.

"I'm not helpless yet, dear," she said with a tired smile. She paused as she worked on slicing the ham, not looking bothered at all by the food shortage, even though Clara knew she was as worried as she herself was. "And stop thinkin' about goin' to work today. I can practically hear you shouting it in your mind."

Clara couldn't help smiling a little. Sometimes, it was like her mother-in-law could read her mind. Perhaps, as a struggling woman who had suffered a loss and was determined to do anything she possibly could to make things even a little bit easier for her family, she could.

"Thank you, May," Clara said.

May waved a gentle hand at her.

"You don't need to be worrying about cooking, anyway," she said. "You have a little boy waiting to go to the creek with you today."

Clara chuckled softly and nodded. And as if on cue, Ben came barreling into the kitchen, throwing his arms around his mother's waist.

"Ma, are we ready to go yet?" he asked.

Clara looked up at May for confirmation that she could handle the meal prep alone. She glanced outside and saw that the sun was beginning to shine brightly from its low position in the sky. By the time she finished helping Ben gather some of his toys and put on his swim clothes, breakfast should be ready. They could eat, and then head on to the creek.

"Let's get you ready to go," she said. "Then, we'll come eat and go."

Ben cheered, jumping up and down.

"Thanks, Ma," he said.

Clara followed her son to his room, where he started wildly rummaging through his toy chest. He pulled out a couple of metal horses, his leather ball, and a jump rope. He held them up to his mother, his eyes hopeful.

"Can I take these?" he asked.

Clara laughed and nodded.

"That's all right with me," she said. "Now, we need to change you into swim clothes."

Ben grinned, putting the toys he planned to take on his still-messy bed. Clara set aside the toys and made up the bed while her son took off his shirt and put on a pair of blue, knee-length cotton shorts. He was ready almost before Clara finished making the bed. He gathered up his toys again and began tugging on her arm.

"Come on, Ma," he said urgently.

Clara laughed. "Slow down. We gotta eat first."

Ben groaned, but he reluctantly agreed. Clara let Ben drag her back through the barren house and to the back door. When they reached the kitchen, May had a small basket in her hands. She smiled sweetly at Clara and handed it to her.

"I made breakfast into a picnic for y'all," she said. "I know how eager certain little boys are to get to the creek."

Ben yelped with delight, making both Clara and May laugh. Clara took the basket, kissing her mother-in-law on the cheek.

"Thank you, May," she said. "I guess we'll be going then."

May nodded, bending down to kiss Ben on the forehead.

"Y'all have fun, and be safe," she said.

Ben grinned up at his grandmother.

"We will, Gramma," he said.

With that, Clara and Ben walked out the back door. Clara had to speedwalk to keep up with her excited son.

"Mama, do you think we'll see any ducks at the creek?" Ben asked, his eyes widening with excitement.

"I'm sure we will, sweetheart," Clara said, her eyes sparkling with a hint of mischief. "Maybe we'll even spot a magical swan that grants wishes."

Ben's eyes lit up at the thought.

"Really, Mama?" he asked. "Can we make a wish if we see one?"

Clara giggled. She knew that Ben knew there was no such thing as a magical swan. But it was wonderful to see him so delighted. It was something she hadn't seen in ages, and it was soothing to her soul.

"Of course, my darling," Clara said with a chuckle. "We'll make a wish together, and who knows, it might just come true."

As they reached the shimmering creek, Clara spread out a blanket on the grassy bank. Ben wasted no time, running toward the water's edge and dipping his toes in the cool, rippling waves. A gasp told Clara that the water might be a bit cold that time of the morning. But he was quick to begin wading out into the water; first up to his ankles, then to his knees, and finally to his waist. Once he was in the middle of the creek, he dunked his head under the water. He was sputtering and laughing when he rose from the water again.

"Mama, come quick," he said, his voice filled with glee. "The water feels so nice."

Clara joined him, slipping off her linen shoes and wading in ankle-deep. The water was refreshing against her skin, and she couldn't help but laugh as Ben splashed around, sending droplets flying through the air.

They spent the morning exploring the creek's surroundings, collecting pebbles, and building crude mud structures. Clara watched as Ben's imagination took flight, as he pretended to be a brave captain, sailing through uncharted waters.

"Mama, look," Ben said, holding up a beautiful pebble. "This one is for you."

Clara accepted the seashell, her heart swelling with love.

"Thank you, my little sailor," she said. "It's the most precious gift I could ever receive."

As the sun climbed higher in the sky, they sat on the blanket, enjoying their picnic feast. Clara listened as Ben chattered away, telling her stories about his adventures on the lake.

"Mama, do you think we can come back here again soon?" Ben asked, his voice tinged with a touch of hope.

Clara smiled, her eyes filled with tenderness.

"Absolutely, my darlin'," she said. "We'll make this our special place, a place where we can create beautiful memories together."

As the morning drew to a close, Clara and Ben packed up their belongings, their hearts full of love and joy. They walked hand in hand back to their cozy cottage, carrying with them the magic of their morning at the lake.

The next afternoon, Clara left work early and headed to the dusty post office of their small Oklahoma town. The wooden floor creaked under her weight as she walked up to the counter, her heart pounding in her chest. She doubted that there would be any letters for her. And if she did, they would just be more rejections. But she *had* sent in that one letter in response to an ad for a mail-order bride. This time, she'd left out any mention of Ben. She felt guilty for having done so, because she was certainly not ashamed of Ben, but she needed to do something to increase her chances of finding a husband.

The clerk, a balding man with a halo of white hair, stepped up to the counter. When he saw her, he gave her a bright smile.

"Ms. Eaves," he said, rifling through a stack of envelopes sitting on the desk behind the counter. "This letter came for you just today."

Clara's heart raced. The letter was there, sealed and promising. Clara's hands trembled as she broke the seal and unfolded the parchment:

Dear Ms. Eaves,

I hope this letter finds you in good health and spirits. Your application to become my mail-order bride has left me both surprised and contemplative. I must admit, the idea of finding love again after the death of my wife, Willa, has long been a distant dream in my weary heart. However, your words have stirred something within me, and after much reflection, I find myself accepting your proposal.

Your willingness to uproot your life and seek a new beginning in these wild western lands speaks volumes about your courage and resilience. It takes an extraordinary woman to embark on such an adventure, leaving behind the familiar comforts of home and venturing into the unknown. I am humbled by your bravery, Clara, and I shall do my best to be deserving of it.

I don't have much to offer, other than a big ranch and a home that needs a lot of tending. But if this letter finds you still of a mind to become my bride, then you are welcome to come to Cattle Creek, Kansas, on the 6th of May. I will be waiting to pick you up from the station that morning. And if you've changed your mind, just write and let me know. Enclosed, you will find the funds for your travels, if you do choose to move forward with this.

Yours,

Roger Banks

Clara had to reread the letter again to ensure that she wasn't dreaming. The letter she had been praying for had finally arrived. A man had accepted her application at last. And to her relief, even enclosed the money for their train journey. She smiled, folding the letter quickly and heading for the door to the post office.

"Thank you, sir," she said as she hurried out the door. Then, she ran home, bursting through the back door, where Ben sat at the table, talking to May as she prepared his dinner.

"I got an acceptance letter," she said, tears of joy and relief filling her eyes.

May whirled around, watching as Clara pulled the letter from her dress pocket. She took the letter from Clara's trembling hands, smiling as she read the words on the page.

"Oh, darlin', this is wonderful," she said. "I am so happy for you."

Clara's smile wilted. "We're gonna miss you very much, though."

May waved her hand, tears filling her own eyes.

"I will write to you every day," she said. "And I will come visit every chance I get."

Clara nodded, turning to Ben, who looked confused.

"We'll be goin' to meet Mr. Roger Banks tomorrow," she said. "And we'll be livin' with him from now on."

Ben looked at his grandmother, then back to his mother. He knew that she had been looking for a husband, and he had seemed fine with the idea. But now that it would be a reality, she had no idea how he would handle it.

"Does that mean that we will have a ranch again?" he asked, sounding hopeful.

Clara nodded, smiling at her son's enthusiasm.

"That's right," she said.

Ben nodded, glancing at his grandmother again.

"What about Gramma?" he asked.

Clara looked at May, who smiled warmly at her grandson.

"Don't you worry about me, honey," she said. "I will still be right here, lovin' you and your mama like always."

Ben thought it over for a minute before nodding again.

"Well, when do we leave?" he asked.

Clara smiled again and stroked her son's head.

"Tomorrow morning," she said.

May blinked, looking surprised.

"Tomorrow?" she asked. "So soon?"

Clara nodded, her heart saddened as she realized just how little time she and Ben had left with the aging woman.

"Yes," she said. "Mr. Banks will be expecting me—us—on the sixth. Tomorrow is the fourth, and it will likely take us two days to get there."

May sighed, her eyes beginning to shine with tears. But in the end, she smiled, blinking away the wetness behind her lashes.

"All right," she said. "Then we need to get y'all ready."

***

The next day, May helped Clara and Ben pack the rest of their things. Clara wouldn't let her family see it, but she was terribly trepidatious. She knew this was the best chance she had of making a better life for Ben.

And yet she knew she wasn't ready to let go of Thomas, or of the life she had shared with him. Marrying again felt like a betrayal to him in her mind, and more than once that morning, she had considered canceling the trip and getting her jobs back in Little Oak. She talked herself out of it each time, however.

She knew that May needed them to stop being a burden on the little money and few resources she had. The aging woman also needed financial help, help which Clara would only be able to offer by marrying this Mr. Banks. She was very reluctant with her decision. But deep down, she knew it was the right thing to do.

May insisted that they eat breakfast, even though the sun would be up in just over an hour, and the train would leave an hour after that. But Clara could hardly reject her offer. It was likely to be the last meal she and Ben would ever share with May. And after everything her mother-in-law had done for her since Thomas died, one last breakfast was the least Clara could do.

After breakfast, May took Ben and Clara to the train station herself in Thomas's old wagon. Even at her age, she drove the wagon with great skill. Her eyesight was still good, and her bones only seemed to be stiff early in the mornings and late at night. Ben talked so much on the way to the train station that May and Clara had little chance to talk. That suited Clara well, however. She was sure that the moment she tried to speak, she would burst into tears.

Her prediction proved itself true when May brought the wagon to a stop at the station. She helped Clara and Ben get their suitcases out of the back of the wagon, then walked them to the ticket window. Once Clara and Ben were set with their tickets, May pulled them both into a fierce embrace.

"I love you both very much," she said, her voice thick with tears. "I'd be lyin' if I said I was happy about all this. But I'm glad that you've gotten a chance for a better life."

Clara hugged her mother-in-law back tightly, her own tears streaming down her cheeks.

"We'll miss you," she said. "We'll write every chance we get, and we'll visit often."

May nodded, kissing first Clara's damp cheek, and then Ben's flushed one.

"We'll be all right, Gramma," he said brightly. "And we know that you'll be all right, too."

Clara's heart squeezed. She was glad to hear her son be so optimistic, especially when she thought that losing his father would have made him afraid to leave behind anyone he loved. But he seemed more excited about the trip than he was afraid, and Clara was thankful. A moment later, the train pulled into the station. May kissed her daughter-in-law and grandson once more, clasping her hands to her chest.

"Y'all take care, you hear?" she asked, her tears also now flowing freely.

Clara nodded, waving to the woman as she and her son headed for the train.

"You, too, May," she called over the sound of the train whistle.

Another moment later, Clara and Ben were seated on the train. And a short while after, it began rolling out of the station. Clara and Ben waved to May until they could no longer see her. Then, braced themselves to embark on their journey to Kansas. She watched the scenery change from plains to thick patches of trees.

She spent the trip staring out the train window, her mind a whirlwind of hopes and fears. Ben, on the other hand, chattered away, his excitement infecting the otherwise somber train car. He spoke animatedly about the ranch they were moving to, dreaming about the animals he would encounter and the insects he could study. Clara found comfort in his enthusiasm and allowed herself to hope that this might be a good home for them both.

The train whistle blew as they pulled into the Kansas station, the loud sound echoing across the vast plains. Waiting for them on the platform was a figure Clara assumed to be Roger. His tall, broad-shouldered silhouette stood out against the setting sun. As they drew closer, she could see his handsome features, the salt-and-pepper hair, and his piercing blue eyes. He was a formidable figure, taller than her late husband, and Clara found her face growing warm under his intense gaze.

"Ma'am," he tipped his hat, his eyes meeting hers. Clara could see curiosity in his gaze, and she felt an unexpected flutter in her heart.

Then Ben stepped out from behind her, his face glowing with excitement. She saw Roger's gaze shift, his eyes widening in surprise as he registered the boy's presence. A rush of heat flushed her cheeks. The familiar pang of anxiety gripped her heart as she held her breath, waiting for his reaction to their unconventional situation.

Chapter Four

Cattle Creek, Kansas

1880

As the dust from the stagecoach settled, Roger stood rooted to the spot, his deep-set eyes wide in disbelief. Before him, a young boy with blue eyes and a mop of blond hair clung to Ms. Eaves' skirts, his gaze filled with a mixture of awe and curiosity. Roger's mind raced; her letters had never mentioned a son.

A wave of anger washed over him. What did this woman think she was doing? She couldn't have thought that he just wouldn't notice when she showed up with a child! He was in utter shock at the turn of events. He was so ruffled that he couldn't think of anything to say.

The trio stood staring at each other wordlessly for what felt like ages. Roger couldn't think of a single word, and Ms. Eaves offered none. That made him angrier, as she was the one who owed him an explanation. He wanted to confront her right then, but the boy was watching Roger warily.

He was half-tempted to send them both back, to tell the driver to turn around, and forget this ever happened. The woman had hidden a very major thing from him, after all. And he was not equipped in the slightest to deal with the situation he now found himself in. He made up his mind right then. He would turn right back around and go home. And the woman and her son could do the same thing.

But before he could act, the boy spotted Ollie. Roger's loyal hound perked up his ears and wagged his tail, sensing the boy's excitement. The child dropped to his knees, and with a joyful yelp, Ollie bounded over, lapping at his face with his large, wet tongue. Laughter bubbled up from the boy, a sound so pure and genuine it pierced Roger's hardened exterior. The sight of them, so innocent, so carefree, touched something deep inside him, and he felt his resolve soften.

While the boy was distracted by Ollie, Roger looked up at Ms. Eaves. Her eyes were sparkling with a mix of apprehension and hope. His gaze lingered on the delicate freckles scattered across her cheeks, the soft reddish-blonde strands escaping her bonnet. He swallowed hard, pushing away the sudden rush of emotions. His shoulders stiffened, and he cleared his throat.

"We better get going," he grumbled, avoiding her gaze.

Ms. Eaves nodded, taking a step toward him. She was clearly scared, and Roger felt that was good enough for her. He wasn't going to hurt her. However, she certainly owed him an explanation. And then, he would likely be sending her home. But it was getting late, and he was already tired, on top of the shock of discovering the son of the woman who was supposed to become his wife.

Ms. Eaves glanced at her son, who was still very much enthralled with Ollie. Then, she looked at Roger again, her voice soft and low.

"I'm sure you have questions," she said. "I will answer them all, I promise."

Roger clenched his jaw. He certainly wanted answers. But even though he wasn't a father, he knew it was not proper to have an argument in front of a child. He gave his head one single shake, giving her a warning look.

"Now's not the time," he said with a cautioning tone. "We'll talk when we get home."

Ms. Eaves looked at him with wide eyes, and she opened her mouth to speak. But Roger held up his hand and shook his head.

"We'll talk when we get home," he repeated.

Ms. Eaves bit her lip, causing it to turn bright pink. Roger's heart fluttered as her cheeks flushed as well. She really was a pretty thing, he couldn't deny that much. But how could she have neglected to tell him that she had a son? He wouldn't have chosen her if he had known she had a child. The boy seemed polite enough, and he looked strong. But after having lost his own baby before he could even name it, he wasn't ready to raise someone else's child.

The ride back to the ranch was a cacophony of sounds as Ms. Eaves' son chattered nonstop, pointing out the colors of the sunset, the shapes of the clouds, the smells of the wildflowers. He was like a sponge, soaking in everything around him. Roger had never met a boy who talked so much. Ollie was in his element, sitting across the boy's lap, basking in the constant attention.

Roger was surprised at Ollie's reaction. Ollie was very wary of new people, at least until he had spent some time around them. And yet, he had taken to the boy as though they had known each other forever. It was a sight to see, to be sure. He just hoped that Ollie didn't get too attached to the boy. Roger didn't know if he could let Ms. Eaves and her son stay long. She had hidden the boy from him, and Roger was in no position to take on a child. But as he watched the boy and Ollie, his heart began to soften.

Once they reached the ranch, Ben hopped down from the wagon, eyes wide with excitement. "Can I look around?" he asked.

Ms. Eaves gave her son a firm look.

"Ben, wait," she said. "Remember your manners, please? This is Mr. Banks's home."

Ben looked sheepish, and he blushed. For a moment, he looked much like his mother, although Roger guessed that he looked more like his father overall. That notion unsettled Roger, and he had to resist the urge to just walk away from the pair before him and leave them to fend for themselves.

"It's all right," he said, giving the boy a nod. "You can go explore. But stay away from the animals and don't get yourself hurt."

Ben's face lit up immediately, and he nodded.

"Yes sir, Mr. Banks," he said, bouncing with excitement. "I will do what you ask."

Roger nodded again and Ben took off running. Ollie followed right behind him, his ears flapping as he raced alongside the boy. Again, Roger was surprised at how well Ollie seemed to like the boy. But he didn't watch them for too long. As soon as the boy was out of earshot, he turned to Ms. Eaves, his expression hard and unyielding.

"What the devil are you playing at, Ms. Eaves?" he demanded, his voice a low growl. The lightness from earlier was gone, replaced by a storm of confusion and anger. "Why didn't you tell me about Ben?"

Chapter Five

Clara's heart was in her throat. She had known she would have to explain about Ben when she arrived in Kansas. And after her rejections from the other men, she knew she shouldn't have expected anything different from Mr. Banks. But she suddenly realized that she had hoped that he wouldn't be upset.

Time stopped as she tried to hold Mr. Banks's firm, cold gaze. He was far from impressed. Only then did Clara realize that he could very well send her and Ben back to Oklahoma. They could go back to May's. But their financial situation would still be dire. And she likely wouldn't be able to get her old jobs back. If he was upset enough with her to send her back home, she and her family would be in real trouble.

Clara looked into Mr. Banks's eyes, a storm of emotion churning within her. She only had one chance to plead her case. If she failed, she would ruin any chance she had of making things better for Ben.

"Please, let me explain," she said, her voice barely a whisper as the wind whistled through the ranch. "I want to tell you why I did this."

He kept his steely gaze on her, his face tense and his jaw clenched.

"What is it?" he asked, his voice carrying the gravelly timbre that echoed the roughness of the frontier life he lived. "Do you wanna talk about how you failed to tell me something as important as you having a kid? Do you have a husband back home who will come looking for you and make trouble for me?"

Clara took a deep breath, her heart pounding in her chest as she took a shaky breath.

"My husband died," she said, her eyes welling up with tears. "Just over a year ago. He was Ben's father. And yes, I hid Ben from you. But please, believe me. I am not playing at anything. I hid Ben because..." she trailed off. The words sounded weak, even to her, as she spoke. She was scared and embarrassed, and she understood she was failing Ben terribly. Tears burned her eyes and she tried vainly to blink them away.

"Because why?" he asked. "Did you really think I wouldn't notice? Did you think I wouldn't care? What made you try to get away with something like this?"

Clara shook her head, more to try to compose herself than to reject the hurtful words Mr. Banks was saying. She knew she deserved to be reprimanded, because she never should have hidden her son from him. But the words cut her deeply, nonetheless.

"Ben and I have been having a hard time since his father died," she said. "My mother-in-law, too. I was working two jobs, and we still struggled for money. And I was afraid... afraid you wouldn't want to marry me if you knew. I couldn't take that risk. Now, I regret not telling you. Please, try to understand..." She lost her words again. But she had said everything she needed to say. Her fate, and Ben's, was now in the hands of Mr. Banks.

Her worst fears were confirmed when he turned his back on her, ran his hands through his salt-and-pepper hair with apparent irritation, and then turned back to her, his eyes blazing. He was silent for a long moment, his gaze fixed on Clara once more. The weight of his silence was heavy, suffocating.

"You lied to me," he finally said, his voice stern and cold. "How can I trust you now?"

Clara felt a stab of fear, but she swallowed it down. She had fought too hard, come too far to back down now.

"Give me a chance, please," she pleaded, her voice trembling. "Let me prove to you that you can trust me. I will never lie to you about anything, ever again. And I can be a good wife."

To her horror, Mr. Banks's expression hardened even further, and he shook his head.

"I don't see how you could possibly expect me to believe you," he said. "I don't even know if I can believe the story you just told me. That could be more lies. Who knows what else you are hiding?" He shook his head again and scowled. "No. I don't think I can marry you now. There's no way that I can trust you."

Clara covered her mouth to stifle a sob. She could see Ben happily playing with the dog, but she didn't want to risk him hearing her cry.

"Please," she begged, clasping her hands together and holding them out to Mr. Banks. "I promise to do anything I must to prove to you that I will never lie to you again. Whatever it takes, I will do it. But please, don't send us back home. I don't know what will become of us if you do."

Mr. Banks was shaking his head before she even finished speaking.

"I'm not sure," he said. "My gut tells me to send y'all right home first thing tomorrow morning."

Clara was losing hope. But she had to try at least one more time.

"Mr. Banks, I am begging you," she said. "Ben is a good boy, and he won't be any trouble. He can even help you around here. He used to work with Thomas, my husband, on our old ranch. And I will be the most dutiful and obedient wife. I used to work at a general store, so I am strong and I can organize things. I can cook, I can clean anything you need me to clean. And I used to do work around the ranch my husband and I owned. Just give us a chance. Please? You're our last hope. Please?"

Mr. Banks stared at her for the longest moment of her life. She knew that he had every right to send her home, as he had said he wanted to. She wished she hadn't made the decision to hide Ben from him. No matter how desperate she had been, lying and keeping secrets was no way to conduct herself. But now that it was done, and Mr. Banks had found out, she could only hope that he could find some way to forgive her.

"All right, Ms. Eaves," he said at last. "I won't send you and the boy home. I will still marry you."

Clara let out a breath she hadn't realized she was holding. "Thank you, Mr. Banks," she said, her voice choked with emotion. "You won't regret this."

Mr. Banks looked at her, his eyes serious.

"Promise me, Ms. Eaves," he said, his voice hard. "Promise me you won't lie to me again. I will not tolerate any more deception from you. Married or not, I will send you and your son packing immediately if you ever do anything like that again."

Clara looked at him, her heart flooded with relief.

"I promise, Mr. Banks," she vowed. "I will never deceive you again."

Mr. Banks nodded, but he looked far from convinced.

"See to it that you don't," he said. "Now, come on inside. There's a lotta work that needs doing."

Clara nodded, grateful that Mr. Banks had decided to accept her and Ben, despite her not being forthcoming. But as she stepped into the small, run-down house that was to become her new home, her gratitude evaporated. Dust coated every surface, cobwebs hung from the rafters, and the furniture was old and battered. Clara sighed, rolling up her sleeves.

There was no time for self-pity; there was work to be done. She considered calling Ben in to help her, or to go help Mr. Banks around the ranch, as she had said that he would. But after the confrontation she'd had about springing Ben on Mr. Banks, she thought it might be best to just let him play with the dog and stay out of the way for that day. She could put him to work the following day, after the wedding. But right then, she felt he would be better off playing and out from under Mr. Banks's feet.

By the time the sun began to set, Clara was exhausted. Her hands were raw from scrubbing, her back ached from lifting, but the house was starting to look like a livable abode again. She freshened up, then went to the kitchen of the house to begin preparing supper.

But when she opened the cabinets and grime-covered ice box, she was once more horrified. The only food to be found was some cold ham that was heavens knew how many days old, and in the cabinet was a chunk of stale bread. Mr. Banks came in just as she was despairing about what to feed the man who was to be her husband.

"You and Ben eat that," he said, pointing to the food she was now holding. "I ain't hungry."

Clara turned to argue and insist that Mr. Banks needed to eat after a long day at work. But the warning in his eyes was enough to silence her.

"All right," she said.

After heating up the food on the stove, Clara put it on a plate and called Ben in for supper. He came bouncing in, with Ollie right at his heels. The dog paused at Clara's feet, sitting to offer her his front paws. Clara giggled, reaching down to scratch the animal behind the ears. Then, he ran over to Ben, who was sitting at the table. He laid down politely at Ben's feet beneath the table.

Clara took him his plate, putting it down in front of him and taking a seat in the chair beside him. Despite her hard day's work, she wasn't hungry. So, she opted for a small piece of stale bread, just so Ben wouldn't worry.

"Ma, you won't believe what happened today," Ben said, his young voice filled with enthusiasm. "Ollie didn't leave me once today. He's the friendliest pup I've ever seen. We played fetch all afternoon, and Ollie even let me give him belly rubs. He loves belly rubs, Ma. And when he got tired, he came and laid across my lap and took a nap." Ben grinned sheepishly. "I fell asleep for a little bit, too. And I woke up to him licking my face. He licked me until I wrapped my arms around his neck. Then, he pulled me off the ground and wanted to play chase."

Clara smiled, her heart warmed by her son's joy.

"I'm glad you had such a great time with Ollie, sweetheart," she said. "I'm sure Mr. Banks will be thrilled that you two are getting along so well."

Ben paused, a curious expression crossing his face.

"Ma, why do you think Mr. Banks seemed surprised when we arrived today?" he asked. "I thought you said he knew we were coming, and that's why we're here."

Clara's heart skipped a beat, and she scrambled to find an answer that wouldn't reveal the truth. She couldn't bear to tell her son that she hadn't mentioned anything to Mr. Banks about him. She reached across the table, gently squeezing Ben's hand.

"Well, darlin', sometimes grown-ups have a lot on their minds," she said. "Maybe Mr. Banks was just distracted by somethin' else, that's all. It doesn't mean he wasn't expectin' us."

Ben frowned, his brows furrowing in thought.

"But you seemed surprised too, when he stepped off the wagon," he said, seemingly trying to make sense of the situation. "And y'all talked real quiet for a long time. Are you sure he knew we were comin'? Did somethin' happen?"

Clara sighed inwardly, realizing that she should have known that her explanation would not be convincing enough. She had to tread carefully, not wanting to burden Ben with the truth just yet. She forced a reassuring smile, brushing her fingers through his tousled hair.

"You know, sweetheart, sometimes expected things can still surprise," she said. "Maybe Mr. Banks just felt surprised, even though he knew we were comin'. Let's not worry about it too much, okay? The important thing is that we're all here now, and we have a new home to share."

Ben's features softened, his innocence shining through.

"All right, Ma," he said. "If you say so. But can we play with Ollie again tomorrow?"

Clara chuckled softly, relieved that her diversion had worked.

"Of course, darlin'," she said. "You can spend as much time with Ollie as you like, though you might be asked to help around here a bit tomorrow. But for now, let's finish our dinner. You need to eat to grow up big and strong, just like a cowboy."

Ben grinned, his appetite suddenly renewed.

"Okay, Ma," he said. "I'm happy to help tomorrow if I need to. I'll finish my dinner, and then I'll go on to bed so I can be ready if I'm needed."

Clara nodded, her heart surging with love for her son.

"That sounds like a perfect plan, my little cowboy," she said.

Right after supper, she took Ben and herself to bed. She chose to curl up with Ben in the cot in Mr. Banks's spare bedroom, their bodies huddled together for warmth in the cool night. Ben fell asleep quickly, cuddled up with his mother.

Clara, however, stared around the room. The room was so barren of décor and furniture that she could see everything, despite the cloudy twilight lighting. Besides the bed, there was a rickety round table on one side of the bed, rather than a nightstand or dresser. The window was caked with dirt and stuck open about half an inch. The curtains were also full of dust, a faded dark green color, and tattered.

She could also see a circle where a rug had once been but had been removed to reveal a circle of floor that wasn't as dull and worn as the rest. There was one very small closet, rather than a dresser, and Clara wondered if anyone had ever used that room.

She allowed herself to relax, taking comfort in her son's small form huddled against her. The following day, her life would change forever once again. She just hoped that she was making the right decision by marrying Mr. Roger Banks.

***

The next morning, Clara's hands trembled as she fastened the buttons of her ivory linen dress, the fabric feeling almost foreign against her fingertips. Her mind was a whirlwind of doubts and uncertainties, for she had only just met Roger Banks, and their first encounter had not gone as smoothly as she had hoped.

The memory of his anger, when he realized that she had hidden Ben from him, still lingered in her thoughts like a dark cloud. She knew she needed this marriage to Mr. Banks to care for Ben. But it didn't help ease her mind at all. In fact, it helped her feel even more like she was making a mistake.

The trip to the church was a silent one. Mr. Banks drove the wagon wordlessly, reaching up occasionally to fiddle with the bowline tie around the neck of his black long-sleeved shirt. There was a hole in the knee of his blue jeans, and his cowboy boots were scuffed and worn. Clearly, he had put as little time into putting together his outfit as Clara had when she left her home in Oklahoma.

She couldn't blame him; their wedding was taking place quickly, and it barely allowed for the time to arrange the ceremony at the little church that served the small town of Weston. Even Ben remained quiet in the back of the wagon, seeming to sense the tension between his mother and his soon-to-be stepfather, solemn even despite the lovely weather and the beautiful birds that flitted overhead as they traveled.

As they approached the small church, Clara's nerves threatened to consume her. The familiar scent of wildflowers that usually brought her solace now seemed suffocating. She cast a quick glance at Ben, who clutched her hand tightly, his own unease mirroring hers. She offered him a forced smile, attempting to hide her own inner turmoil.

Her son looked the best-dressed of all of them, wearing a clean blue jean shirt with a dark blue vest and blue jeans to match. May had made him the vest, just to make him feel special for having something so nice. He looked handsome, but just as pensive as she felt.

The wooden doors of the church creaked open, revealing a sight that momentarily stole Clara's breath away. The intimate space was adorned with wildflower bouquets, carefully arranged by the townsfolk, no doubt to bring a pleasant atmosphere to their place of worship. The sunlight, streaming through the stained-glass windows, cast a kaleidoscope of colors on the worn floorboards, lending an air of serenity to the place.

The elderly reverend, a kindly man with gentle eyes, stood before them, his voice resonating with reassurance. Clara and Roger faced each other, their eyes meeting for the first time since their clash the day before. The silence between them seemed to stretch endlessly, filled with the weight of awkwardness and regret. Mr. Banks—Roger—averted his gaze just as quickly as he locked eyes with her. Clara's heart sank. It was clear that Roger didn't wish to marry her. She prayed that she wasn't making the wrong decision.

Still, as the reverend stopped with the first part of the ceremony and smiled at Clara and Roger, Clara steeled herself to commit herself to the man in front of her. The reverend looked at Mr. Banks and nodded. Roger gave a nod back and began the vows portion of the ceremony.

"I, Roger Banks, take you, Clara Eaves, to be my lawfully wedded wife, to have and to hold from this day forward, for better or worse, for richer or poorer, in sickness and in health, until death do us part."

Clara kept her expression unchanged, but her heart was breaking as Roger spoke. All she could think about was Thomas's and her wedding day. They had gazed lovingly at one another as they recited their vows, and she had been giddy with anticipation for the part where she would at last kiss Thomas as his wife. Now, she dreaded the end of the ceremony, where she would be another man's wife.

But when the reverend turned to her, she just gave a small smile.

"I, Clara Eaves, take you, Roger Banks, to be my lawfully wedded husband, to have and to hold from this day forward, for better or worse, for richer or poorer, in sickness and in health, until death do us part."

The rest of the ceremony passed in a blur. Clara was only vaguely aware of Roger putting a wedding ring on her left ring finger. Everything felt so surreal that Clara almost felt detached from her body. She felt both relieved and saddened when it was over.

It was far too late, but Clara began to question herself. Would she ever be happy as Roger Banks's wife? Would he ever be happy as her husband?

Chapter Six

The dust of the wedding hadn't yet settled before Roger began to wonder if he made a mistake. He found himself in an emotional whirlwind. The presence of Clara and her son stirred in him an odd brew of comfort, relief, and an aching sorrow. They were a stark reminder of the life he could've had, should've had, with his wife and child who were now but a memory, swept away in the cruel river of time.

As the reality of his new family set in, Roger swallowed hard. His eyes drifted toward a ball lying near the edge of the porch, a constant reminder of Ben's presence. He could supposedly handle horses and cattle, even rustlers if the need arose. But a seven-year-old boy with questions in his eyes and a heart longing for a father's love terrified him more than a stampede. Would he be able to provide Ben the guidance he needed, the steady presence of a father he longed for?

Roger led Clara and Ben to the ranch's kitchen. He wasn't surprised to find Hiram already in there, looking around the kitchen thoughtfully. When they walked in, Hiram turned and smiled at them. Roger turned tensely to his new wife, gesturing to Hiram.

"Miss... Clara, this is my ranch hand, Hiram Massey," he mumbled. "Hiram. This is Clara."

Hiram tipped his hat, walking over to take her hand in both of his.

"It sure is a pleasure to meet you, Mrs. Banks," he said. "And congratulations on your weddin'."

Roger noticed how uncomfortable Clara was at the kudos from Hiram. But she gave him a warm smile, and Roger thought she blushed a little.

"Thank you kindly, Mr. Massey," she said, pulling Ben closer to her. "And this is my son, Ben."

Hiram put his hands on his knees and leaned down to look the boy in the eye. He held out one of his hands, waiting until the child took it timidly.

"Well, what a strapping young fellow you are, Ben," Hiram said brightly. "I'm delighted to meet you as well, sir."

Ben slowly beamed at Hiram, clearly grateful for the kindness. Roger couldn't help feeling a twist of guilt when he realized that he had been less than welcoming to the boy. But he reminded himself that he hadn't known to expect him. Besides, he couldn't get attached to Ben when he had lost his own child. He shifted his gaze nonetheless when Hiram looked up at him questioningly.

"Pleased to meet you, too, Mr. Massey," Ben said politely.

Hiram chuckled softly.

"Call me Hiram, son," he said, looking at Roger again, who pretended to be studying a scuff on his boots.

The awkward silence that followed turned Roger's stomach. He hadn't had the chance to tell Hiram that his new wife came with a son. He knew his ranch hand was full of questions. He also knew that Hiram would wait until they were alone to ask them. Somehow, that made him even more uncomfortable. He was just ready for life to get back to normal, and to try to forget that Clara and Ben existed for the most part.

Clara was the next to break the silence.

"Why don't I prepare us a nice lunch?" she asked. Roger could tell she was nervous, and once more he felt bad. He didn't know if it was proper to expect a wife to cook on her wedding day. But he was no good in the kitchen, and he didn't care anything about food right then, anyway.

Hiram gave him one more judgmental look before smiling at Clara again.

"That sounds like a lovely idea," he said. "We can let Roger take a load off, and I'll show you where everything is around here. Ben here can join us, if he'd like to."

Ben's face lit up and he nodded.

"I would love to see the place," he said. "It's gonna be my new home now, after all."

Roger winced at the boy's words, and he tried to hide his grimace. From the corner of his eye, he could see Hiram give his head a shake. But then, he turned back to Clara and Ben and gestured to the back door.

"Well then, let's get to it," he said.

Roger waited for the trio to go out the back door. Then, he practically ran out the front of the house. His mind was reeling. He had never been so uncomfortable and awkward in his own home. He had no idea what he had just done by marrying Clara. Nor did he know what he was going to do. He sighed, running his hands through his graying hair, and looking up to the heavens. Had he done the right thing? Would Willa ever forgive him for his decision?

Roger sat on the weathered porch of his ranch house, his gaze trained on the dusty trail winding through the scrubland toward town. His heart throbbed a heavy rhythm in his chest, threatening to break free from its ribbed cage.

The morning sun was still fresh, glistening against the tall grass, glinting off the worn wooden rails. That day, Clara and her son had turned his solitary existence on its head. He still wasn't sure if he could trust Clara after she kept Ben from him. And his heart still ached for Willa, and he had yet to convince himself that he had done the right thing by remarrying.

But it was done now. His new wife was in his—now their— kitchen, making their post-wedding feast. He was glad that Hiram had offered to stay and help her find everything she would need to cook. In his frustration with her the previous day, and with the rush to get to the church that morning, Roger hadn't taken the time to do that himself.

He tried to remind himself that he didn't want any of it in the first place, that it had been Hiram's idea and that he should be the one to show the unwanted woman and her child around. But something in his heart tugged. He had agreed to marry Clara, even despite his reservations. Didn't he owe it to her to try to be a little nicer to her?

"Roger," Hiram called, startling him so bad that he jumped. The foreman chuckled, shaking his head. "Are you gonna sit out here and brood all day, or are you gonna come eat?"

Roger tried to look calm and steady his wild thoughts.

"It's ready?" he asked casually.

Hiram chuckled again.

"Nope," he said. "I thought I'd invite you in to eat the food raw."

Roger snickered at his friend's sarcasm.

"It'd still be better than what I've been eating lately," he said as he rose. "I'm coming."

Hiram nodded, opening the door, and gesturing for Roger to go ahead of him. Even before he was inside the doorway good, the smells hit him. It smelled like a feast he would expect at a wealthy man's house. He followed the smells to the kitchen, where he stood, staring dumbfounded at what he saw. The table was indeed set with hearty fare—roasted chicken, freshly baked bread, a salad with tomatoes bright as sunset, and a pot of coffee brewing on the stove. The smell of the food was intoxicating, a welcome change from the meager meals Roger had grown accustomed to since inheriting the ranch.

Clara, who hadn't even changed out of her simple white cotton dress, turned to him, and gave him a timid smile.

"I hope you like it," she said. "And I hope that I didn't go too overboard. I just wanted to make this meal special for you."

Roger nodded, but he was looking at the food again.

"It looks wonderful," he said.

Clara waited for everyone to be seated at the table. Roger realized with chagrin that there were only three chairs in the small kitchen. Hiram seemed to notice at the same time and gave Roger a pointed look.

"Y'all go on ahead and sit," he said. "I don't mind standin' to eat. And tomorrow, I'll get on makin' another chair to put in here."

Clara shook her head, looking sheepish and embarrassed, as though it was her fault there wasn't a fourth chair.

"That's not necessary," she said. "Ben can sit in my lap while we eat. Really, it's fine. We used to do that all the time back home."

Hiram looked at Ben, who took his mother's hand and beamed at her.

"I like to sit with Mama," he said. "Besides, I wouldn't want you and Mr. Banks to not have a chair."

Hiram gave Roger another look that he ignored. Then, he nodded to Clara and Ben, smiling sweetly.

"That's mighty kind of you," he said. "Well, if that's the way you want it, then I will take the other chair."

Ben grinned and nodded. Clara looked relieved as she put her son in her chair.

"I'll get lunch served up," she said. "Y'all go on and get comfortable."

Roger hung his head as he took the chair on one end of the table. Ben sat between him and Hiram, who sat on the other end. When Roger looked up at his friend, the ranch hand was giving him another knowing look. Roger sighed and shrugged slightly, as if to say, 'what do you want from me?' Though he knew what Hiram wanted—to put him in his place and to be grateful that he had two new people in his life.

Roger, however, knew he could never do that. At best, he could learn to tolerate their presence so that they didn't constantly annoy him.

Clara served the food, saving her place for last so that she could pick Ben up and put him on her knee. Roger was impressed. For being so small and wispy, she lifted the seven-year-old child with ease. He supposed she was used to it. But it was still impressive to him. As they began to eat, Roger nearly fell out of his chair.

A single bite of the chicken made him forget all his worries. It was perfectly cooked, seasoned with salt and pepper, and, he thought, might have had a garlic clove put inside of it. He hardly glanced up from the plate until Clara spoke to him.

"Do you like it?" she asked.

Roger nodded, looking up at his new wife with awe.

"This is the first decent meal I've had in weeks," he admitted, a small, appreciative smile on his face.

Clara arched an eyebrow at his confession. "Really? I'm surprised you don't have freshly butchered meat every single day."

Roger shrugged. "I was a blacksmith in Oklahoma until a few months ago. Didn't know much about running a ranch. This place... it was my father's. Haven't seen him in years, and when I did, it was through the lens of a lawyer's letter, saying he'd left it all to me. I'm still getting used to the ranch life. Including butchering meat."

Hiram chuckled good-naturedly and nodded.

"Any meat that gets butchered out here is done by me," he said. "And I don't mind. Roger is real generous, and he gives me my fill of anything I slaughter."

Clara looked at Roger with a look of approval on her face.

"That's mighty sweet of you," she said.

Roger blushed at the praise, a smile creeping onto his face. Seeing Clara smile reminded him of how beautiful he thought she was when he first saw her. And her praise made him feel good. It was something he hadn't heard since Willa was alive, and he was surprised at how proud it made him feel.

"It's nothin'," he said. "Besides, the meat would spoil if it didn't get eaten fast. And if anyone deserves good meat, it's Hiram."

Hiram gave him a big smile and a nod.

"It's still mighty kind of ya, boss," he said. "And it's sure appreciated."

Ben, sensing the change in the air around him, began chatting excitedly about his favorite foods. To Roger's surprise, the boy liked many of the same things he did. They both apparently preferred beef roast to pork, but they liked roasted chicken better than the other two. They also liked veal stew, especially during the winter, and they both preferred white bread to cornbread. Ben's favorite pie was peach, whereas Roger's was apple. Roger found himself wondering what a peach-apple pie would taste like.

Just as they were finishing their lunch, the sound of a horse's hooves beating against the arid ground echoed through the air. A figure soon loomed in the doorway— Jeremiah Banks, Roger's uncle. His face was weathered from the sun and wind, his eyes as hardened as the land he'd been driving cattle across for the past six weeks. Roger quickly excused himself from the table and went out the back door to greet his uncle.

Ollie, who Roger had missed until he came trotting out of his bedroom, bolted out the open back door and barked loudly at Jeremiah's arrival, earning himself a warning shot fired into the air from Jeremiah's pistol. Roger gritted his teeth, wanting to clock the man for shooting at his beloved dog. It wasn't as if Jeremiah didn't know Ollie was there. But with Clara and Ben inside, he didn't want to create a confrontation.

"Come on in, Uncle Jeremiah," Roger said, standing aside as the heavyset bald man waddled up to the porch.

Jeremiah grunted, walking into the kitchen hitching up his pants. His gaze then landed on Clara and a look of surprise crossed his craggy face.

"A woman? Here?" he grumbled, his confusion evident.

Roger quickly intervened.

"Clara and I, we're married," he announced, his voice steady despite the pang of uncertainty he felt at his uncle's reaction.

Jeremiah looked Clara over with a disgusted expression. Then, he sneered at Roger, shaking his head.

"Married? Without waiting for me?" Jeremiah's asked, his voice gruff with disapproval. "I might've been delayed, boy, but I wasn't dead."

Roger sighed. He couldn't have guessed that his uncle would care whether he got married. And why was he so upset? Roger would have thought his uncle would be glad that there would be more help in getting the place sorted out then.

"It was a quick decision we made," he said. "Just got married this morning, in fact. Clara and her boy just got here last night. And I didn't know when you might be by again."

Hiram cleared his throat, breaking the strange tension in the kitchen.

"I'd best get back to work," he said curtly. Then, he softened, looking at Ben with a smile. "Would you and Ollie like to come play outside?"

Ben, who had been startled by the gunshot, suddenly brightened again. Ollie, who had cowered at the boy's feet, also seemed excited by the idea.

"Can we?" he asked.

Hiram chuckled and nodded, deliberately avoiding Jeremiah's gaze.

"Sure can," he said. "Come on, boys."

Roger watched as the three of them headed out the front door, making sure to avoid Jeremiah. Roger knew that Hiram and Jeremiah had a long, bad history, and the men hated each other. Jeremiah didn't seem at all bothered, however. As soon as the three were gone, he collapsed heavily into one of the chairs, making it groan under his weight.

"Are you gonna serve me, woman?" he demanded, turning his steely gaze on Clara.

With a small nod, Clara obliged, trying to keep her face neutral despite the harshness of his tone. As she moved, Roger could smell the whiskey on Jeremiah's breath, an odorous testament to his uncle's notorious love for the bottle. He sighed inwardly, steeling himself for the inevitable conflict that was sure to follow. He didn't have to wait long. Jeremiah's next words burned Roger more than a cattle brand.

"You decided to marry, and you chose this one?" the rude, heavyset man said, sneering at Clara.

Chapter Seven

Clara turned her back both to avoid speaking out of turn and to hide her anger with the man's words. She didn't even know him, and he had come in barking orders at her. And even though she barely knew Roger, she felt that he should do something to defend her. But then again, it was a woman's job to serve a man when he came into her home. Shouldn't she have a reasonable expectation of some manners, though? And why had Hiram left the room as soon as the man arrived?

Roger cleared his throat loudly, and Clara could sense that he was as tense as she was.

"Uncle Jeremiah, this is Clara," he said in a clipped voice. "Clara, this is my uncle, Jeremiah Banks."

Clara turned around just long enough to dip her head at the crude man.

"Charmed, Mr. Banks," she said, turning back to the food to make a plate for Mr. Banks.

The fat man snorted and wheezed out a cough, sending a pungent blast of liquor scent through the air.

"That makes one of us," he said snidely.

Clara clenched her jaw, throwing some food onto the man's plate. Her own plate sat abandoned, half-eaten, but her appetite was truly destroyed. As quickly as she could, she served him his meal.

"Clara," Roger said when his uncle had his food in front of him. "Why don't you go freshen up and put away Ben's and your things, if you want."

Clara felt weak with relief, and she gave her husband a genuine smile for the first time.

"All right," she said. "Just holler if you need me again."

Roger nodded. "Thank you, Clara."

Clara was too happy to get away from Roger's uncle. He was horribly rude, especially considering he had only just met her. But more than that, it was clear that no one in the Banks household liked Jeremiah. Her nerves were already raw from the wedding, and all the emotions she felt. Jeremiah's intimidating presence and the tension between him, Roger, and Hiram amplified her anxiety. She was determined to focus on her duties from then on.

She had promised Roger that she would be an obedient and dutiful wife. And if that involved serving her new husband's strange uncle, she would do it without complaint, even though the man didn't seem to care at all for her or Ben.

While Roger talked in the kitchen with his uncle, Clara went to the room she had shared with her son the previous night and changed into a plain, old gray dress that she used to wear when she helped Thomas with the ranch. Her wedding dress was nothing special.

But she didn't want to get it permanently dirty while she tended to her chores. She hung up her dress in her small closet. Then, she walked around the front part of the house, trying to decide where she should start. She knew the house was in a terrible state, despite the work she had done the day before.

But as she examined it more closely, she was horrified. The furniture she had first thought was gray was all just coated in thick layers of dust. The curtains were dully colored for the same reason. Even the barren walls looked like they were stained with dirt and clay.

What have I gotten myself into? she wondered as she looked around in exasperation. It would take her the better part of two days to clean the whole house properly. It was already late afternoon, and she was exhausted from the day's events.

She wouldn't need to make dinner, since she had made such a big lunch. She hoped her new husband wouldn't be angry with her for not beginning the cleaning right away. She decided that she would go find Ben, and then figure out how and when she would start such a big job.

She went out the front door to avoid Roger's uncle. Until he warmed up to her and Ben, she wanted to keep her distance. She spotted Ben right away. He was rolling in the grass with Ollie on the right side of the front yard. Ben was laughing in a way she hadn't heard him do since before Thomas died.

She stood and watched for a minute, savoring the sound of her child's happiness. She was so focused on Ben that she didn't hear Roger come up behind her.

"That was a wonderful meal, Clara," he said, startling her.

She gasped, turning to face him, fearful that he would be angry with her for shirking her duties.

"I'm very glad you liked it," she said. "I was just checking on Ben before I got to work cleaning."

Roger chuckled and shook his head.

"Don't worry yourself about cleaning today," he said. "It's been a long day. You can pick that back up tomorrow. Rest and enjoy some time with Ben. I gotta go back out to the ranch for a couple hours. Just wanted to compliment you again on the wonderful food."

Clara blushed. Roger's kindness was unexpected, especially when he was so angry with her the day before. But rather than argue or insist, she nodded.

"That's mighty kind of you," she said. "I'll do that. And I will make you an extra plate of food before I put everything away, so you have it when you come back in later."

Roger nodded and smiled. She couldn't believe how much younger he looked when he smiled. Her heart skipped, and the heat in her cheeks intensified.

"Thank you, Clara," he said. "See you in a couple hours or so."

Clara nodded, stepping aside so that Roger could move past her and head out to the ranch. Roger didn't seem like he was always such a hard man. She could see some goodness in him, and he seemed to want to be nice to her, at least right then. She began to wonder if maybe things might be okay married to him after all.

***

Clara woke early the next morning, her senses prickling with unease. She could still feel the tangible tension between Roger and his Uncle Jeremiah from the night before. Jeremiah's face was a hard, weathered canvas of stern lines and narrow eyes, a true testament to a life lived in the harsh Wild West.

His gaze had lingered on Clara and her son, Ben, with an unspoken judgment that was hard to ignore. Despite his stern demeanor, Clara held on to a hope, like a frail daisy in the desert, that with time, he'd come to understand and appreciate them. She dressed quickly in the same gray dress she had worn after her wedding the day before, then went and made breakfast.

The morning sun was barely peeking over the horizon when she finished cooking. Roger had already gone out to the ranch, so it would just be her and Ben. She made Ben's plate, preparing to wake him to eat. But just as she set his plate on the table, he came walking sleepily into the kitchen.

"That smells great, Ma," he said, rubbing his eyes.

Clara smiled fondly at her son, ruffling his hair.

"Eat up, honey," she said. "Roger might need your help outside today."

Ben beamed, the notion waking him up rather quickly. Like his father, he loved being outdoors and working on a ranch. Clara didn't know how much Roger would let him do to start, or how much Hiram would be able to teach him when Roger was busy. But she knew that Ben would love to learn, and that he would do very well. As she had told her new husband, Ben was bright and strong. If Roger would just give him a chance, he would be a grand asset to the ranch.

When breakfast was finished, Ben took off outside with Ollie right on his heels. Clara marveled at how well those two got along. Ben had never had a pet of his own, though his father's ranch dog would sometimes follow Ben and Thomas around while they were working with the horses.

Ben was good with Ollie, and the dog seemed to love the boy as though they had been friends for years. Clara began her chores, determined to make the best of the situation. She cleaned, swept, and tidied, her hands moving with a sense of purpose and resolve.

Everything was going well until around lunchtime. She was preparing the leftovers from lunch the day before so that Roger and Ben would have lunch. But a large shadow covered the kitchen window, and her heart dropped when she saw who was there. Jeremiah Banks had returned, and he was looking in the window at her. His eyes were cold, and his lips were curled up into a silent snarl. She calmly finished reheating the food and called to Roger and Ben to come eat.

Ben came, but Roger did not. She saw him in the paddock, however, so she guessed that he intended to work through lunch. Mr. Banks, however, would do no such thing. He entered the kitchen, without a word to her, and plopped down in the same chair in which he had sat the night before.

She groaned inwardly, making him a plate with her portion of the meal, and serving it to him without a word. Then, she went about cleaning the kitchen as she had the rest of the house.

She tried to pretend that Mr. Banks wasn't there. But every now and then, Clara would catch Jeremiah's hard gaze on her. His suspicious eyes would follow her around the room, scrutinizing her every move.

Each time, she'd simply offer him a warm smile and continue with her tasks, choosing not to let his skepticism dampen her spirits. She wished she could flee the room and work somewhere else in the house. But she didn't want him to see how uneasy he made her. Besides, she wanted to have the kitchen spotless before she started dinner that night. She had overheard Roger and Ben talking the day before, and she wanted to make beef roast with white bread, and both a peach and apple pie for dessert.

In the afternoon, after a long day of cleaning and adjusting, Clara, Ben, and their loyal dog, Ollie, went for a stroll. It was a lovely afternoon, with the sun sitting lazily just above the horizon of the hills in the distance, and clouds drifting like sleepy tufts of cotton.

Ben had found a whole strip of wildflowers at the edge of the property, where it met the bush, and on the other side were big clusters of berry vines. His eyes sparkled with unadulterated joy as he pointed out interesting rocks, peculiar insects, and hidden paths that wound through the rough landscape.

The sight of her son, so full of life and wonder, made Clara's heart swell with joy. Seeing Ben so happy, so eager to explore and learn, gave her a sense of accomplishment. It felt as if, after a year filled with hardship and loss, she'd finally managed to do something right for her son.

"And guess what else, Ma?" Ben was saying, pulling her out of her reverie.

Clara giggled at her son's enthusiasm. "What, honey?"

Ben pointed to the far corner of the ranch to a small clearing just at that edge of the bush.

"There's a small creek out there," he said. "I hope we can talk Mr. Banks into taking us out there one day. Or maybe Hiram will take us. I didn't get too close, but I could hear it running. And it looks like it's in the shade, so that water will be nice and cold."

Clara nodded, her smile wilting a little. Roger had been nicer to her recently. But he still seemed to be avoiding her. She didn't want to put pressure on him about spending time with Ben. But nor did she want to crush her son's hopes about visiting the creek.

"I'm sure Hiram will take you one day while y'all are out here working," she said.

Ben continued chatting as they walked back to the homestead. Clara looked at the setting sun, her heart filled with a newfound determination. The road ahead was uncertain, with the looming presence of Jeremiah and the unforgiving harshness of the Wild West. But as she watched

Ben chase Ollie around their new home, she knew that she would face any obstacle to ensure the happiness and safety of her son.

Chapter Eight

Ever since Roger had set foot on the ranch, life had been a continuous uphill climb. The fences needed mending, the cattle required tending, and the barn roof had a habit of leaking whenever the heavens decided to open. A man with lesser resolve might have packed up and left, but Roger was not that kind of man.

He harbored a stubborn determination, as steadfast as the granite in the nearby mountains. He'd left his old life behind, and he had every intention to make this work. Besides, he hoped Clara's arrival would bring a breath of fresh air, that her presence would somehow make the labor less arduous. And if their wedding feast, and the cleaning she had done the day before, were any indication, it likely would.

That next morning, Roger woke with a start. He smelled something cooking, and he forgot about his new wife for just a moment. He flew down the hall, stopping just outside the kitchen doorway when he saw Clara, still in her robe, with her strawberry hair hanging down her back in wisps. The sun was just starting to rise, and Roger realized he had slept later than he usually did. He let his heartbeat slow again before he entered the kitchen.

"Morning, Clara," Roger said, already enraptured with the smells coming from the stove.

Clara turned to give him a small smile.

"Morning, Roger," she said. "I got a later start than I meant to. But breakfast shouldn't be too much longer now. I hope that's all right."

Roger nodded.

"That's fine," he said. "I'll take some coffee, though, if it's ready."

Clara nodded, rushing to get him a cup. She filled it with fresh, hot coffee and brought it to him just as he sat down at the table.

"Here you go," she said, giving him another timid smile.

Roger raised the cup to his lips, relishing the first taste of the strong, hot drink. It had been ages since he had coffee in the mornings. He was instantly more alert, and he wasn't completely dreading the day ahead as he normally did.

"Thank you," he said.

Clara nodded before going back to work on the food. Roger watched as she expertly tended to the eggs and bacon, cleaning as she went. Roger remembered that she had said she was married once, before him. It was clear that she was, indeed, a very helpful wife. He felt a twinge of guilt for having doubted her when she surprised him with Ben. It hadn't been a good way for them to start their lives together.

But now, he was beginning to understand why she would have been so reluctant. He was also starting to believe that her actions then were no representation of who she really was. He still wasn't sure if he should have rushed into marrying her. But he was slowly coming to accept the idea that he needed to truly give her a chance.

And as it had turned out, Ben really was a good helper. There wasn't anything as of then that Roger had asked of him that he couldn't do. Moreover, he seemed to find real joy in helping around the ranch.

The only thing was that Ollie rarely followed Roger around anymore. Now, he spent most of his time with the young boy. Roger had been irritated by that at first. But he was gradually becoming okay with it. It seemed to bring joy to both Ben and the dog. And Roger had to admit that their growing bond was touching to him.

When breakfast was finished, Clara brought him a plate. He started to protest and remind her that he only wanted coffee. But then, he saw that not only had she made the eggs and bacon, but she had also toasted some leftover bread and put a generous helping of butter on it, and she had added a piece of the apple pie from the night before. Roger could hardly wait for the plate to touch the table before he started eating.

Clara joined him shortly with her own plate. He looked up from his to find her watching him with anticipation. He swallowed the giant bite of food he had to give her a sheepish grin.

"This is delicious," he said. "And I guess I was hungrier than I realized."

Clara smiled sweetly at him, looking relieved and pleased.

"I'm glad to hear it," she said. "What do you feel like for supper tonight?"

Roger stared at her for a long moment. He hadn't had the time to plan dinner since before Willa died. But with Clara there to prepare the food earlier in the day and collect everything needed for meals, he figured he could have anything he wanted.

"Would a stew be all right?" he asked. "Maybe some veal stew?"

Clara smiled again at him.

"That's just fine," she said. "Ben loves veal stew, too."

Roger kept eating, but he nodded. *I know,* he thought, surprised at himself. *I remember.*

After breakfast, Roger went out to the barn to load up the supplies he would need for the day. He and Hiram had repaired the chicken coop and set the new fence posts, but they would need to be painted, and Roger needed to tend to his saddle. He fetched the feed, paint, and his saddle and the polish. He was whistling to himself and didn't hear Hiram come up behind him.

"Well, ain't you in high spirits?" he asked.

Roger whirled around, nearly hitting his friend with a can of paint, and earning him a hearty laugh.

"You gotta quit sneaking up on people, Hiram," he said.

Hiram chuckled again.

"Well, I reckon I've done you a mighty favor by suggesting that mail-order bride business," he said. "Ain't she a fine woman, that Clara?"

Roger paused for a moment, trying to hide the blush in his cheeks.

"I suppose, Hiram," he said, trying to sound casual. "She sure can cook, and that's more than I can say for myself. I can't deny that her culinary skills have been a blessing around here."

Hiram chuckled again.

"That's what I've been tellin' you, Roger," he said. "A man needs a good woman to keep things in order. And from what I've seen, Clara's got a knack for cleanin' too. House is lookin' better than ever, ain't it?"

Roger nodded, continuing to load up the supplies in his wooden wheelbarrow.

"Indeed, it is," he said. "She's been puttin' in the effort, I'll give her that. I ain't never seen this place so tidy before. Makes me feel like I'm livin' in a whole new world."

Hiram grinned, clearly pleased with himself.

"See?" he asked. "I told you she'd bring some sunshine into your life. It ain't easy findin' a woman who can cook and clean like Clara. You're a lucky man."

Roger sighed.

"I suppose I am," he said. "But you know, it's just... I can't help but feel like this whole situation happened too fast. We barely know each other, and yet, here we are, husband and wife. And Willa still takes up so much of my heart. I don't know if I can ever get attached to Clara the same way I loved Willa."

Hiram shrugged.

"Sometimes, love ain't about how long you've known someone," he said. "It's about findin' that spark, that connection. I believe you two got it, especially since y'all both know the pain of losin' a spouse. And if it's meant to be, it'll grow with time. You just gotta give it a chance."

Roger shook his head. He was glad for Clara's help. But love seemed like too farfetched of a notion to him.

"Grab some feed, and let's get to work," he said.

Hiram chuckled once more, but he headed to the back of the barn where the feed was stored.

"Yes, boss," he said.

Roger and Hiram set off for their tasks for the morning, and Roger tried to put the conversation at the back of his mind. Sure, it had been a good idea to get a mail-order bride. But Hiram was talking crazy about the whole love thing. The only woman he could ever love was Willa, and Roger knew that would never change. However, perhaps, he and Clara could become friends. Clara had promised him that he wouldn't regret giving her and Ben a chance. And he was beginning to believe that.

As he often did, Roger worked through lunch. Under the vast canvas of the clear blue sky, Roger found himself engrossed in the meticulous task of cleaning his saddle. His fingers worked diligently, massaging oil into the leather, when he saw a dust cloud approaching. As it neared, the figure of Jeremiah, his uncle, came into view. Jeremiah had a rugged exterior, like the landscape he'd inhabited his whole life, but his eyes held a harsh light.

"Roger," Jeremiah said, his tone gruff, "We need to talk."

Roger placed his saddle aside and straightened, meeting Jeremiah's gaze.

"Of course, Uncle. What's on your mind?"

Jeremiah sneered, pulling a flask from his pocket, and taking a long pull of it. Roger turned his head so his uncle wouldn't see him making a face. Roger enjoyed an occasional drink, too. But his uncle seemed to be drinking every time he saw him.

"I ain't too happy 'bout this marriage of yours," Jeremiah said, his voice carrying a note of resentment. "You bring a woman I don't know and her boy into my home, this place I've known all my life. And you didn't even have the decency to talk to me 'bout it."

Roger felt a pang of guilt. He didn't know his uncle well, but he was the only kin he had left. The man seemed to be hard, inside and out. Roger couldn't think of three times that Jeremiah Banks had been anything but callus and mean since he'd met him. But the last thing he wanted was to create a rift.

"Uncle Jeremiah, I apologize," Roger said. "I should've talked to you. But I believe Clara and her son can help us. They can make this place better."

Jeremiah chortled, coughing as he did so. He took another drink, shaking his head and glaring at Roger.

"Women ain't nothin' but trouble, Roger," he said. "Especially women you don't know. I would have expected better of my own kin. You shoulda talked to me before you ran off and got married."

Roger began to bristle. He knew his uncle was upset. But Roger was a grown man. And the ranch now belonged to him, not Jeremiah. If Roger wanted to move a wife and stepchild into his life there on the ranch, he didn't see why he needed Jeremiah's permission.

"Try not to judge her before you know her," he said carefully. "Havin' her here has allowed me to get much more done."

Jeremiah snickered again, and he wiped his bald head with a cloth. But before Jeremiah could respond, a shout echoed from the stable, followed by the rapid patter of small feet. Out rushed Ben, brandishing a monstrous spider in his hand, its legs writhing wildly. Jeremiah's face drained of color as he stumbled backward, nearly tripping over his own boots in his haste to escape the creature.

"Look what I found," the child exclaimed, clearly very pleased with himself for the discovery. "It was spookin' one of the horses, so I took it outta the stall."

Jeremiah looked like he was turning green, and Roger swallowed his laughter, fighting to keep his features composed. But his uncle's reaction had been priceless. Jeremiah, however, glared at him, looking as mad as a rattlesnake.

"This is exactly what I'm talkin' about, Roger," he barked, his voice shaky. "This ain't no place for the likes of them. Especially if they gonna go playin' with spiders."

Roger glanced at Ben, then back at his uncle.

"I promise, Uncle, things will get better," he said.

Jeremiah regained enough of his composure to straighten himself and storm off. Ben watched him go before turning back to Roger with wide eyes.

"Did I do something wrong?" he asked.

Roger looked at the spider in the child's hand, biting back another bout of laughter.

"No, Ben," he said, unable to stifle a snort. "You didn't do nothin' wrong." *In fact, keep on goin'...*

Chapter Nine

It took another three days, but Clara finally began to feel more comfortable in her new house. She had been married, for the second time in her life, for less than a week, and the days had been filled with unending work. She was not one to shy away from hard work, but the dilapidated state of the house had been more than she had bargained for.

Still, as she began to fall into a routine that felt familiar to her and was less stressful than working two jobs had been, she found a sense of contentment. For the most part, Roger was gone from after breakfast until dinnertime, and he usually retired for the night immediately after he finished his last meal of the day. But when they shared meals together, they had pleasant conversation, and he seemed to have let go of his anger with her about keeping Ben from him.

However, six days after her wedding, she realized that she was making real progress. She moved through the rooms methodically, scrubbing, dusting, and sorting until she was satisfied. It was clear that the house had suffered neglect when it came to repairs, as well as with cleaning.

But she thought she could at least detract from the old wood by making little tablecloths and doilies to sit atop all the furniture, and maybe start putting vases full of fresh wildflowers throughout the house, if Roger gave her permission to do so.

Clad in a worn cotton dress, her hands and face smeared with a layer of grime, she was elbow-deep in the stove's belly when she heard the front door creak open. Without turning, she recognized the heavy footsteps of Jeremiah.

It was all she could do to not groan aloud. She hated every second she had to spend around the heavyset man. She had thought that with time, he would warm up to her. But it seemed that, more every passing day, he only seemed to dislike her more.

When she didn't turn around to face him the instant he walked into the kitchen, he made a strange grumbling, throat-clearing noise.

"Woman," he called out gruffly. "Make me some coffee, would you?"

Clara glanced over her shoulder at him, pulling a grimy hand through her mussed hair. "Can't you see I'm filthy? It wouldn't do to get grime and grease in something I serve someone."

Jeremiah looked her over, looking utterly disgusted.

"So?" he asked. "A man asked you to do something. I think you best do it."

Clara stared at the man, her mouth open. She couldn't believe he could be so disrespectful to her in her own house. She knew that she was new to the family. But she had done nothing but serve him every time he entered the house. Why would he be so rude when he could see that she was cleaning?

"I need a moment to clean myself off," she said, a bit more sharply than she intended. "I can't do anything with this stuff all over my hands."

Jeremiah snorted, shaking his head as he did his typical collapse into the kitchen chair.

"You're gonna to have to earn your place here, woman," he sneered. "It ain't a free ride."

Clara bristled at the implication.

"I've been working since sunup, Mr. Banks," she said, not hiding the disdain in her voice as she addressed him. "I'm not afraid of a little hard work."

He merely raised a skeptical eyebrow at her.

"Then make me that coffee," he said. "Now."

Clara held his gaze firmly, not wanting to relent so easily.

"Would you like something to eat, too?" she asked, not withholding her sarcasm.

Jeremiah looked at her, bewildered by her question. But instead of answering it, he sneered at her again.

"And that boy of yours," he said. "He's gotta work, too. Ain't no free rides for anyone around here. Not even snot-nosed little boys."

Clara had to wrestle to control her temper. It was one thing for the man to insult her. But now, he was going after an innocent child. *Her* innocent child.

"Ben works just as hard as any grown man," she said. *Any grown man but you, you cad,* she added silently.

Jeremiah sneered again and shook his head.

"Until he can wrangle cattle on his own, he ain't worth the dirt beneath his feet," he said.

Clara balled up her fists, but she turned back to the stove and set about making the man his coffee. She secretly hoped that some of the soot would drip down into the drink. Maybe then, he wouldn't press her so hard the next time she was grimy from such hard work.

The soot held in place on her skin, though, and she managed to pour a cup of coffee without contaminating it, much to her dismay. She took it to the table and set it down in front of the fat, cruel man, not caring if some of it splashed onto him.

The only thanks she got was a bitter grunt as he grabbed the cup. But before she turned back to the oven, she saw him sipping from the flask he had retrieved from his coat pocket. She could see the dark amber liquid of whiskey being poured into his coffee cup. She turned away, making a face. She wondered if Roger knew that his uncle was so fond of the drink.

"Gotta earn your keep," the man repeated, starting to slur his words. "That boy, too."

Clara turned around with her hands on her hips, but Jeremiah wasn't even looking at her. He was examining the cup of coffee, probably thinking of what she said about getting soot in it.

Feeling the sting of his doubt, Clara set her jaw, her eyes flashing defiantly.

"I will earn my keep," she said before turning back to the stove. "And so will my Ben."

Jeremiah Banks snorted again, but he didn't say anything else. Her blood was boiling, and she was glad to not have to talk to him. She desperately wanted to leave the kitchen, but she was determined to finish her task. As she worked, she could feel his gaze on her, the silent judgement burning into her back.

But she was determined to prove him wrong. When she finally did finish the stove, she left the kitchen. She was fairly sure she saw the heavy man passed out at the table. But she didn't waste the time checking to see.

She hurried out of the kitchen and went to the washroom to clean herself properly. Maybe, if Roger found him in that state, he would do something about his horrible uncle.

Later that day, Clara was out in the yard, the scent of fresh laundry filling her nostrils as she hung sheets on the line. The blue in the sky was littered with white tufts of clouds, and the sun shone warmly over the yard. Yet her heart was nowhere near as warm.

She was irked, she was hurt, and more than a little confused. Her gaze shifted from the clothesline toward the house. Try as she might, she couldn't forget the conversation she had with Jeremiah earlier that day. His hands were as calloused as his demeanor, his face was lined, and his eyes unkind.

Clara was sure he was a proud, hardworking man, but his words toward her and her little Ben were as sharp as cactus thorns. Clara was quickly developing the sense that Jeremiah Banks was going to be a world of trouble, despite him being Roger's kin.

She thought of Ben. Her sweet, brave, little boy. He was, even right then, working hard, doing anything Hiram and Roger needed him to do. He worked every bit as hard as Clara had told Roger he would every single day, and he seemed to love it more every day.

His laughter, his bright spirit, a beacon of light in the arid, harsh plains. To her, Ben was a source of pride, a source of her strength and resilience. He was her reason to push on, to face every dawn with hope. Why then, did Jeremiah regard her precious boy with the same coldness he showed her? Why did he discount Ben's hardiness, his spirit, his joy for life?

The peaceful rhythm of her work was broken when the sound of angry voices carried over from the adjacent property. Recognizing Roger's voice, she hastily dropped the sheet in her hand and hurried over. The sight that met her was that of Roger, his face red and angry, arguing with a man she didn't recognize.

His sharp, intimidating voice filled the air, a stark contrast to the gentle man she had come to know. Fear mixed with curiosity spurred her closer, her heart pounding in her chest. Who could Roger be having trouble with, and what could it be about?

Chapter Ten

Roger's face was as red as the Kansas sunset and his demeanor as prickly as the cacti that surrounded his humble ranch. The seed delivery man stood by with a look of bewilderment, holding a sack of seeds that were useless to him.

"How could you have gotten the order so far wrong?" he asked. "I wrote it all down myself."

Immediately, Roger realized what must have happened. Normally, Hiram wrote out those orders. But he had gone to run other errands the day the order was made. Roger had been the one who handled writing down the order. And his handwriting was illegible on a good day and could be outdone by chickens with coal on their feet on a bad day. But he couldn't bring himself to admit the mistake. Now, as well as angry, he was embarrassed. He turned his back to the man just in time to see Clara approaching.

Roger was shocked at the state of her. She was wearing an apron over one of her old dresses, but the skirt was streaked with soot. Her hands were clean, but there was soot on her sleeves, too. And her hair was wildly poking out from beneath a white bonnet. If he hadn't been so agitated, he would have found her appearance comical. He turned back to the man, trying to figure out what he should do. When Clara reached them, she looked from the flustered Roger to the confused delivery man.

"Is everything all right?" she asked.

Roger scoffed.

"No," he said bitterly. "I ordered seeds a few days ago. This man brought me the wrong ones. Now, I have a big problem."

And worst of all, it's all my fault, he added with silent bitterness.

Clara wiped her hands on the singular clean spot on her apron. She approached the delivery man slowly and gave him a warm smile.

"May I see the order?" she asked gently, extending a hand adorned with her new wedding ring.

The delivery man looked at her as though trying to assess if she was going to fly off the handle at him as well. When she maintained her kind smile, he handed her a crumpled piece of paper. Roger's handwriting was sprawled across it in a hurried, uneven scrawl, the letters barely distinguishable from each other. It was a mess of lead and nonsense that would make any schoolmaster wince. Roger barely suppressed a groan. Now, his wife would know that he could barely write. He had never been so mortified in his entire life. He stood with his head hanging, awaiting her ridicule.

"Ah," Clara said after a moment, her voice carrying a note of understanding. She turned to Roger, her blue eyes softened with empathy. "Have you got a pencil, Roger?"

Almost mechanically, he reached into his vest pocket and handed her a stubby pencil, its lead worn to a dull point. Clara accepted it, her gaze never leaving the paper as she began to decipher the hasty handwriting. She worked carefully for a couple of minutes, working around the pathetic excuse for penmanship that Roger had used and scribbling expertly on the page.

She wrote out the correct order beneath his original attempt, her script neat and firm, and the order was completely correct, even though she couldn't have known what it was he meant to write without asking him. It was clear she was accustomed to this, her hand moving with the confidence of someone who had spent years managing a ranch.

"Here," she said, handing the corrected order back to the delivery man. "I apologize for that, sir. I fear that first order sheet was my fault. I got too careless and sloppy. Please, forgive me."

Roger stood watching his wife, stunned. Not only had she managed to fix the issue that Roger himself would have never been able to fix, but she was now taking the blame for the ruined order. He wanted to speak up and tell her that wasn't necessary. But the words stuck in his throat, and all he could do was watch to see what the delivery man did next.

He looked over the sheet, his face beginning to relax. Clearly, Clara's writing was much clearer, and the words were understandable to him.

"I see now," he said, still sounding a little nervous. "It's all right, Mrs. Banks. These things happen. But it's too late for me to fix the order issue today."

Clara touched him with a hand as gentle as her smile and shook her head.

"That's all right," she said. "Again, it was my mistake. Would you be able to bring the right order tomorrow?"

The man nodded, relief washing over his face. "Sure, ma'am. First thing in the morning."

Clara gave him another of her sweet smiles. Now that he was calming down, Roger noticed how much her face brightened each time she gave such a smile.

He noticed again just how beautiful she was. Not only that, but she was apparently good with tasks on the ranch. She had told him that she was apt when she first arrived. Roger hadn't put much stock in her words because of her deception. But now, he realized that she had been telling the truth.

"Thank you very much, sir," she said. "We'll be ready for the delivery as soon as you arrive."

The man smiled at her, seeming almost as surprised as Roger that she understood the situation and was able to fix it.

"I'll see you then, ma'am," he said.

The man pulled away in his wagon a moment later, and Roger just stared at his wife. Now that the man was gone, he felt uncomfortable. He knew she had seen his horrible handwriting. And he didn't know what she would say to him now that it was just the two of them.

As the dust from the delivery man's wagon settled, Clara turned to Roger.

"I used to help my husband with the ranch orders," she explained, her voice barely above a whisper. "He had terrible handwriting too, so he taught me how to do stuff like that when I was real young. I'm sorry if I embarrassed you by stepping in for you. I just didn't wanna see the problem escalate, and maybe scare the man off for good."

Roger shook his head, suddenly not wanting her to feel nervous or timid, especially after having helped him so much.

"No, Clara," he said, giving her a small smile. "You did right. Much obliged."

Clara nodded, visibly relaxing.

"I didn't know you had trouble with your handwriting," she said. "The letter you sent to me was written very well. I would have never guessed."

Roger's cheeks reddened further as he managed a grateful nod.

"I... I broke my hand when I was a boy," he said. "Never healed right, so my writing's a bit of a mess. And I wasn't the best student either... Spelling's never been my strong suit. It's something I'm a bit embarrassed about, if I'm honest. I had to have Hiram write that letter to you, in fact. I couldn't bear the thought of sending a letter that you couldn't even read."

Clara smiled gently at his confession.

"Well, Roger, if you ever need help with your writing, I'd be glad to assist," she said. "I help Ben with penmanship and spelling all the time. It's no trouble, really."

His weathered face softened at her offer. He had never noticed before, but she was as kind as she was lovely and adept at household work.

"Thank you, Clara," he said. "I sure do appreciate that. Hiram isn't always around, and I wouldn't want my uncle to think I can't manage a simple order."

He noticed that her face darkened at the mention of his uncle, and he thought he could guess why. Jeremiah Banks was a hard man, and Roger had already seen the way he spoke to Clara.

He made a mental note to speak with his uncle about that. It wouldn't do for him to go upsetting Clara. She deserved respect, just the same as anyone else. He didn't say anything to Clara, though. He didn't want to make her uncomfortable by questioning her about it.

"Oh, I almost forgot," she said, holding out the pencil. "I need to give this back to you, before I lose it."

Roger looked down, blushing as he realized that he had already forgotten about the pencil himself.

"Thank you, Clara," he said, reaching out his hand.

As he took back his pencil, their fingers brushed against each other. Roger nearly dropped the pencil, his heart pounding like a stampede in his chest. He looked into Clara's eyes, finding a warmth there that both comforted and excited him. The moment was fleeting, yet it held a promise, a hint of a future that was slowly coming into focus under the harsh but hopeful sun of Kansas.

He stood frozen, staring at his wife, unable to move and not unhappy about it. For the first time since he married Clara, he felt something for her other than comfortable indifference. How was it that she was making him feel in such a way?

Chapter Eleven

Clara stood in the warm, cozy kitchen, a comforting aroma of simmering spices filling the air as she prepared a hearty dinner for her small family. The rhythmic clinking of utensils against pots and pans accompanied her gentle humming, creating a peaceful atmosphere. Nearby, seated at the wooden table, Ben was engrossed in his beloved sketchbook, his nimble fingers gracefully bringing the pages to life with every stroke of his pencil.

Suddenly, a loud crash resonated from the floor above, accompanied by an alarmed shout that shattered the tranquility of the moment. Clara's heart skipped a beat as she exchanged a worried glance with Ben, both freezing in place, their senses attuned to the commotion upstairs.

Before they could fully comprehend the situation, the kitchen door flew open, revealing Jeremiah, his face contorted with anger. His entrance was as abrupt and jarring as the noise that had preceded it, casting an ominous shadow over the room.

"What'd you think you were doin'?" Jeremiah bellowed, his voice dripping with venom. His gaze fell upon Ben, accusatory eyes narrowing, as if he had already decided who was to blame for the disturbance.

Clara, her heart pounding in her chest, managed to gather her composure.

"Jeremiah, what's the matter?" she asked, trying to mask the trepidation in her voice.

Jeremiah stormed toward them, his face flushed with indignation.

"That wretched boy of yours deliberately put a spider in my bed!" he said, spitting the words and pointing a quivering finger at Ben. "I know it was him. He's always causing trouble."

Ben looked up from his sketches, eyes wide with surprise and confusion.

"I swear, Uncle Jeremiah, I didn't put any spider in your bed!" he said, his voice trembling with innocence. "It must have escaped from my room. I would never do something like that."

Jeremiah's sneer deepened, his anger reaching a boiling point.

"You expect me to believe such nonsense? I found the vile creature crawling on my pillow. Disgusting! I took care of it, though," he said, a cruel satisfaction glimmering in his eyes as he mimicked a crushing gesture with his hand.

Ben's face fell, his youthful features marred by crestfallen disappointment. Tears welled up in his eyes, and Clara watched him fight an overwhelming sense of loss.

"But... I didn't want it to get hurt. I never meant for this to happen," he whispered, his voice cracking.

Clara's heart ached for her son, her protective instincts surging forth. She stepped between them, her voice firm but tinged with compassion.

"Jeremiah, Ben is telling the truth," she said. "I know my son. He would never intentionally harm anyone or anything. Accidents happen, and it's our responsibility to handle them with understanding, not anger."

Jeremiah's scowl remained etched upon his face, his hostility lingering like a dark cloud.

"He needs to learn his place," he hissed, his voice oozing disdain as he sneered at Ben.

Clara's resolve solidified, her eyes narrowing as she stood up to her uncle-in-law.

"No, Jeremiah. It is you who needs to learn compassion and forgiveness. I won't allow you to bully Ben or treat him unfairly," she said with determination.

Jeremiah looked at her with all the poison that had been in his every word since he burst into the kitchen.

"I told you that y'all both needed to learn your place, woman," he said. "And I'ma tell you right now, I won't tolerate a skirt talkin' to me that way. Now, you better deal with that son of yours. Or I'm gonna."

Clara instinctively stepped toward Ben, putting a protective arm around him. She couldn't believe that Jeremiah had made a direct threat to her son, especially with her right there in the room. She didn't know what his idea of dealing with Ben was. But she didn't intend to give him the chance to find out.

"I'll talk to him," she said, narrowing her eyes at him as she pulled Ben closer. "In private, if you don't mind."

Jeremiah glared at her for another second. Clara's heart raced as she realized that she and Ben would be helpless if he were to begin his tantrum again and got violent. But after another brief moment, he mumbled something under his breath and turned to leave the kitchen in the same huff in which he had entered. Just then, Roger stepped in the back door, pausing in the doorway to survey the three of them.

"What's going on, Clara?" Roger asked with wary concern as he glanced around the room, taking note of the disarray and the residual traces of a tumultuous encounter.

Before Clara could respond, Jeremiah strode across the kitchen, his face still contorted with anger.

"Roger, you won't believe what's been happening in this house," he said, the words thundering through the room. "It's turnin' into a blasted zoo."

Roger's brow furrowed, perplexed by his uncle's outburst. He looked to Clara, a silent query for an explanation, seeking to understand the cause of this sudden upheaval.

Clara took a deep breath, praying that her voice was steadier than it had been minutes ago.

"Roger, it was Ben's spider," she said, quickly recounting the events that had unfolded in his absence.

Jeremiah interrupted, his voice dripping with disdain.

"That boy planted it in my bed on purpose," he said, his fury unabated. "He's wreaking havoc in this house, I tell you."

Roger's gaze shifted from his uncle to Ben, who stood quietly beside his mother, his eyes downcast but his spirit unbroken. Something flickered within Roger's expression, a blend of contemplation and determination.

"Uncle Jeremiah, that's enough," Roger said, his voice firm yet calm. "It's just a spider. Accidents happen, especially with young ones around. Ben is a good boy, and I won't tolerate unfair accusations against him. If Ben says it was an accident, then that's all it was."

Clara's heart swelled with both surprise and relief, her admiration for her husband deepening in that moment. To have his support, to see him defend her son, was a relief. Not even two weeks prior, he hadn't even wanted Ben. Now, he was standing up for him, just like a father would.

Jeremiah's face reddened, his anger simmering beneath the surface. He muttered a few choice words under his breath before turning on his heel and storming out of the kitchen, his departure punctuated by the slam of the door.

Clara couldn't help but feel a tinge of worry lingering in the wake of Jeremiah's exit.

"Do you think this will be the end of it, Roger?" she asked fretfully.

Roger approached Clara, gently placing a hand on her shoulder, his touch a reassuring anchor.

"I can't say for certain, Clara," he said. "But I believe y'all. You let me worry about Jeremiah." He paused, removing his hand from Clara's shoulder, and kneeling down to put it on Ben's. "Are you all right, my boy?"

Ben sniffled, but he seemed to be considerably comforted by Roger's touch. He nodded, giving his stepfather a small smile.

"I am now," he said. "Thank you for believing me."

Roger gave him a warm smile, ruffling the boy's hair as he stood back up.

"Of course I believe you," he said. "I know how much you love animals. You never woulda put it somewhere that it would get hurt on purpose."

Ben nodded firmly. "I sure wouldn't. I'm sad that Uncle Jeremiah killed it."

Roger's jaw locked into a tight clench at the news. He patted Ben once more, turning his face away from the boy. Clara understood immediately that Roger was angry about his uncle killing Ben's pet. There was a moment of silence before Roger turned to Clara. His eyes blazed with anger, but his jaw had relaxed, and he offered her a weak smile.

"I'll make this right, Clara," he said. "I promise you that."

Clara nodded. She was still not convinced that Jeremiah was finished raging about the incident. But she trusted Roger, and she knew that he would do what he said.

"Thank you, Roger," she said. "Dinner'll be ready in about an hour or so. Y'all can go wash up and relax, and I'll call you when it's done."

Roger nodded, and Ben mimicked him.

"Yes, Ma," he said. "I'll wash up and then read for a little while."

Roger tipped his hat to her silently.

"I might do the same," he said as he and Ben headed out the door that led to the hallway of their home.

As the sun dipped below the horizon, casting a golden hue over the western landscape, Clara found a moment of solace in the quietude of the kitchen. Dinner preparations simmered on the stove, their savory scents filling the air, while her family got cleaned up for the meal.

She was still upset by the way Jeremiah had accused Ben of trying to upset him on purpose with the spider. She had known that Jeremiah was not an amiable man.

However, with each passing day, she became more convinced that it was much worse than she thought. She knew he was Roger's kin. But she was rapidly becoming uncomfortable being in the house alone with Jeremiah when Roger was out working.

Her thoughts were interrupted by Ben, who walked in with a very long face. He sighed heavily, looking at her with his father's gray eyes.

Sensing the need for a heart-to-heart conversation, Clara beckoned Ben to join her by the window, where the dying light painted their faces with warm hues.

"Ben," Clara said, her voice gentle yet resolute. "I want you to know that what Jeremiah said about the spider is not true. You didn't do anything wrong. Maybe I should have helped you find something sturdier to put it in so that it wouldn't escape. But I know you wouldn't do what he said you did."

Ben's troubled gaze met his mother's, uncertainty clouding his young eyes.

"But he squashed it, Ma," he said. "And then, he put it in my bed."

Clara's fingers delicately brushed against her son's cheek as she tried to swallow the sudden wave of rage that came over her. Who could be so evil as to put a child's dead pet in their bed?

"I'm sorry, honey," she said, trying to give her son a reassuring smile through her boiling temper. "Sometimes people say and do hurtful things out of anger or frustration. You didn't deserve Jeremiah's accusations, and him putting it back in your bed was wrong. But Roger and I won't let him bother you about it again."

Ben's tension was apparent as soul-weary hurt filled his eyes.

"But why did he get so angry, Ma?" he asked, clearly confused and wounded. "Why does he treat us like that? It's not even just about the spider. He's always mean to us. Especially to you. And I don't like it."

Clara took a moment to choose her words carefully, mindful of her son's tender heart, and of the fact that Jeremiah could be listening.

"Sometimes, people carry their own burdens and struggles," she said. "It can make them bitter, and they might try to hurt others to make themselves feel better. But it's important not to let their negativity define how we see ourselves. We know the truth, Ben, and we won't let their words bring us down."

A fleeting smile graced Ben's face, a spark of resilience rekindling within him.

"You're right, Ma," he said. "Uncle Jeremiah doesn't really know me or you. And I won't let his words get to me anymore. Except when he's being mean to you."

Clara smiled fondly at her son, her heart aching. He sounded so much like his father as he defended her. She embraced him, kissing him on top of his head.

"Don't you worry about me, sweetheart," she said. "He doesn't hurt my feelings one bit."

Ben pulled back, his brow furrowed. He clearly had more he wished to say. But Roger joined them just then, freshened up and ready for their evening meal. Clara squeezed Ben's hand.

"Everything all right?" Roger inquired, his voice tinged with concern.

Clara met her husband's gaze, her anger still bubbling. She told her husband what Jeremiah had done with the dead spider, and Clara watched as Roger fought strongly to control his own temper.

"I'll talk to him," he said, his voice hard and cold. "But I'll do it tomorrow, so nothing happens to spoil our dinner."

Clara nodded, comforted by the way Roger seemed to be becoming more protective of Ben. But she was also worried. What would happen when Roger confronted his uncle? Would that solve the issue, or make things worse, especially on Ben?

Roger took a deep breath, trying to calm himself. He gave Clara a smile, walking over to the table and pulling out the chair beside him.

"Come here, Ben," he said warmly. "Tell me about your recent lessons and let your mama finish up with supper."

Ben's face lit up and he left his mother's side. He plopped down in the chair beside Roger, his distress over the spider melting as he talked about the new words he had been learning. Clara smiled, trying to push aside her anger with Jeremiah. Roger was right. There was no reason why Jeremiah's attitude and behavior had to ruin their meal. What was done was done. And Clara knew it was best for Roger to take some time to calm down before confronting his uncle.

When Jeremiah reentered the kitchen a few minutes later, the tension was temporarily thick enough to resist a slice with a bayonet. The big, shaggy man sneered at everyone in the kitchen, seeming to relish the silence that his entrance induced. But a minute later, Roger turned back to Ben, giving him a brilliant smile.

"Tell you what, Ben," he said. "If you ever find another critter you wanna keep as a pet, let me help you make something to keep it more secure."

Ben grinned, his tension melting immediately.

"Thanks, Roger," he said. "I'd sure appreciate that."

Jeremiah, his countenance as stormy as the skies before a downpour, grumbled to himself as he sat at the head of the table. He brooded, falling uncharacteristically silent. Clara served the men and her son, barely resisting the urge to accidentally drop Jeremiah's hot food in his lap. He picked at his food with a disinterested air, his appetite seemingly absent.

Instead, he reached for one of the beers, which Clara hadn't seen him carrying. Her stomach churned as she sat down with her own plate. She sometimes thought he would be a nicer man if he drank less. But after what he had done that day, she was no longer so sure.

"Oh, Ben, I almost forgot," Roger said, turning his attention to the boy. "I was planning on heading to the river tomorrow to check the water levels and see what we might need to do for the upgrades. Would you like to come along?"

Ben's eyes sparkled with excitement, his youthful enthusiasm shining through.

"You bet," he said with another grin. "I'd love to see the river and help you with the work."

Roger smiled, once more showing Clara just how handsome her husband really was.

"Great," he said, tussling Ben's hair. Then, he looked up at Clara with an inquisitive glint in his eye. "Would you like to come with us, if you have some spare time tomorrow?"

Clara's heart leapt. Roger never invited her to join him to do anything. She thought about how the outing would be a good opportunity for the three of them to bond.

"I'd love to," she said. "I'm sure I can get some spare time."

Jeremiah, unable to contain his discontent, muttered under his breath, his words sharp yet barely audible.

"Slacking off again, I s'pose," he said. "Can't keep a proper home if she's gallivanting around."

Clara's breath caught in her throat, the sting of Jeremiah's words grazing her spirit. But she refused to let his negativity overshadow the prospect of a day spent with her family, embracing the beauty of their surroundings.

Roger's eyes locked with Clara's, a silent understanding passing between them. With a steady but icy tone, he addressed his uncle.

"Clara has as much right as anyone to enjoy some time outside," he said. "And she don't slack off at all. We all work hard, and it's important to find moments of respite. Besides, there ain't nothing here that won't keep for a couple hours."

Jeremiah rolled his eyes, but he went back to his meal. Clara glared at him as he wolfed down the food. For a woman who slacked off, she seemed to make meals edible enough for him. She forced herself to eat some of her own food, mainly because Ben was watching her with worried, nervous eyes. She smiled at him, reaching over, and patting her son on the arm.

She wouldn't let Jeremiah get to her. Despite his hateful rudeness, she had plenty to be grateful for. Her little family would have a lovely time the following day, working on strengthening their relationships together. And nothing Jeremiah said or did would take that away from her.

Chapter Twelve

As the sun began its ascent over the vast expanse of his ranch, Roger took a deep breath, readying himself for the day ahead. The familiar rhythm of morning chores beckoned, offering the chance to clear his mind in the midst of the turmoil that had unfolded within his family.

With a heavy heart, he stepped into the barn, the scent of hay and livestock embracing him like an old friend. Roger began his routine, feeding the horses, their gentle snorts reminding him of the innocence of his young stepson that had been tarnished by Jeremiah's vile behavior the night before.

Roger couldn't shake the image of Ben's bewildered face, his tears falling as he faced an accusation he could never have committed.

The weight of anger coursed through Roger's veins as he moved on to shoveling the manure, his muscles working mechanically while his mind grappled with the heartlessness his uncle had displayed.

How could he crush Ben's pet spider, a creature so small and insignificant in the grand scheme of things, and place its corpse in the young boy's bed?

It was an act of cruelty that shook Roger to the core. He had known that Jeremiah was a hard man ever since he moved into the ranch house. But he would have never guessed that his own flesh and blood could do something so mean to a child.

Or to Clara, he said to himself as his thoughts shifted, dwelling on the venomous words Jeremiah had spewed at his wife. The insult to her homemaking skills angered Roger deeply, for he knew the passion and dedication she poured into creating a good home for their blended family.

How dare he belittle her efforts and call her a slacker? Roger would not stand idly by while Jeremiah's toxic presence threatened the harmony that Clara was fighting so hard to build.

As he continued with the chores, mending fences and tending to the cattle, Roger tried to find solace in the simplicity of the tasks at hand. The rhythmic clanging of hammer against metal, the comforting aroma of wood shavings, grounded him amidst the chaos of emotions swirling within.

With each swing of the axe, Roger channeled his frustrations, his determination to protect Clara and Ben growing stronger. Jeremiah's actions would not define them, nor would they continue to make Ben and Clara feel unwelcomed or worthless. What Jeremiah had done was wrong. But if he could keep his wits about him, Roger felt sure he could speak with his uncle and prevent any future abuse from the haggard old man. He hoped, at least.

As the morning sun reached its zenith, casting a warm glow over the ranch, Roger wiped the sweat from his brow and surveyed the work he had accomplished. The physical exertion had served as a catharsis, clearing his mind, as he had hoped, and allowing him to focus on the steps he needed to take.

But right then, there was a more pressing matter. He had promised his new family a trip to the river that day. And he knew they were all looking forward to it. Much to his surprise, he found that he was excited, as well.

It was the first time he, Clara, and Ben would do something as a real family, and that brought him a great deal of delight. He was determined to make it the best day for his wife and stepson that he possibly could.

When he reached, the house, he was greeted at the front door by a very excited Ben.

"Roger," the boy said, throwing his arms around him and then producing a jar from a little pack he had made. "I'm so excited to go to the river. I even have this jar, in case I find something I wanna keep as a pet."

Roger chuckled, ruffling the boy's hair.

"I see that," he said. "What about your mother? Is she ready yet?"

Clara entered the living room then, smiling softly at her husband.

"I'm here," she said. "I'm ready whenever y'all are."

Roger looked at his wife, noting the slight flush in her cheeks that made the freckles across her nose and the top of her cheeks stand out. Her blue eyes shone with excitement, and her strawberry blond hair was tied back in a neat bun, with delicate wisps having fallen loose and framing her beautiful, pale face. Roger had to catch his breath, giving her a crooked smile as he opened the front door away.

"I guess we're all ready, then," he said.

Ben put his jar back in his little sack. Then, Roger led him and Clara outside. He called Ollie, who was running to greet the family almost before Roger finished saying his name. He leaned down to pet his dog, and then he and his small family turned toward to the right of the house that would take them to the river.

Ben hummed happily to himself as he skipped just ahead of Roger and Clara with Ollie beside him, the events of the previous day seemingly forgotten. Roger took a minute to appreciate the beauty of the afternoon.

The sky was as blue as Clara's eyes, and completely clear, with only pale streaks of clouds scattered sparingly. The ranch pasture slowly gave way to sycamore and black walnut trees.

When they reached the entrance of the path that would take them to the river, bluebirds and squirrels scattered, flitting and running, respectively, from the trees closest to Roger and his family to others that were a safe distance away from the humans, but close enough that the curious animals could watch the people as they tracked along the dirt path. Ben noticed, looking at them with wonder.

"Look, Ma," he said with the same enthusiasm he always used when he spoke of things that brought him joy. "Those birds are pretty."

Clara smiled lovingly at her son and nodded.

"They sure are, honey," she said.

Roger grinned at her.

"Just wait until we get to the river," he said. "There's bluebirds and redbirds and robins that hunt worms and bugs, and sit right on the edge and drink, no matter who's there."

Ben ran over, moving between Roger and his mother, looking utterly enthralled.

"Really?" he asked. "I can't wait to see them."

As they reached the riverbank, a burst of energy consumed Ben, and he dashed off toward the water's edge, Ollie bounding beside him. Roger saw Clara watching them with a smile, her heart clearly warmed by the bond that had formed between Ben and Ollie.

"It really is beautiful here," she said, turning her attention to Roger.

Roger smiled and nodded.

"Do you wanna sit and watch them play by the water here?" he asked. "Or do you wanna come with me while I assess the infrastructure that Hiram and I are gonna need to come work on?"

Clara glanced back at her son and Ollie, who were rolling around in a clearing just a few paces away from them.

"I'll come with you," she said. "I would like to explore a bit more."

Roger nodded, surprised at how happy he was that she had chosen to walk with him.

"Let's get to it, then," he said.

Roger guided Clara along the river, his hand protectively holding hers. She didn't complain, and he was glad. He told himself that he was holding her hand to keep her upright, should she slip or step in a hole. But something deep down tried to tell him there was more to it than that, evident by the way that the soft, smooth feel of her warm, pale skin made his heart skip beats.

The first structure they came to was the first of two bridges. That one was a little newer than the second bridge, which Roger had help his father build when he was a young boy. Roger had had to make minor repairs to it over the years.

However, the last time he and Hiram had worked on it together, he saw that replacing boards was no longer sufficient. The bridge before them was in better shape, though clearly affected by heavy rains and floods. It sagged in the middle of the bridge, and the ropes holding the bridge up on either side were fraying and strained.

Clara saw it, stopping to look at it with wary curiosity.

"That bridge was very well-built," she mused. "It looks a little beaten. But I bet between you, Hiram, and Ben, y'all could get it good as new in no time. The boards are largely still strong, with the exception of those that are the most waterworn. And the posts it's attached to on either side of the river might need a little varnish, but they look sturdy."

Roger looked at his wife in surprise.

"You seem to know a lot about infrastructure," he said.

Clara blushed and shrugged.

"I had to help Thomas a time or two," she said shyly. "Mostly, I went to help with Ben, in case he got bored while Thomas was trying to teach him to work on things. But I watched everything he did, and I helped out when he needed me to."

Roger nodded in approval.

"That's good to know," he said, giving her a wink. "I'll be sure to come get you if Hiram and I need your help."

Clara nodded eagerly.

"I would be happy to help," she said.

The assessment was almost exactly the same at the two dams along the river and the old watermill. The mill was a bit more rundown than the dams, which were more worn and fragile than the first bridge had been. Roger chewed his lip, deep in thought, making mental notes of the supplies they would need to fix everything, and of how long he expected it to take them.

When they reached the second bridge, Roger's heart sank. He had expected it to be in bad shape. But it was one of the last pieces of his late father that he had. It still hurt his heart to see it in such bad shape. *It was gonna need to be rebuilt sometime,* he told himself. *Eventually, the past always gets replaced.*

Clara's eyes widened with curiosity and he watched her face light up as she spoke.

"Roger, imagine what we can do here," Clara said, her voice filled with excitement as she spoke of ideas that had just come to her. "This place has so much potential, but it needs a touch of modernization and improvement."

Roger nodded, his gaze fixed on the structures in need of repair.

"I've been thinking the same," he said. "The river can provide us with not only a beautiful view, but also the means to better our lives. We can upgrade so that we can get more fresh water to collect more easily for the house and the animals, build sturdier bridges, and use better technology for the watermill."

Clara's eyes sparkled with admiration for her husband's vision.

"That would be wonderful," she said. "I believe that would be one of the best things you could do for the ranch."

Roger nodded, his cheeks heating at her praise. He realized that when she was passionate about something, her whole face lit up, and she looked at least five years younger. His heart skipped, and he had to force himself to tear his eyes away.

In the distance, Ben's laughter carried on the wind as he and Ollie played behind them along the riverbank. Roger was thrilled that the child was enjoying himself so much. He had wanted to help Ben forget about his bitter uncle, and it seemed the mission had been a success.

Just as Roger was thinking of turning back to collect Ben and head back to the ranch, a gentle breeze rustled through a nearby sycamore tree, causing its sturdy branches to sway proudly. Roger bit his lip, knowing full well what was under that tree. In the same moment he had the thought, Clara stopped, looking at the ground beneath the tree. His heart sank as he followed Clara's gaze to a pair of crosses. Memories of the past flooded his mind, unearthing emotions he had buried deep within.

"What are those?" Clara asked, looking up at him curiously.

He took a deep breath, his voice slightly trembled as he spoke.

"Clara," he began, his words filled with a mixture of sadness and longing. "Those crosses... they are a memorial for my late wife and child."

Clara's eyes softened, her hand reaching out to touch Roger's arm gently.

"Oh, Roger," she whispered, her voice a comforting melody. "Do you want to talk about it, or tell me about them?"

Roger opened his mouth to firmly say no. But he realized that he didn't mind. In fact, since Clara had shared her trauma with him, he felt it was about time that he told a little more about himself. And Willa had been such a wonderful wife and woman, her memory deserved to be shared, especially with a woman who was turning out to be pretty incredible herself.

Roger's gaze turned distant as he recalled the bittersweet memories.

"My wife, Willa, was a kind and gentle woman," he said. "She had a smile that could brighten the darkest of days. And our child... I never even knew what we were having. The baby didn't make it into the world before Willa died." He paused, his mind traveling back to the painful day they were ripped away from him. "It was a tragedy that shattered my world."

Clara looked at him with surprise, and plenty of empathy. She released his hand to put hers on his back, giving him a sympathetic look.

"Are they buried there?" she asked softly.

Roger shook his head.

"No," he said. "They died in Oklahoma, where we lived until she died. Their real graves are there. I just made these little memorial crosses for them here, behind the ranch. They're made from honey locust wood, because that was Willa's favorite tree. She loved the sweet-smelling flowers that grows on them. I thought I owed her at least that much. And I couldn't bear the thought of completely leaving them behind. I wanted them with me, even if only in spirit."

Clara's eyes filled with tears as she listened to his story. The depth of his loss was immeasurable, and he realized then that she herself knew a great deal of the strength it took for him to carry such a heavy burden.

"Thank you for sharing that with me, Roger," she murmured, her voice filled with tenderness. "I can't begin to imagine the pain you've endured."

Roger's eyes met Clara's, gratitude and vulnerability shining through.

"It means everything to me that you understand, Clara," he said. "I mean, I'm not happy that you suffered losing a spouse, too. But it helps the hurt in my heart to know that I have someone in my life who really knows how I feel."

Clara nodded, her eyes still misting with unshed tears. She reached out and took Roger's hand again, intertwining their fingers.

"I do," she said, her own emotion thick in her voice. "And I'm here to help you through it."

Roger nodded, reaching out with his free hand to tuck a long strand of strawberry hair behind her ear.

"Same goes for you, honey," he said quietly.

As they stood together, Roger looked over the crosses that represented the lives of the two most important people in his life. He glanced over at Clara, his heart filling with a new appreciation and affection for her.

He looked in the other direction and, even though they were too far away to see Ben, he could hear Ollie's excited barks echoing off the riverbank. Willa and their unborn child had been his most cherished people. But now, Roger was beginning to see that he might have room in his heart for two more people.

Chapter Thirteen

Clara stood on the riverbank, her gaze fixed on the gentle flow of water. The setting sun cast a warm glow over the landscape, painting everything in shades of gold. She couldn't help but feel a tinge of sadness as she thought about her late husband, Thomas. Their love had been a storybook romance, but fate had taken him away too soon.

Beside her stood Roger with his hand still in hers. It was still strange to think of him as her husband. They had met under unexpected circumstances, and they were now bonding through their shared losses.

Clara had lost her beloved Thomas, and Roger had experienced the heart-wrenching pain of losing both his wife and his child. She glanced at Roger, his strong features etched with a mixture of sadness and acceptance. She couldn't help but feel fortunate, even amidst her own sorrow. While she had lost Thomas, she still had Ben, her young son, by her side. Roger, on the other hand, had been left completely alone in the world.

Her heart ached for him, and without thinking, she reached out and gently placed her hand on his arm. Roger turned to look at her, surprise mingling with gratitude in his eyes. For a moment, they shared a silent understanding, a connection that went beyond words. For a moment, something happened to Clara that she could have never anticipated. She found herself getting lost deep into Roger's blue eyes. Her heart raced, and she couldn't help wondering what it would be like to kiss him.

But just as quickly as the moment had appeared, it was interrupted by the exuberant voice of Ben. He had wandered off and now excitedly rushed toward them, his small hands cupping a jar filled with water. Inside, there swam a whole cluster of tadpoles, wriggling and darting around.

"Ma!" he shouted excitedly as he and Ollie ran up to where Roger and Clara stood. "Look what I found."

Clara couldn't help but smile at her son's enthusiasm. She let go of Roger's arm and turned her attention to Ben, marveling at the small wonders he had discovered. The tadpoles seemed insignificant in the grand scheme of things, but they represented the beauty of life's simple joys.

"That's impressive, sweetheart," she said. "I'm not sure if you can keep them, though. We would need a pond much closer to the house than this river is. It wouldn't be long before they outgrew that jar."

Ben nodded, not looking at all fazed. In fact, he was still smiling sweetly at his mother, looking from her to the tadpoles and back again.

"I know," he said. "I wouldn't try to keep them. I just wanted to watch them for a little while. I'll put them back when we get ready to leave here."

Clara reached out and stroked her son's hair. Every time she thought she couldn't be prouder of him, he went and proved her wrong.

"Good boy," she said.

Roger joined them, leaving his post on the riverbank in front of the crosses. He put his hands on his knees, peering into the jar.

"That was a good job, collecting those little guys without hurting them," he said, sounding truly awed at the boy's gentle hands. "Did you find a grown frog? We might be able to take him or her if you found one."

Ben shook his head, looking at Roger with great pride.

"No, I didn't see a grown one," he said. "Besides, I don't wanna take their mom or dad away from them."

Clara's heart squeezed. Ben never ceased to amaze her with how kind and considerate he was. It was hard to believe that a man the likes of Jeremiah could ever think anything bad about such a sweet child.

"That's very noble of you, sweetheart," she said.

Ben nodded, his grin widening at his mother's praise.

"Okay, Ollie," he said, turning on his heel. "Let's get ready to put these little guys back."

Ollie barked in happy agreement, and the foursome began slowly making their way back up the riverbank the way they came from.

As they watched Ben's excitement unfold, Clara couldn't help but steal a glance at Roger. Their hands brushed against each other for a brief moment, and Clara hoped more than anything that their shared understanding would continue to grow, just like the tadpoles in Ben's jar.

At last, the small family made their way back home. The sun was descending in the sky, casting a warm glow over the countryside. The air carried the scent of wildflowers and the promise of an idyllic evening. For the first time since Thomas's death, Clara was no longer overwhelmed with her sadness. In fact, she was finally starting to see a bright light in the future of her little blended family.

As they approached the homestead, Ben and Ollie raced ahead, their laughter and barks echoing in the distance. Clara couldn't help but smile at the sight of her son and their furry companion playing together. The carefree joy they shared was a balm to her soul.

"Looks like those two are having the time of their lives," Clara remarked, her voice filled with affectionate amusement. "They're like two peas in a pod."

Roger's eyes twinkled with fondness as he glanced at Ben and Ollie.

"Indeed, they've become fast friends," he said. "Ollie seems to have taken more of a liking to your son than he did to me. And who can blame him? Ben's quite the charmer."

Clara's heart swelled with warmth, grateful for the easy camaraderie that had developed between the two of them. She reveled in the simplicity of the moment, engaging in pleasant small talk with Roger as they walked alongside each other. They were no longer holding hands, but the memory of Roger's fingers around hers would linger forever. They spoke of the beautiful day and the promising future that awaited them.

Amidst their conversation, Clara noticed Roger stealing glances in her direction. She could feel his gaze upon her, a mix of curiosity and fondness, similar to that which she was beginning to feel. It stirred something within her, a blossoming connection that went beyond mere companionship. It was as if the barriers that had guarded her heart were slowly crumbling down, making room for a new chapter in her life.

However, as they reached the homestead, the tranquility was shattered by the sight that awaited them. Smoke billowed from the kitchen chimney, carrying with it the acrid scent of burnt wood. Panic surged through Clara's veins as she realized something was terribly wrong.

In the same instant, she realized that Ben and Ollie were no longer anywhere in sight. She glanced back at Roger, who looked as worried as she felt. She ran ahead of her husband, rushing toward the smoke that was wafting from the back of the house. She ran in blindly, having little regard for the danger that might be waiting. Nothing mattered except making sure that Ben and Ollie weren't in trouble.

As Clara entered the kitchen, her heart sank. The fire had ravaged the room, leaving behind a charred mess and a sense of devastation. Black smoke was streaming from the oven, and flames had ruined the wall behind it, as well as the wall beneath and around the window above the sink. The cabinets had also caught fire, and the flames had practically devoured them.

Her eyes searched for any signs of danger, relief flooding her when she realized that no one besides her and Roger, who came in right on her heels, was in the kitchen. She also noted that the fire itself seemed to have been extinguished before they arrived, which meant there was no rush to put out any more flames. However, the damage was extensive, and the whole room would require significant repairs.

Roger's face contorted with a mix of frustration and concern. He stepped forward, surveying the damage with a heavy sigh.

"We'll probably need to rebuild the whole room," he stated firmly, frustration lacing his words. "But what happened in here?"

Clara shook her head as she stood amidst the charred remnants of what was once their kitchen, her heart heavy with a mix of regret and frustration. The fire had taken a toll on their home, leaving behind not only physical damage but also a lingering sense of discord.

Roger paced back and forth, his brow furrowed.

"How could this have happened, Clara?" he asked again.

Clara looked at her husband, just as baffled as he was.

"I don't know, Roger," she said. "I have no idea what could have happened. I was with you all afternoon."

Roger bit his lip, glancing around at the damage. Clara was startled by a slam against the back door, and she looked up to find Ben teetering in the doorway, carrying a bucket of water that was clearly way too heavy for him.

"Is it still burning?" he asked, panting.

Even though Clara had seen that he had not been in danger of being consumed by a still burning fire, she was still relieved to lay eyes on her son's face. She hurried over, taking the bucket of water from him and setting it in the sink.

"No, sweetheart," she said. "Go back outside. There's still too much smoke in here, and I don't want you breathing it in."

Ben exhaled heavily, nodding.

"Yes, Ma," he said. "I just wanted to make sure the danger was over."

Clara nodded. But before she could answer, a soot-covered Jeremiah came in the other door to the kitchen, his eyes narrowed into tiny slits.

"No thanks to you, boy," he growled. "And no thanks to your mama, neither."

Clara's mouth fell open, and she stared at her uncle-in-law, stupefied.

"What?" she asked weakly.

Jeremiah sneered at her, moving so close that he was almost directly in her face. Roger stepped between them just in time to make Jeremiah move back a couple paces.

"You heard me, woman," he said. "This is your fault. Goin' off and leavin' a pot on a hot stove." He paused, glaring at Roger. "I told ya you didn't need to let her slack off. And now, look."

Roger looked at Clara in disbelief and shame. Clara's heart sank as she realized that he believed what Jeremiah was saying.

"Clara, how could you do such a thing?" he asked, sounding wounded. "Leaving a pot on the stove unattended... it's dangerous."

Clara's eyes narrowed as she defended herself.

"I didn't leave a pot on the stove, Roger," she said. "I haven't cooked anything since breakfast. And we would have known if there was still a hot pot on the stove when we left to go to the river."

The words hung heavily in the air, fueling the embers of an argument waiting to ignite. Even Jeremiah fell briefly silent as he considered the point she had just made. Clara and Roger locked eyes, the tension palpable between them. It seemed that the remnants of the fire had cast shadows on their once-blossoming relationship.

Jeremiah snorted. "Well, ain't no one else comes in here and cooks. That's a woman's job. Which means that when something like this happens, it's the woman's fault."

Clara whirled around to face her accuser, prepared to give him a piece of her mind. She and her little family had had such a lovely day, and Jeremiah was destroying the last bit of lingering joy they had shared.

But before the sparks could fly, Roger intervened, his voice firm but measured.

"Enough," he said. "Blaming each other won't solve anything. What matters now is that we find a way to move forward and rebuild."

His words echoed through the room, urging them to set aside their grievances and focus on the task at hand. Clara felt a pang of guilt for the rising heat of their disagreement. But there was no way she could let Jeremiah blame her for something she knew she hadn't done. He seemed bent on finding things to blame on her and Ben. And she intended to put a stop to it right then.

Taking a deep breath, Clara turned her attention to the surroundings, searching for answers within the ashes. However, her gaze shifted involuntarily toward Jeremiah, who brushed against her rudely as he walked past her to the far fringes of the room. She caught a whiff of alcohol on his breath, a familiar scent that had become all too common.

Her thoughts raced, grappling with a cocktail of emotions— disgust with Jeremiah and frustration at the accusations, and a growing determination to prove her innocence. But in that moment, Clara knew that the most important thing was making plans to rebuild the kitchen.

As Clara turned to face Roger once more, she met his gaze with a mix of resolve and vulnerability. She wanted to protest Jeremiah's accusations again.

But Roger's expression was firm, and she knew that continuing to press the issue right then would only anger him. She gave Jeremiah a pointed look, however, one which he pretended to not see. Whatever it took, she would get to the bottom of what really happened in the kitchen, and show Jeremiah that it wasn't her fault, after all.

Chapter Fourteen

Roger stood in the center of the kitchen, his disappointment mingling with a tinge of frustration. The room looked like a war zone, with cracked tiles, charred countertops, and a lingering smell of burnt wood. How could Clara have let this happen? She had to know that leaving unattended cooking food or boiling water would create problems. And now, it would take a considerable amount of money and time to restore the kitchen to its former state.

As he surveyed the damage, Roger let out a sigh. He clenched his fists, trying to contain his frustration. This was not how he envisioned the start of their new life together. Was Clara really capable of being so careless? He found it hard to believe that she would leave a boiling pot unattended, but the evidence before him was undeniable. Perhaps he didn't know her as well as he thought he did.

He looked at his wife with weary eyes.

"Is there any way you can fix something tonight for any kind of supper?" he asked.

Clara wrung her hands tightly in front of her, but she nodded.

"I think there's some chopped beef in the ice box," she said. "I can make sandwiches."

Roger nodded, running a hand through his graying hair.

"Do that, then," he said. "I'll figure something else out until we can get this fixed. Uncle Jeremiah will go into town tomorrow and get supplies to start rebuilding, but I expect that to take weeks."

Clara nodded. She looked like she wanted to say something else. But Roger was exhausted and still upset with her. He just gave her a curt nod and turned on his heel, leaving the kitchen.

He could have sworn that he heard Jeremiah mutter something else under his breath about Clara. But when he glanced over his shoulder, Jeremiah was drinking from his flask. Roger shook his head, turning down the hallway and heading for the stairs. He would have to give Clara a proper talking to about what she had done. But he saw no sense in doing it in front of Jeremiah.

***

The next day, Roger and his uncle climbed into the wagon and rode into town. Their destination was the local general store, the only place where they could find the supplies they needed to repair the kitchen. The old man grumbled under his breath, a constant commentary on Clara's supposed shortcomings.

"I tell ya, Roger, that girl of yours is nothing but trouble," Jeremiah muttered, his voice filled with disapproval. "Leavin' a pot on the stove like that. She'll be the ruin of this homestead, mark my words."

Roger's brows furrowed, a mixture of frustration and defensiveness rising within him. He couldn't fathom why his uncle seemed so fixated on finding fault with Clara. True, she had made a mistake, but it didn't mean she was incapable of taking care of their home.

"Now, Jeremiah, let's not be too hasty in passing judgment," Roger replied, his tone measured. "We all make mistakes, and Clara is still adjusting to her new responsibilities. She'll learn, given time."

Jeremiah scoffed, his weathered face wrinkling with disapproval. "Learn? The girl needs more than just time. She needs someone to show her how things are done. I've seen it all before, Roger. These young women think they can run a household without a clue. Just you wait and see."

Roger's patience wavered, but he knew arguing with his uncle wouldn't achieve anything. Instead, he focused on the task at hand, steering the conversation away from Clara's perceived shortcomings. As they reached the general store, Roger couldn't help but wonder if there was more to his uncle's grumbling than met the eye. Was there some unresolved issue between them, or was it merely the stubbornness of old age?

Amidst the aisles filled with tools and supplies, Roger meticulously selected the materials they needed to repair the kitchen. Hammer in hand, he contemplated the task ahead, knowing that it would take considerable effort to undo the damage caused by a single careless mistake.

And in that moment, he silently vowed to himself that he would not let this setback make things any worse. Roger would do whatever it took to get his home back in order, no matter how unhappy the men were around each other. Besides, surely, they could set aside differences to get such an important thing accomplished, couldn't they?

Upon their arrival back at the ranch, Roger wasted no time in gathering Hiram, his head ranch hand, to assist with the construction. When the two men rejoined Jeremiah in the kitchen, Roger examined the damage, now that the charred wood was no longer hot, gently pressing places with his fingertips.

He was relieved to find that, apart from burned beams and boards, the skeleton of the room seemed to be mostly intact.

He stepped away, facing the other two men, who were standing as far as they could from each other.

"Hiram, measure to make sure the beam wood is the right size," he said. "Uncle Jeremiah, I need you to do the same with the boards. If there are any discrepancies, I will trim and fix them. Then, we will work to demolish the ruined parts one section at a time, on one wall at a time. We will see where we need to go from there."

Hiram nodded, tipping his hat. Jeremiah grunted, looking like he resented the project. Roger ignored him, however. He spread out the tools, apart from the ones the other two men needed right then, on the burned table, setting them on display for the three of them. Then, he surveyed the room once more, trying to figure out the fastest way to make a semi-sturdy structure that would be serviceable until they could properly finish the repairs.

As the men toiled away, a heavy silence hung in the air, punctuated only by the occasional clatter of tools or the muffled sound of muttered words. Roger could feel the tension simmering between his uncle and Hiram, their animosity barely concealed. He wished they could set aside their differences for the sake of this shared endeavor, but he knew it was easier said than done.

Jeremiah grumbled under his breath, shooting Hiram a sharp glare as they argued over the placement of a beam. Roger's heart sank, the strain between the two men becoming a stark reminder of the fractures within their makeshift family. He had hoped that this project would bring them together, but it seemed that some rifts ran too deep to be easily mended.

Finally, Jeremiah slammed down his measuring tape. He glowered at Hiram, breathing heavily.

"You got somethin' to say to me?" he asked.

Hiram sneered at him.

"Might, if you could understand it," he hissed back.

Jeremiah, his eyes bloodshot and voice laced with a bitter edge, took a swig from his flask before pointing an accusing finger at Hiram.

"You've always had a bone to pick with me," he said. "Never respected me, have you? Always questioning my judgment."

Hiram, his stance firm and unyielding, clenched his fists.

"Jeremiah, you've had one too many drinks," he said. "Again. Don't you dare try to pin your mistakes on me. I've been loyal to this ranch longer than you can remember."

Roger stepped forward, his voice laden with authority, a desperate attempt to quell the rising storm.

"Enough, both of you," he said. "We have work to do. We need to focus on rebuilding, not tearing each other apart."

Neither man acted as though they had heard him. They moved closer to one another, Jeremiah teetering slightly as he raised his empty fist in the air.

"I don't care how long you been here," he said. "This place is rightfully mine. Y'all ain't runnin' it worth a hog's hair. And you got no right treatin' me like I'm manure on your boot. Now, spit out your problem with me or get off it."

Hiram snarled at him.

"And you could do so much better?" he asked. "You ain't gonna find ranch supplies or repaired fences at the bottom of that flask of yours. And you treat everyone like they owe you somethin'. You don't even show Roger any respect."

Roger shook his head, not pointing out that his friend was currently disrespecting him, as well. His hands tightened around the handle of his hammer, the metal cool against his palm. With a sudden burst of determination, Roger raised his voice, cutting through the chaos.

"That's it," he said. "I won't stand for this bickering any longer. If you two can't put your differences aside and work together, then I'll find someone else who can."

The threat hung heavy in the air, the weight of it palpable. For a moment, silence reigned, broken only by the sounds of their ragged breaths, the echoes of their heated words lingering.

Hiram broke the silence first, removing his hat and hanging his head in embarrassment.

"Sorry, Roger," he said. "I won't say nothin' else. I promise."

Jeremiah snickered, giving Hiram a look of pure venom.

"Yeah, right," he said. "You're too stupid to fix any of this right, and you have less respect for Roger than I do."

Hiram's face turned red, and Roger was sure a fight would commence. But Hiram just sniffed, turning around and going back to his task. When Jeremiah realized that he wouldn't get the fight he was expecting, he stormed to the other side of the kitchen and went back to work. Roger sighed again. Would they even manage to get through the day, let alone the next few weeks working together?

Roger shook all his thoughts away, especially those pertaining to Clara. The work would help him not think about how hard it was to believe that the woman he was growing rather close to could be so careless as to start a fire. Nor could he take the time to wonder if maybe Jeremiah was wrong about what started the fire. The job at hand was more important. He would have to figure everything else out later.

The men worked for the rest of the day. To Roger's relief, the other two men did everything they could to stay away from, and ignore, each other. As the moon began to rise, casting a pale glow over the ranch, the makeshift structure finally stood tall and sturdy. It was far from perfect, but it would serve its purpose until they could fully restore the kitchen. Roger wiped the sweat from his brow, feeling a mix of exhaustion and pride.

"We did it," he murmured, his voice filled with a quiet triumph. "Tomorrow, we'll begin the repairs on the kitchen itself. We'll make it even better than before."

Jeremiah grunted, a reluctant nod indicating his approval. Hiram simply nodded, his gaze avoiding eye contact with Jeremiah. Roger knew that the tension between the two men wouldn't magically disappear, but for now, they had set it aside in the name of progress.

As they dispersed, ready to rest their weary bodies, Roger couldn't help but hope that this shared effort would be the catalyst for a deeper understanding and eventual reconciliation. However, with the way Jeremiah acted, especially around Clara and Ben, Roger thought he might be expecting a little too much.

As Roger sat outside on the porch, lost in his thoughts, Clara emerged from the shadows, her expression a mix of concern and determination. Her steps were hesitant, her voice gentle as she approached him.

"Roger," she said softly, "I need to talk to you about something important. It's about the fire in the kitchen."

Roger turned his attention toward his wife, his gaze filled with curiosity. He couldn't help but wonder what she had to say, her words stirring a mix of apprehension and anticipation within him.

Clara took a deep breath, her eyes meeting his with a sincerity that struck him to the core.

"I didn't leave a pot on the stove, Roger. I swear it," she said. "I wouldn't be so careless."

Puzzlement etched across his face, Roger furrowed his brow as he tried to make sense of the situation.

"If it wasn't you, then how did the fire start?" he asked. "It doesn't make sense, Clara."

Clara's eyes flickered with a mixture of frustration and concern.

"I don't know, Roger, but something doesn't add up," she said. "I was with you all afternoon. If I had left a pot on the stove, the whole house would have gone up in the time we were out. I think we should consider other possibilities. Maybe someone else was involved, or perhaps it was an accident unrelated to me."

Roger's thoughts churned, his mind racing through the various scenarios. He knew that Clara's words held weight, and he couldn't dismiss the idea that there might be more to the story. The lingering question of how the fire ignited gnawed at him, and he knew he needed answers.

"You're right," he said. "I still don't know who else could have done it. Jeremiah is right, he doesn't cook. And Hiram was out on the ranch all day, covering for me while we checked out the bridges and stuff. Could Ben have lit the stove or something before we left and forgot?"

Clara's jaw twitched, and Roger instantly regretted his words. Even he knew how pathetic it sounded. But someone had to have left something on to burn. The stove didn't just light itself on fire.

"No," she said firmly. "But what if Jeremiah missed something because he drinks so much?"

With a heavy sigh, Roger shrugged.

"He… he drinks more than is good for him," he admitted. "I know that for sure."

Clara's brows furrowed in concern, her eyes filled with a mix of empathy and understanding. "I've noticed," she said. "Should you intervene? At the very least, it's bad for him. And if it's causing him to miss important things or forget about something, it's a real problem."

Roger nodded, grateful for Clara's understanding. "You're right. But it's not really my place to step in and try to stop him. Especially since he and I have only known each other for a few months."

Clara blinked, clearly surprised. He realized he had never told her was how Jeremiah came to be at the ranch.

"I only met Jeremiah after I took over this ranch a few months ago," he explained. "I didn't even know that my father had a brother when I was a kid. He looks like a bigger, harder version of my pa, though, so it's obvious that we're kin. I took him in, thinking it would be nice to have some family, after everything I lost. I didn't know he was a drunk, though. I might have reconsidered if I had."

Clara's frowned, looking thoughtful. Roger was starting to feel guilty. Everything Clara said made more sense than the idea that she had left something on the stove. But he still couldn't figure out what might have happened that Jeremiah didn't know about.

"Why don't you talk to Hiram about it?" she asked at last. "He's been with the ranch for years, and he probably knows your uncle better than anyone. Hiram might have insights or advice on how to handle the situation."

Roger's lips curled into a small smile, appreciating Clara's wisdom.

"Again, you're right, as always. Hiram has been a steady presence in my life, and I trust him implicitly. I'll seek his guidance, and I'll see if we can find a way to help Jeremiah."

Chapter Fifteen

As they sat together, Clara felt a renewed sense of determination. She wouldn't let Jeremiah's deceit poison the small bit of happiness that she and her family were finally starting to find. She knew it likely wasn't wise.

But she thought that, if she approached Jeremiah with kindness and understanding, he might be able to tell Clara that he was just mistaken. As horrible as Jeremiah was, she wanted to believe that he hadn't just told a blatant lie. Even though the other strange happenings niggled at her mind, she vowed to not think the worst of the man.

Roger turned to Clara, his eyes filled with understanding and a touch of regret.

"Clara, I want to apologize for ever doubting you," he said. "I know now that you would never leave something on the stove that could harm us or our home."

Clara's heart swelled with a mixture of relief and affection. She took Roger's hand in hers, intertwining their fingers as she looked into his sincere eyes.

"Roger, I'm grateful that you believe me now," she said. "It hurt deeply when you doubted my intentions, but I understand why. The story that Jeremiah told you was convincing, and it took time to disprove it. I am sure that he didn't mean to lie, though. I believe he is simply mistaken."

To her surprise, however, her husband shook his head.

"I'm not sure," he said. "I still can't make sense of it all. I can't shake the feeling that Jeremiah is purposely trying to blame other people for things for some reason. I just haven't figured out why."

Clara nodded, feeling another wave of relief. She wasn't the only one who thought that there was more to Jeremiah's story than a simple misunderstanding. But what could have happened that he wanted to hide?

Clara shook her head. Roger had had a long day, and she didn't want to make his night longer by continuing to talk about Jeremiah and his tall tales.

"So, how much longer do you think it will take to fix the rest of it?" she asked, changing the subject.

Roger shrugged again.

"Hard to say yet," he said. "Most of the bones of the kitchen are still good. Means it's not a total loss. But we gotta work on it while still doing all the regular chores. So, there's really no telling. No less than a month, that much I do know."

Clara sighed.

"I'm sorry this has happened," she said, looking at her husband sadly. "I hope you can get it fixed with as little trouble as possible."

Roger looked at her with tired eyes.

"Thank you, Clara," he said with an exhausted smile.

Clara rose, smiling sweetly at Roger.

"Do you want a sandwich or something?" she asked.

Roger shook his head slowly.

"No, thank you," he said. "Too tired to eat. I think I'm just gonna sit out here a little while longer and have another drink or two. I'll be up sooner or later, though."

Clara nodded, smiling once more.

"All right," she said. "But holler for me if you change your mind."

Roger gave her an appreciative look, but he only tipped his hat that time. Clara left him in peace, going upstairs and straight to their room. She peeked into Ben's room on the way, finding him already asleep. She felt bad that things had been so chaotic the past few days. She hoped it wouldn't have any long-term effects on her son.

She changed into her nightgown, then sat down on her side of the bed. She massaged her temples, behind which a firm headache was building. She understood why Roger had believed his uncle at first. Truthfully, the entire night before, she had tossed and turned, questioning if there was a chance that Jeremiah could be right.

The more she tried to recall everything she did before she went to the river with Roger and Ben, the muddier the memories got. She knew that was silly, however. And now, Roger knew it, too. She was grateful that he believed her. But that meant there was something far worse going on. And neither she nor Roger could figure out what it was.

***

The early morning sunlight streamed through the kitchen windows, casting a warm glow over Clara as she bustled about, preparing a hearty breakfast. She moved with grace and purpose, her apron tied securely around her waist. The scent of freshly brewed coffee mingled with the aroma of sizzling bacon, filling the room with a tantalizing allure and covering the fading stench of the smoke.

The men had done an impressive amount of work in the short time since the fire. The walls were almost completely rebuilt, and Roger had started to paint the two parts that were finished. The counters had been sanded and primed for a layer of varnish. And Hiram had even replaced the table from wood Roger had bought to cut up and use to repair the fence.

Just as Clara reached for a spatula to flip the pancakes, she heard the creak of footsteps on the staircase. She turned her head, expecting to see Ben, but her breath caught in her throat as Roger descended the stairs, his bare torso on full display.

Her heart skipped a beat, and Clara's eyes widened as her gaze traced the lines of Roger's sculpted abs. She couldn't help but be captivated by the way the sunlight played across his tanned skin, highlighting his well-defined muscles. A faint blush crept onto her cheeks, the heat of her embarrassment competing with the warmth of the kitchen.

Roger, seemingly unaware of Clara's flustered state, approached the table with a casual air. His tousled hair, still damp from a recent wash, added to his rugged charm. His eyes met Clara's, a puzzled glimmer flashing within them as he took note of her flushed cheeks.

Clara averted her gaze, her hands trembling slightly as she attempted to regain her composure. She felt a mixture of exhilaration and shyness, unsure of how to react to the sudden surge of desire that coursed through her veins.

Clearing her throat, Clara busied herself with flipping the pancakes, grateful for the excuse to avert her eyes. She could sense Roger's presence behind her, his warmth permeating the air, and it took every ounce of self-control to focus on the task at hand.

"Good morning, Roger," she said, her voice cracking.

Roger was quiet for a moment, and Clara dared a glance over her shoulder. He was opening some of the cabinets, which made her a bit puzzled. Why was he in the kitchen shirtless, rummaging through cabinets when she was cooking?

"Good morning, Clara," Roger greeted, his voice carrying a hint of confusion. "Have you seen any of my shirts?"

Clara glanced back at Roger, her eyes widening in surprise. "Your shirts? No, I haven't seen them. They should be in the closet, right?"

Roger shook his head, disappointment crossing his face.

"I checked the closet and they're not there," he said. "The dresser, too. It's like they've vanished into thin air. I can't fathom what happened to them. I was hoping you had them all in the wash or something."

Clara's brow furrowed as she contemplated the strange turn of events. How could a set of shirts simply disappear? It seemed perplexing, almost as if some mischievous spirit had meddled with their belongings. Determined to find a solution, Clara composed herself and met Roger's gaze.

"Well, we'll find a way to sort it out," Clara said, even though she didn't have the first clue how. She would go look for his shirts when she was finished making breakfast. But if Roger said they weren't in the closet or dresser, she knew they wouldn't be there. But how could that possibly have happened?

Roger let out a sigh.

"I sure hope so," he said, utterly mystified. "I will never know how six shirts could have just gotten up and walked away."

Clara bit her lip, chewing thoughtfully. She couldn't understand how it was possible, either. But clearly, that was the case.

Clara couldn't help but sympathize with Roger's frustration. It was indeed a peculiar occurrence, and the absence of his shirts only added to the mystery. She watched as Roger made his way back up the stairs, his steps carrying a mix of confusion and mild exasperation.

As Clara continued to prepare breakfast, her mind churned with questions. What could have happened to Roger's shirts? Was it a simple case of misplacement, or was there something more sinister at play? Her thoughts raced, forming theories and speculations as she tried to unravel the enigma.

Roger returned a few minutes later, wearing one of his uncle's shirts. The fabric hung slightly loose on his frame, accentuating his broad shoulders. He walked over to Clara, a faint smile tugging at the corners of his lips.

"I borrowed one of Jeremiah's shirts," he said. "I appreciate your support. It's just so strange that my own shirts went missing like that."

Clara nodded, her eyes filled with determination.

"I'll keep an eye out for them, Roger," she said. "We won't let this mystery dampen our spirits. Perhaps there's a logical explanation, one that will soon reveal itself."

Roger nodded, but he looked as doubtful as she felt deep down. He sat down, his face belying the puzzled racing his mind was doing. Clara couldn't blame him. No one had their clothes disappear that way. And with the rest of the unexplained events that had happened lately, Clara couldn't convince herself that it was a coincidence.

She and Roger at breakfast in silence, both of them clearly thinking on the issue with the shirts. She decided that she would go double check the closet and dresser, and then she would ask Ben if he had borrowed them to play dress up, like he once did with some of Thomas's old shirts. She was sure he would never do it without asking. But she had to rule out every possibility.

Ben entered the kitchen just as Roger was leaving. Roger tussled the boys hair, giving him a tired smile. Ben smiled warmly up at him, nothing about his expression betraying that he would know anything about missing clothes.

"Morning, Roger," Ben said brightly. "Have a good day."

Roger smiled fondly at him, tipping his black Stetson.

"Thank you, Ben," he said. "You, too."

Ben grinned, joining his mother at the table. Clara rose, putting away her plate and making one for her son. She gathered her courage, trying to be sure she worded her question carefully. She would never want Ben to think she would accuse him of something, like Jeremiah would.

"Thanks, Ma," Ben said, greedily digging into his pancakes.

Clara patted him on the head, sitting down slowly beside him. She glanced around at the kitchen, which was still very blackened. But the work the men had been doing was evident, and it already looked considerably better.

Clara took a breath, putting on her best, sweet, motherly smile.

"Poor Roger came downstairs without a shirt this morning," she said, hating herself for blushing again at the thought. "He seems to have misplaced all his shirts."

Ben lifted his head, his entire expression the epitome of confusion and curiosity.

"How'd he do that?" he asked.

Clara searched her son's face, looking for any indication that he might know what happened to the shirts. But there was none. The boy looked genuinely baffled, not even amused at the notion that someone could lose half their clothes.

"I'm not sure, honey," she said. "But if you see them, please, come and let me know. I'm sure they simply got misplaced. But he's gonna need them for work."

Ben grinned again, nodding early.

"Sure thing, Ma," he said. "I'd do anything to help you and Roger."

Clara's heart ached. There was no way her Ben had taken the shirts. And she felt bad for even thinking he did. She rose from the table once more, rubbing her son's shoulders.

"I'm gonna go look upstairs for them again," she said. "After you finish your breakfast, you can go play outside. We won't pick up your lessons again until they finish with the kitchen."

Ben nodded.

"Thanks, Ma," he said through a mouthful of pancakes.

Clara giggled as she headed back up the stairs. With determination in her heart, she set out to uncover the truth. She made her way to the bedroom, the wooden floor creaking softly beneath her feet.

A quick glance told her that the shirts were not, in fact, in the dresser or closet. She peeked in the other three rooms upstairs, but no luck. And to be sure that she hadn't been wrong about the wash, she rummaged through every piece of laundry that she had done the past couple days, and the clothes she intended to wash later that week.

There was no sign of Roger's shirts. She was beginning to go from baffled to concerned. It was not possible for clothing to just disappear like that. So, where were they?

Later that day, while dinner was simmering, Clara carried a basket full of fresh laundry back upstairs. She put away some clothes in Ben's dresser, scolding herself when she peeked inside, checking for Roger's shirts. Of course, they weren't there, just as she knew they wouldn't be.

Then, she took the basket and put it on the bed of what was now Roger's and her room, now that she and Roger were getting more comfortable with one another. Or they had been, at least, until the fire incident. She hoped they wouldn't go back to the cool distance that had existed between them before their walk along the stream.

She pulled out a pair of jeans belonging to Roger, and something fell out of the pocket and hit the floor with a loud clink. *A coin,* she thought frantically. *I can't let him lose money, too.* Kneeling down, she reached under the edge of the bed, her fingers grazing against nothing but wood at first. There was no sign of the coin, so she reached further. She nearly jumped out of her skin when she touched fabric. Her heart skipped a beat as she pulled out the missing shirts, her confusion deepening.

How had they ended up in such an unusual hiding place? Clara racked her brain, trying to piece together the events of the day. She couldn't fathom how the shirts had slipped out of sight, buried beneath the bed. The mystery only grew thicker, and Clara yearned for answers.

Lost in her thoughts, Clara emerged from the bedroom and made her way to the supper table. The aroma of a hearty meal filled the air, but her mind was consumed with the enigma that surrounded the hidden shirts. She couldn't keep this revelation to herself; she had to share it with Roger and the others.

As they gathered around the table, Clara cleared her throat, capturing the attention of those present.

"I found Roger's shirts, everyone," she announced, her voice laced with a mixture of perplexity and concern. "They were hidden under our bed."

A chorus of surprised gasps and curious glances filled the room. All eyes turned to Clara, awaiting an explanation for this unexpected discovery. Jeremiah cleared his throat and interjected, his tone laced with accusation.

"Sounds like a prank," Jeremiah said, his voice tinged with skepticism. "Perhaps young Ben here thought it would be amusing to hide his stepfather's shirts."

Clara's eyes narrowed, her protective instincts rising. She looked at Ben, who sat beside her, his innocent gaze meeting hers. She knew him well, knew the goodness that resided within him. There was no way he would have played such a foolish prank.

"No, Jeremiah," Clara said firmly, her voice holding an undercurrent of conviction. "Ben wouldn't do something like that. He's a good boy, and I trust him completely."

Ben, his eyes filled with a mix of confusion and hurt, spoke up.

"It wasn't me, Ma," he said, sounding distressed. "I promise. I would never hide someone's things like that."

Jeremiah's gaze shifted uncomfortably, realizing that his blame had fallen on innocent shoulders. He cleared his throat, attempting to salvage the situation.

"Well, then, if it wasn't Ben, perhaps it was a mischievous ranch hand. We'll have to look into it."

Clara nodded, her gaze steady. She had made up her mind, and no amount of deflection or false accusations would sway her. She would uncover the truth behind the hidden shirts, ensuring justice and protecting the integrity of her family. She was all but sure that Jeremiah had something to do with the shirts. But she also knew she would need evidence to confront him. And she would stop at nothing to get her proof.

Chapter Sixteen

Roger was silent throughout the rest of the meal after Clara's announcement. He knew that he had combed every inch of Clara's and his room that morning, and those shirts weren't there. So, not only had the shirts been missing when he got up, they had found their way back by the time Clara looked under the bed.

He thought about the look on Jeremiah's face when he once again blamed Ben for something going wrong. Roger could no longer deny it. There was nothing coincidental about all the incidents, and Jeremiah seeming to be quick to pin them on anyone. Anyone, that was, except for himself.

After dinner, Roger gave Clara a pointed look.

"I gotta go to bed early," he said deliberately. "Hiram and I have a big project tomorrow before we start working on the kitchen again. I wanna be up as early as possible to make sure we get everything we need done."

Clara nodded, giving him a smile that told him she understood what he was saying.

"All right, Roger," she said sweetly. "I will be up, too, as soon as I clean up the kitchen."

Jeremiah snorted, muttering some remark that was too quiet and too alcohol-slurred for it to be intelligible. Roger wasn't interested, anyway, though. He was focused on his upcoming conversation that he realized then was long overdue. He actually didn't anticipate being able to sleep. But the next thing he knew, it was morning. The sun was already rising, and he was surprised that he slept so long. He got out of bed and dressed, slipping out of bed carefully, without waking Clara.

Roger felt a knot forming in his stomach as he approached Hiram's cabin. Clara's words echoed in his mind, urging him to confront Hiram about his uncle's drinking problem. He knew it wouldn't be an easy conversation, but he couldn't ignore the truth any longer.

Taking a deep breath, Roger knocked on the cabin door, the sound echoing through the quiet afternoon. Hiram opened the door, his face creased with worry.

"Roger, what brings you here so early?" he asked, his voice laced with curiosity. "Am I late for work?"

Roger shook his head. Even with the sun already rising, Hiram usually wasn't on the ranch for another hour. At his age, Roger tried to not require more of the man than he could handle. He was still strong and fit, but he had more trouble getting going in the mornings than Roger and the younger ranch hands did.

"Can we talk, Hiram?" Roger replied, his voice steady but tinged with a hint of anxiety. "It's about Jeremiah."

Hiram's expression grew guarded, and he shifted uneasily on his feet. "What about him?"

Roger took a moment to choose his words carefully, not wanting to accuse Jeremiah without any evidence.

"Clara mentioned that you might have some concerns about Jeremiah. I wanted to know if there's something I should be aware of."

Hiram's gaze fell to the floor, and he hesitated before speaking.

"I've known Jeremiah for a long time, and I've never trusted him entirely," he confessed, his voice barely above a whisper.

"He drinks too much, gambles away his money, and he's not someone I would leave in charge of this ranch."

Roger felt a surge of disappointment mixed with relief at Hiram's words. Disappointment because he had hoped to hear otherwise, that his uncle was just misunderstood and cranky. Relief because his instincts had been right all along.

"Why didn't you say anything before, Hiram?" Roger asked. "Why keep it a secret?"

Hiram's shoulders sagged, and he looked weary. "I didn't want to cause any trouble, Roger. Jeremiah is family, and I didn't want to create tension between us. But I can't keep silent anymore. It's not fair to you or anyone else."

Roger nodded, his jaw set with determination. "Thank you for telling me the truth, Hiram. I appreciate your honesty, even if it's hard to hear."

Hiram cleared his throat, shifting his weight again. Roger could see he seemed nervous, and the dread grew in the pit of Roger's stomach.

"There's more," he said. "There was a time when Jeremiah was blind drunk. I heard him ranting to himself about how he should have gotten the ranch instead of you, and that you didn't deserve to be runnin' it. He said…" Hiram took a shaky breath, shaking his head. "He threatened to burn the whole place to the ground, before he would let you keep it."

Roger stared dumbly at Hiram, his mind racing.

"You don't think he set the kitchen on fire, do you?" he asked.

Hiram shrugged. "I don't know what I think. But I know that wife of yours and her boy didn't do it."

Roger nodded, disbelief setting into his brain.

"I know that, too, Hiram," he said.

Hiram placed a hand on Roger's shoulder, a gesture of support and concern.

"Just be careful, Roger," he said. "Keep an eye on Jeremiah. He may not be the person you think he is."

Roger gave his ranch hand a curt nod. He supposed he should have been upset with Hiram for keeping something so important from him. But then, wasn't Roger just as much at fault for sweeping Jeremiah's drinking problem under the rug and pretending it didn't exist?

As Roger left Hiram's cabin, his mind swirled with conflicted thoughts. He couldn't ignore the warning he had just received, yet a part of him still clung to the hope that Jeremiah could change. He vowed to keep a close watch on his uncle, unwilling to let his trust be betrayed any further.

The dusty wind whistled through the ranch, carrying with it an eerie sense of foreboding. Roger walked aimlessly back toward the ranch house, his gaze fixed on the horizon, lost in a labyrinth of thoughts.

Roger couldn't ignore the strange occurrences that had been plaguing them recently. The kitchen fire that erupted seemingly without cause, the disappearance and reappearance of his shirts tucked away beneath his bed, and Ben's pet spider lurking in Jeremiah's bed. These incidents had been dismissed as mere accidents or coincidences, but Roger couldn't shake the feeling that there was something more sinister at play.

Jeremiah's demeanor had transformed into a harsh, bitter facade, leaving Roger disheartened and disturbed. Roger regretted that he hadn't met Jeremiah when Roger was a boy. He had no basis of comparison for his uncle's personality.

It was possible that Jeremiah Banks had once been a kind, upstanding man. But all Roger saw before him was a cruel, verbally abusive older man who drank way too much. And then, there was the threat to burn down the whole ranch...

As Roger grappled with this realization, he was interrupted by a sudden burst of energy and excitement. Ben came bounding from around the back of the house, a delicate butterfly perched gently on his outstretched hand. His eyes sparkled with delight, and he eagerly beckoned Roger to come closer.

"Roger, look what I found!" Ben exclaimed, his voice filled with wonder. "Isn't it beautiful? I've been watching it flutter around the garden. It's like a little piece of magic."

Roger couldn't help but smile at Ben's infectious enthusiasm, a temporary respite from the weight of his worries. He crouched down to Ben's level, studying the delicate creature perched on his small hand.

"It's a magnificent butterfly, Ben," he said. "How did you manage to catch it?"

Ben's face lit up, pride evident in his voice.

"My father taught me about animals and nature," he said. "He used to take me exploring, showing me all the wonders of the world. I think he'd be proud of me for capturing this beauty."

Roger's heart swelled with emotion as he listened to Ben's words. He could see the deep longing in the young boy's eyes, the yearning for his father's presence. It struck a chord within Roger, reminding him of the importance of family bonds and the legacy that lingered even after loved ones were gone.

"I have no doubt your father is mighty proud of you, Ben," Roger replied softly, placing a hand on the boy's shoulder. "I believe he's watching over you, guiding you through every step of your journey. Keep exploring and cherishing the wonders of nature. It's a precious gift."

Ben beamed at Roger's words, a sense of comfort and reassurance enveloping him. In that moment, Roger understood the power of hope and love, even in the face of darkness. The shadows cast by his uncle's actions couldn't extinguish the flicker of light that burned within their hearts.

As the butterfly took flight, its wings carrying it away on a gentle breeze, Roger couldn't help but feel a glimmer of optimism. The challenges ahead remained daunting, but with love, understanding, and the beauty of the natural world, he knew they would find the strength to navigate the treacherous path that lay before them. Clara and Ben had shown him that the world didn't have to stay dark and painful after Willa's and his unborn baby's deaths. He was grateful to them. And he intended to get to the bottom of the strangeness on the ranch, and then start working on making the three of them a real family.

Chapter Seventeen

Clara sighed as she briskly moved around Jeremiah's room, a cloud of dust rising from the old furniture with each stroke of her feather duster. It seemed that no matter how hard she tried, the room never stayed clean for long. Her thoughts drifted back to the recent kitchen fire, a constant reminder of the misfortune that seemed to follow her and her son.

Jeremiah's voice echoed in her mind, his accusatory words ringing in her ears. He always found a way to blame her and Ben for any mishap that occurred within the household. Clara couldn't help but feel the weight of his disapproval press down on her shoulders, and she longed for a moment of respite from his constant scrutiny.

As she made her way toward the bed, carefully pulling the sheets taut and smoothing out the wrinkles as she set about making it, Clara couldn't help but notice the lingering scent of alcohol in the room. It seemed to be a constant companion for Jeremiah, the fumes wafting from his breath like a dark cloud.

She shook her head, hoping that Roger would find a way to mend the strained relationship between them. But as she adjusted the mattress, something fell onto the ground—a letter that had been hidden beneath the mattress.

She knew she should put the letter back. But curiosity overtook her. She turned the envelope over in her hands, noticing that it was sealed. It appeared to be a letter written by Jeremiah. But it looked worn, as though it had been written weeks ago. Why would he not go post it? Why would he have it hidden under his bed?

Lost in her thoughts, Clara froze as she heard the creak of the door opening behind her. Her heart raced, terrified to let Jeremiah see that she had a letter of his in her hand. She quickly tucked it into her apron pocket, hoping that he hadn't seen it.

"Clara," Jeremiah's gravelly voice broke the silence, "what are you doing in here?"

Clara turned to face him, her expression one of feigned innocence.

"I was just tidying up, Jeremiah," she said. "The room was in need of some cleaning."

He eyed her suspiciously, his gaze lingering on her apron. Clara's hands instinctively tightened around the crumpled letter in her pocket, her mind racing with a mix of curiosity and anxiety.

"Well, make sure you do a thorough job," Jeremiah grumbled, his disapproval evident in his tone. "I won't tolerate any half-hearted attempts at cleanliness."

Clara nodded meekly, her eyes averting his gaze. "Of course, Jeremiah. I'll do my best."

She expected Jeremiah to leave, grumbling to himself and stumbling drunkenly, as he always did. But instead, he stood in the doorway, leaving Clara no way to escape his distrustful gaze. She tried to ignore him, hoping he would go away.

But when it became clear that he intended to remain there, watching her, her nerves got the better of her. She pretended, as casually as she could, to give the room one final check for cleanliness. Then, she gathered up the basket of the remaining clothes, carefully approaching the door.

"Forgive me, Jeremiah, but I have to finish putting away this stuff," she said.

Jeremiah's piercing gaze bore into her, his imposing figure blocking the doorway. Clara's heart raced as she struggled to find her voice. The tension between them crackled in the air, and she couldn't shake the feeling of his presence being more threatening than usual. She averted her eyes, praying for a way out of this uncomfortable situation.

Finally, Jeremiah stepped aside, granting her passage out of the room. Clara wasted no time, hurrying downstairs in a mix of relief and unease. She descended the stairs in a rush, her heart pounding in her chest. However, in her haste, she'd failed to notice Roger's presence at the bottom of the stairs.

In a near collision, Clara stumbled to a halt, her eyes widening in surprise as she caught herself just in time. The sight of Roger's concerned expression offered her a moment of solace amidst the chaos. She reached out to steady herself, grateful for his sturdy presence.

"Clara, are you all right?" Roger's voice carried a hint of worry, his hand gently gripping her arm.

Clara took a deep breath, trying to steady her racing heart. "I... I'm fine. Just a little startled, that's all."

Roger's gaze searched her face, concern etched in his features. "Did something happen? You seem shaken."

Her mind raced, contemplating whether or not to share her discovery with him. The weight of the hidden letter in her pocket pressed against her thoughts, urging her to confide in her husband. But caution held her back, and she decided to keep her finding to herself, at least for now.

"No, it's nothing," Clara responded, her voice tinged with a hint of unease. "Just a small mishap in Jeremiah's room. Nothing to worry about."

Roger's brows furrowed, but he nodded, accepting her explanation. "All right, just be careful. I'm here for you, Clara, whatever you need."

Clara smiled weakly at her husband. "Thank you."

Before he could say anything else, Clara excused herself from Roger's concerned gaze, determined to convince him that her encounter with Jeremiah had not affected her. She put on a brave face, reassuring him that she was unbothered by the menacing presence of his uncle. But deep down, Clara couldn't shake the unease that lingered within her. She pondered over Jeremiah's behavior, unable to fathom why he would be so menacing toward her.

As she continued her tasks around the house, Clara resolved to do everything in her power to avoid any further confrontations with her uncle-in-law. She moved with a newfound caution, keeping a watchful eye on her surroundings, hoping to evade Jeremiah's presence. She didn't understand the source of his animosity, but she vowed not to let it overshadow her happiness with Roger.

It was only when evening descended upon the house that Clara's memory sparked, and she remembered the hidden letter. A pang of guilt washed over her as she realized she had neglected to return it. She sneaked down the hall, hoping that Jeremiah was still out. But to her chagrin, she found the door locked, indicating that he was holed up inside. She went back to Roger's and her room, retrieving the letter from her apron pocket and carefully placing it on her dressing table, vowing to herself that she would promptly return it to its rightful place as soon as Jeremiah was away from his room again.

The evening air held a sense of calm as Clara sat at her dressing table, her reflection gazing back at her with a mixture of weariness and determination. She knew she couldn't let Jeremiah's presence continue to cast a shadow over her life. It was time to confront the secrets hidden within the walls of this house and bring about a resolution that would grant her the peace she so desperately sought.

As she extinguished the candle on her dressing table, Clara cast one last glance at the letter. It lay there, a testament to the mysteries that lurked within their home. She made a silent vow to herself, promising to return it to its rightful place as soon as the time was right. Right then, however, she had a couple things left to do for the day.

As the sun began its descent, casting warm hues across the landscape, Clara finished her tasks and decided to seek out her son. She quietly made her way to his room, a small smile tugging at the corners of her lips. Finding him engrossed in a book from Roger's collection brought a sense of joy to her heart.

"Ben, supper will be ready soon," Clara gently announced, leaning against the doorframe.

Startled, Ben looked up from his book, his eyes wide with anticipation.

"Oh, Ma," he said. "I didn't realize how late it had gotten. I'm sorry."

Clara shook her head, her affectionate gaze fixed on her son.

"No need to apologize, sweetheart," she said. "I just wanted to let you know. But tell me, how are you finding the book?"

Ben's face lit up with excitement as he eagerly shared his thoughts.

"It's wonderful, Ma," he said. "Roger said I could borrow it, and it's been so captivating. I can't put it down."

A mix of emotions washed over Clara, her heart swelling with both happiness and a twinge of melancholy. She understood the weight that memories of her late first husband, Thomas, carried, and she knew Ben wrestled with his own feelings about embracing a new father figure in Roger.

"You seem to be getting along really well with Roger," she said. She wasn't sure if that was the right time to start such a conversation with her son. But she had already started it. She just hoped that it didn't make him uncomfortable.

Ben's brows furrowed in contemplation, his eyes searching Clara's face for understanding.

"I miss Pa," he said. "But sometimes I feel like... like it's okay to let Roger into our lives. He's been kind to us, and he defended me against Uncle Jeremiah. Is that all right, Ma? Is it okay to like Roger and see him like a father?"

Clara's heart swelled with pride and warmth, realizing the depth of Ben's understanding. She enveloped him in a tender embrace, cherishing the bond they shared.

"You're absolutely right, darling," she said. "Roger has shown us kindness and support. He cares for us deeply, just as we care for him. Opening our hearts to love again doesn't diminish the love we had for your father. It merely expands our capacity to care. I believe it's perfectly all right for you to like Roger and consider him like a father."

Ben nodded, looking up at his mother, still looking rather serious.

"Do you think it's okay with Roger?" he asked.

Clara thought about the way Roger was so quick to defend Ben against Jeremiah. He had not been thrilled when she first showed up to Cattle Creek with the son she hadn't mentioned to him. But just a couple weeks later, Clara had seen Roger warm very quickly to Ben. She hadn't been brave enough to ask Roger, but she felt confident as she answered her son.

"Yes, honey," she said. "I am sure it's fine with him, too."

Ben nodded again, nestling into his mother.

"It feels good to be happy again," he said.

Clara nodded, tears stinging her eyes as she held her son close.

"It sure does, sweetheart," she whispered. "It sure does."

In that moment, Clara allowed herself to acknowledge the warmth that Roger's presence had brought to their lives. She recognized the delicate balance between holding on to cherished memories and embracing the promise of a future filled with love and companionship.

With each word spoken, Clara's heart grew lighter, the weight of the past slowly releasing its grip. It was a gentle reminder that moving forward didn't mean forgetting, but rather honoring the past while embracing the present. She had just assured her son that it was okay to care for Roger. Maybe now, it was time to reassure herself of the same thing. There was nothing wrong with her budding feelings for her husband, or with the developing relationship between the two of them. Perhaps, it was time for her to embrace her new marriage, and the love she was starting to feel for Roger.

Chapter Eighteen

Roger wiped the sweat off his brow as he worked alongside Hiram. The sun beat down relentlessly, casting long shadows across the vast expanse of the property. The rhythmic sounds of horses neighing and the clinking of tools provided a comforting backdrop to their labor. Yet Roger's mind was preoccupied.

Hiram's words from two day's prior echoed in his mind, replaying like a broken record. He couldn't forget what his friend had told him about Jeremiah. The image of Jeremiah, intoxicated and threatening to burn down the entire estate rather than relinquish it to Roger, haunted his thoughts. It had been hard enough growing up without a father, but to discover an estranged uncle who seemed to harbor such animosity was disheartening.

Jeremiah had returned to town a few months ago, bringing with him a glimmer of hope for Roger. The notion of family had sparked excitement within him, visions of shared laughter and stories around the fireplace. But after Roger invited Jeremiah to live under the same roof, Roger couldn't help but question his true intentions.

And what, exactly, did Jeremiah do all day? He was either locked in his room or completely missing most of the time. Roger had to practically hold him at gunpoint to get him to help with ranch chores. Where did he go?

As they worked in tandem, Roger stole glances at Hiram, searching for guidance in his weathered face. Hiram had always been a voice of reason, a steady presence in his life. Perhaps he could shed some light on the situation, provide reassurance or offer a perspective that Roger hadn't considered.

"Hiram," Roger finally spoke up, breaking the silence that had settled between them. "I can't stop thinking about what you told me about Jeremiah. About how he threatened to burn it all down."

Hiram paused in his tasks, his gaze meeting Roger's troubled eyes. There was a somberness to his expression, as if he carried the weight of the world on his shoulders.

"I reckon Jeremiah's got demons of his own, Roger," he said. "The bottle ain't kind to a man's soul. It can twist even the kindest hearts. And a man with a dark heart already is bound to be even more apt to find himself with such demons."

Roger nodded, the truth of Hiram's words sinking in. He understood that people were capable of change, that their past didn't define their present. But the uncertainty still gnawed at him, the fear that Jeremiah's presence could disrupt the fragile peace he had built. Especially when his uncle seemed intent on doing just that.

"I just... I thought having an uncle would be a blessing, Hiram," Roger confessed, his voice tinged with trepidation. "But now, I don't know if he really wants to be a part of my life. Maybe I'm just a reminder of a past he'd rather forget. Or maybe I'm in the way of a prize he believes should have been his."

Hiram rested a hand on Roger's shoulder, offering a silent show of support.

"You can't blame yourself for another man's demons, son," he said. "It ain't your burden to bear. Jeremiah's got his own journey to reckon with. But don't let misplaced guilt and a sense of duty cloud your judgment. Sometimes, a man is just cold and cruel, without any demons to use as an excuse."

Roger mulled over Hiram's words, finding solace in their wisdom. He had tried to let go of his apprehensions and give his uncle a chance. But since he had married Clara, Roger had seen nothing but malignance and brutal words from his uncle.

It was hard for Roger to believe that the man was brothers with his beloved father, who was as far opposite of Jeremiah as any man ever could be. For the first time, Roger wondered if it was worth it to keep running a ranch that his only last living relative clearly wanted. He had always done better as a blacksmith. Would it really be so bad to let Jeremiah have the place, and go back to doing what he loved?

And the question of Jeremiah's whereabouts and usefulness around the ranch continued to plague him. He suspected he would regret it. But he decided to find out what Hiram knew.

"Do you know what my uncle does all day?" he asked.

Hiram snorted, shaking his head.

"Only speculation," he said. "But given what everyone knows about his drinking, I don't think I'm too far off. I rarely see him working on anything, aside from an occasional cattle drive. And on nights where I work late, I see him dragging his tail up the drive, stumbling over specks of dust. Best I can figure, he hides out at the saloon all day most days. I even found him passed out in the barn on the hay bales a couple times."

Roger sighed. The revelation should have angered him. It certainly displeased him. But it didn't surprise him at all. And truthfully, if it wasn't for Jeremiah being so cruel, Roger wouldn't care much. Jeremiah was old, coming to the end of the strength most men had in their younger years.

He never expected Jeremiah to do much anyway, unless the job was too big for Roger, Hiram, and the other ranch hands. But it did irritate Roger to learn that his uncle wasted what was left of his usefulness in the bottom of a bottle.

As the day wore on, Roger couldn't shake off the lingering doubts entirely. But he made a silent promise to himself—he would confront Jeremiah, speak from his heart, and see if they could forge a genuine connection. In the depths of uncertainty, he held on to the flickering hope that family ties could withstand the test of time and heal wounds that had long festered.

The warm, golden rays of the setting sun bathed the ranch in a soft glow as Roger and Hiram finished their duties of feeding the cattle. The weary but satisfied smile on Hiram's face hinted at a job well done, but Roger's attention was quickly captured by a figure in the distance.

Squinting his eyes against the fading light, Roger recognized Ben standing near the edge of the ranch. A pang of guilt tugged at his heart as he recalled the blame Jeremiah had placed on the young boy whenever pranks went awry. Roger knew deep down that Ben was innocent, yet his uncle's accusations had taken their toll on his relationship with both Ben and Clara.

With a small smile, Roger strode purposefully toward Ben, his boots crunching against the dry earth. As he closed the distance, he noticed the boy's intense focus on a cluster of ants diligently building their intricate tunnels. Curiosity piqued, Roger halted beside Ben, his gaze shifting from the boy's intent expression to the captivating world of the ant colony. The tiny creatures scurried about, their teamwork and intricate patterns mesmerizing to observe.

"Hey there, Ben," Roger greeted, his voice gentle yet laced with concern. "Mind if I join you?"

Startled, Ben looked up from his study, surprise mingling with apprehension in his eyes.

"Uh, sure, Roger," he said. "You just surprised me. I was just watching these ants. They work together, building their home."

Roger crouched down, his curiosity mirrored in his stepson's gaze.

"You know, ants are fascinating creatures," Roger said. "They may be small, but their determination and unity make them mighty. Just like a family, you know?"

A flicker of understanding crossed Ben's features as he contemplated Roger's words. The boy seemed to have been longing for acceptance, to be seen beyond the misattributed pranks that could have tarnished their relationship. Roger felt a pang of guilt at having spent so much time avoiding the child.

"Yeah," Ben replied softly, a hint of vulnerability seeping into his voice. "I wish Uncle Jeremiah could see that. He always blames me for stuff I didn't do."

Roger sighed, a mix of frustration and sympathy coursing through him. He had to do something to get Jeremiah to lay off Ben, to ensure that the weight of undeserved blame didn't crush the boy's spirit.

"I know it's been tough for you, Ben," Roger admitted, his voice tinged with regret. "But I want you to know that I believe you, and I'm sorry for everything you've had to endure. Let's find a way to make things right."

Ben's eyes widened, a glimmer of hope igniting within them. It was a pivotal moment, one that held the potential to redefine their relationship and create a bond based on trust and understanding.

Together, they watched the ants diligently carry out their tasks, each contributing to the well-being of the colony. It served as a poignant reminder that true strength lay in unity, in standing together against the challenges that life threw their way. They watched the ants until the sun was low enough in the sky to cast long shadows over the ground where they were sitting.

Even though an hour passed, it felt like mere moments. Roger realized then that he had spent so much time distancing himself from Ben, he hadn't considered how it might feel to be more of a father figure to him. And he certainly hadn't known how much he would love the feeling of bonding with the young boy.

Roger rose, giving the boy a warm, fatherly smile.

"We best get inside, my boy," he said. "I'm sure your mother will have dinner ready soon."

Ben scooted away from the ant colony slowly, only standing when he was sure he wouldn't step on any of the ants.

"I'm famished," he said, grinning up at Roger. "That's a word I read in that book you loaned me. I found out what it means by myself, and I like that word."

Roger chuckled, wholly impressed with the boy's intelligence.

"It's a mighty fine word, indeed, Ben," he said.

As Ben's small hand slipped into his, Roger felt a surge of optimism wash over him. Their journey toward understanding had just begun, but he knew that with patience, empathy, and the unbreakable bond they were forging, they could overcome any obstacle and build a brighter future together.

Roger and Ben made their way back to the ranch house, their steps filled with a newfound ease. The weight of unspoken words had been lifted, replaced by a growing connection that bloomed between them. The early evening air carried a sense of serenity as they walked side by side, a comfortable silence enveloping them.

Roger marveled at the beauty of the landscape surrounding them, the tall grasses swaying gently in the breeze, and the distant silhouette of grazing cattle. Nature seemed to echo the harmony that was beginning to settle within their hearts.

"Ben," Roger began, breaking the silence with a gentle smile. "I must say, I've been enjoying our conversations about nature. You've taught me a thing or two about ant colonies, and it's fascinating."

Ben's face lit up with excitement, his eyes shining with the joy of sharing his newfound knowledge.

"Yeah, ants are like a big family, like you said," he said. "They all work together and do their parts to keep their colony strong. I think it's pretty great."

Roger nodded, appreciating Ben's enthusiasm. It was moments like these that revealed the depth of the boy's spirit, reminding Roger of the resilience hidden beneath the weight of past hardships.

"You know, Roger, I'm glad my mom is happier now," Ben said. "I can see it in her eyes and in the way she smiles. I didn't like it when things were hard for her and me. But now, things are getting better. And I believe we have you to thank for that. I'm sure grateful for you, Roger. I know you're not my father. But you feel like a good father figure, anyway."

The boy's words resonated deeply within Roger. His heart swelled with a mixture of tenderness and admiration for the boy's perceptiveness. He hadn't fully comprehended the struggles Clara and Ben had faced before their paths intertwined. The realization struck him, bringing a sense of responsibility to his role as a husband and a stepfather.

Beneath the fading light, Roger turned to face Ben, a warm smile gracing his lips.

"Ben, you're right," he said, wrestling to keep his emotions at bay. "I may not be your real father, but I promise to be the best second father I can be. I'll always be here for you and your mom."

Ben's eyes sparkled with affection as Roger ruffled his hair, a simple gesture that spoke volumes. It was a testament to their growing bond, proof that acceptance and love could overcome initial reservations.

In that moment, Roger caught a glimpse of Clara watching them from the porch, her eyes glistening with tears and a radiant smile on her lips. The sight tugged at his heart, a gentle reminder that he was slowly but surely becoming a part of this new family, a family he had initially been reluctant to embrace.

Roger's gaze met Clara's, and he mouthed a silent "thank you" for bringing them together, for showing him the joy and fulfillment that could be found in opening his heart to the unexpected. He has been very reluctant the first time he laid eyes on Ben. Now, he didn't think he could have any kind of life without the boy. When they reached the back door, Roger's steps grew lighter, his heart filled with a newfound sense of belonging. The journey toward building a family had its share of challenges, but in that moment, he realized that the reward was immeasurable.

Chapter Nineteen

Clara stood on the porch, watching as Ben and Roger walked back to the house together, their laughter carrying on the gentle breeze. The sight brought a warm smile to her face, for it had been far too long since she had seen her son so happy. Ever since the untimely passing of his father, Thomas, a shadow had lingered over young Ben's countenance, stealing away the light that once danced in his eyes.

But now, as he hugged Clara tightly, she felt some of that brilliant spirit returning to her son. Joy filled her, and she gave her son a big kiss atop his head.

"I had such a good time, Ma," he said. "I told Roger all about the ant colony. And we had a whole big, special conversation, too."

He paused, looking at Roger and giving him the kind of wink only a young child could. Roger returned it, and Clara got a good look at the way Roger was looking at her son. It was the same look Thomas always had when he looked at Ben. Her heart swelled with joy. She couldn't help but notice the genuine mirth in Ben's voice, a sound that had been absent for far too long. The newfound companionship between her son and her new husband was like a balm to her soul.

With a loving pat on Ben's head, Clara smiled.

"I'm so glad, my sweet boy," she said. "It warms my heart to see you happy again." She brushed a strand of hair behind his ear, her gaze lingering on his face. How much he had grown since his father's passing, both in height and resilience. It was a testament to the strength he had inherited from his parents.

Ben excused himself, stating that he wished to retreat to his room to indulge in his favorite pastime—reading. Clara watched him disappear into the house, his steps light and filled with a newfound spring. She felt a mixture of pride and relief. It was as if a weight had been lifted from his small shoulders, allowing him to once again embrace the simple pleasures of childhood.

As Ben disappeared from sight, Clara turned her attention to Roger. The man stood tall and strong, a pillar of support in her life during these trying times. She admired his unwavering patience and kindness, understanding that he had brought a ray of hope into their lives when darkness threatened to consume them.

"A special conversation, huh?" she asked, smiling sweetly. She didn't expect him to divulge anything they discussed. Truthfully, she didn't need him to. The way they were interacting now and the way Ben looked at Roger with idolization and admiration told her everything she needed to know.

Roger blushed and looked away, but the biggest smile broke out across his face.

"Just some guy talk," he said, glancing up at Clara.

Clara walked over, putting a hand on her husband's arm.

"Well, I think that is wonderful," she said. "Thank you for being so good to Ben. And to me, as well."

Roger cleared his throat, the redness spreading along his neck. But the smile never left his face, even as he turned his back on her.

"I gotta go to town before dark," he said. "I need to place an order that will be delivered either tomorrow or the next day at the latest."

Clara clasped her hands together, looking at her husband hopefully.

"Roger," Clara said sweetly. "I need to go into town also, to post a letter to my mother-in-law. Would you mind if I accompanied you?"

Roger met her gaze, his eyes brimming with affection.

"Not at all, my dear Clara," he replied, his voice warm and reassuring. "It would be my pleasure to have your company."

Clara's heart skipped a beat at his words. The way he called her "my dear Clara" sent a shiver down her spine, igniting a flicker of something more profound. She marveled at the tenderness in his eyes, a stark contrast to the pain she had known all too well in the past.

"I'll go ask Ben if he wants to come with us," she said, blushing just as her husband had.

Roger nodded, gesturing for her to go ahead of him.

"We can both ask," he said. "Together."

Clara's heart was singing as she and Roger walked to her son's room. He was reading, just as he had said, and he smiled up at them when they entered the open door.

"Roger and I are going into town, sweetheart," Clara said. "Would you like to go with us?"

Ben thought it over for a moment before shaking his head.

"No, thank you," he said. "I was gonna go call Ollie and see if he would like for me to read to him."

Clara giggled, and Roger walked over and gave him a tight hug.

"That's fine, my boy," he said, the affection in his voice so thick that it nearly brought Clara to tears. "Just don't wander too far from the house when we're not here, all right?"

Ben nodded.

"Okay, I won't," he said.

Roger nodded, looking at Clara with a very similar doting affection.

"Are you ready then, darling?" he asked.

Clara shivered again, loving the way her husband was starting to call her pet names.

"I sure am," she said.

As the wagon rumbled forward, Clara's heart overflowed with gratitude for the gentle hand of fate that had brought Roger into their lives. With every passing mile, she clung to the hope that their newfound happiness would only deepen, forever erasing the painful memories of the past and paving the way for a brighter tomorrow.

The town bustled with activity as Clara and Roger rode, holding hands, along the main street. The sun cast a warm glow, highlighting the colorful storefronts and filling the air with the scent of freshly baked bread. It was a welcome respite from the daily routine at the ranch, a chance for Clara and Roger to enjoy a few stolen moments away from the responsibilities that life had bestowed upon them.

As they meandered through the town, Clara couldn't help but steal glances at Roger. He walked with a confident stride, his broad shoulders framing a kind face that held a hint of sorrow. The lines etched around his eyes spoke of a life filled with both joy and hardship, much like her own.

As they continued their leisurely walk, Clara couldn't help but feel a surge of warmth and contentment. She turned to Roger, overwhelmed with affection and happiness.

"Roger, I want you to know how much the time we've spent getting to know each other means to me," she said, her voice quivering with sincerity. "You have been a pillar of strength, and I'm falling in love with the ranch and the life we are building together. Ben loves it, too. It does my soul so much good to see him so happy. I am grateful to you for that."

Roger's face softened, and he brought Clara's hand to his lips, pressing a gentle kiss upon her knuckles.

"Clara, honey," he murmured, his voice filled with tenderness. "You have done an incredible job with the house, keeping it tidy and turning it into a home. And your cooking... well, it warms my heart and fills my stomach with delight. I am grateful every day for the love and care you bring into our lives. And that boy of yours must be the best kid in all of Kansas."

Clara blushed at his words, a rush of warmth spreading through her cheeks. She had never expected such praise and adoration, and it made her heart flutter with a newfound sense of belonging.

"He's a better child than I had any right to hope for," she said, smiling dreamily as she thought of her son.

Roger nodded, gently squeezing her hand.

"I feel the same way," he said.

As they made their way back toward the wagon, Roger stopped by the general store to order some supplies. Clara took the opportunity to post the letter to her mother-in-law, May, hoping it would bring some comfort to the grieving woman. She sealed it with a tender kiss, entrusting her words to the hands of fate.

It was a lovely evening, backed by the song of the cicadas, and even the silence that fell between Clara and Roger as they headed back home felt comfortable and pleasant. Clara was happy, for the first time in far too long, and she felt sure life would only continue to get better.

However, when they arrived back at the ranch, Hiram stood near the porch, his weathered face etched with worry. Clara's heart clenched, a sense of foreboding washing over her. Something was amiss.

"Hiram," Clara called out, her voice trembling slightly. "What's wrong? Where is Ben?"

Hiram's gaze met hers, filled with concern.

"I was hoping he was with you," he said. "I thought I heard a troubling shout just a couple minutes ago, so I went to see if Ben was in his room. But he wasn't. And I haven't seen him anywhere since. I thought it might have been one of the other ranch hands, but they already went home for the night."

Clara felt the world spin around her. Panic and fear gripped her heart, threatening to choke her. Ben, her precious son, was nowhere to be found. Thoughts raced through her mind, imagining all the possible dangers that awaited him. She clutched onto Roger's arm, seeking solace and strength in his presence. In that moment, Clara's world was turned upside down, her newfound happiness shattered by the raw fear that enveloped her. She knew that she had to be strong, to keep faith alive, and pray that Ben would return unharmed. But the panic was strong, and it was all she could do not to collapse in hysteria.

The vast expanse of the ranch spread out before them, casting long shadows in the fading light of day. Clara, Hiram, and Roger, their faces etched with worry, fanned out, their steps quickening as they scoured the land in search of Ben. Panic gripped Clara's heart, each passing moment amplifying her desperation to find her beloved son"

"Ben!" Clara's voice rang out, carried on the wind. "Ben, where are you?"

Hiram's grizzled features mirrored Clara's concern as he called out, "Ben! Come out, son! It's time to come home!"

Their pleas echoed through the canyons and across the rolling plains, but there was no response. She tried to make sense of why Ben would wander off, but she just couldn't. Her hands trembled, and her mind raced with worst-case scenarios. She couldn't bear the thought of losing Ben, not after everything they had been through.

Just as desperation threatened to consume her, Roger's voice pierced through the haze of fear.

"Clara, you and I will go check the house," he said, his urgency evident. "Hiram, you patrol the perimeter of the property, near the trees. We'll find him. Even if we have to split up and comb the woods around here."

Hiram gave a short nod before trotting off to the edge of the ranch. Clara nodded, her voice choked with worry.

"Please, Roger," she said. "Help me find him. Help me find my baby."

Roger nodded silently. With a determined stride, Roger led Clara toward the house, his footsteps heavy with anticipation. Clara didn't want Roger to leave her, not with her as petrified as she was. But she knew they had to split up to find her son. She couldn't cling to Roger like a helpless damsel when her son was missing.

Clara and Roger met at the bottom of the stairs, their footsteps becoming more frantic with each passing moment. When they established that they both had no luck, they rushed back outside. They combed through the stables, the barn, and every hidden nook and cranny on the ranch. It was beginning to look like they would have to comb the woods, as Roger had suggested.

And then, a glimmer of hope emerged from the darkness. Ollie, Roger's loyal and trusty dog, broke the silence with a series of urgent barks. Clara and Roger exchanged a knowing glance and raced toward the sound. Clara's heart was working its hardest to leap from her chest. But she forced herself to remain focused. She had to find Ben. Nothing else in the world mattered.

Chapter Twenty

Roger, Clara, and Hiram trudged through the dense forest, their steps guided by the urgent barking of Ollie. The hound's voice echoed through the trees, laden with fear and distress. Roger's heart pounded in his chest, his mind racing with worry for Ben.

"I'm sure he's fine, Clara," Roger said, his voice tinged with forced reassurance. "Ben is a tough young lad, and Ollie wouldn't let anything happen to him."

Clara nodded, her face pale with worry. She clutched Roger's arm tightly as they pushed forward, each step bringing them closer to Ollie's frantic barking. The sound seemed to grow louder, more desperate, and Roger's intuition told him that something was terribly wrong.

As they neared the source of the commotion, the forest began to thin, revealing a small clearing. Roger's heart skipped a beat when he saw what lay before them. Ben's limp figure lay on the ground, his foot ensnared in a cruel steel trap. Panic surged through Roger's veins, and he rushed forward, his fatherly instincts overriding all else.

"Ben!" Roger cried out, his voice laced with anguish. He dropped to his knees beside his unconscious son, his hands trembling as he assessed the situation. Blood stained the ground, evidence of the cruel grip the trap had on Ben's leg. Fear gripped Roger's heart, but he fought to maintain a semblance of composure.

"Clara, stay back," Roger urged, his voice tight with worry. "Hiram, go fetch the doctor. We need him here, now!"

Hiram nodded, his face etched with concern, and hurried off through the trees, leaving Roger and Clara alone with their injured loved one. Roger gently cradled Ben's head in his hands, his eyes flickering with a mixture of fear and determination.

"You'll be all right, son," Roger whispered, his voice wavering slightly. "We'll get you out of this trap and get you the help you need. Just hold on, Ben."

Clara knelt beside them, her hands pressed against her trembling lips. Tears welled in her eyes, but she refused to let them fall. Roger admired her strength, even in the face of such distress.

Together, they worked to free Ben from the steel jaws that held him captive. Roger's hands shook as he carefully manipulated the trap, desperately trying to release its grip without causing further harm. With a sudden, desperate yank, the trap finally sprang open, and Ben's whole leg, from knee to ankle, was freed.

Roger cradled Ben in his arms, his heart breaking at the sight of his unconscious child. Ben's face was pale, his breathing shallow. Blood stained his clothes, evidence of the ordeal he had endured. Roger kept his arms out of view of Clara, so she didn't see what he saw. Everything about the boy's physical state was a grim reminder of the danger his stepson had faced, and how critical his condition was.

As Roger held Ben close, he couldn't shake the nagging feeling of guilt that weighed heavily upon him. He hadn't seen anything wrong with leaving Ben alone at home. Now, Ben was injured, and he felt like a failure. Determination flared within Roger, vowing to do whatever it took to ensure Ben's recovery.

Roger held Ben in his arms, the weight of his unconscious stepson pressing against his chest. The journey back to the house felt agonizingly long, each step weighted with worry and a desperate need for answers. He didn't want to say it to Clara, but it was evident that Ben had lost a great deal of blood. Roger prayed that it wasn't too much, and that he could be saved.

Just after they entered through the front door, Hiram returned, the doctor in tow, breaking the somber silence that had settled over the clearing. The doctor hurried to examine Ben, his face grave. Roger's gaze followed their every move, his mind racing with a mixture of fear, hope, and the burning desire for justice.

As the doctor tended to his injured stepson, Clara let out a sob. He led her out of the room, taking her out onto the front porch. With a silent nod, Roger confirmed that Hiram would sit with Ben and the doctor until he was finished tending the boy. He held Clara close as she cried, making a silent vow. He would find the one responsible for setting that treacherous trap, and they would face the consequences. No harm would befall his family again, not if he had anything to say about it.

"Clara, it's going to be all right," Roger murmured, his voice tender and filled with reassurance. "The doctor's here now, and he'll take care of Ben. We just need to stay strong for him."

Clara nodded, her tear-streaked face buried in Roger's shoulder. He could feel her trembling against him, her fear and anguish consuming her. Roger knew that he needed to be her anchor, her source of strength, even as his own worries threatened to overwhelm him.

His thoughts turned to Jeremiah. The man had vanished, leaving behind a wake of resentment and tension. Jeremiah sometimes left and stayed gone overnight. Sometimes, for a day or two. But one of the horses or the smaller wagon would have been gone if he had gone to the tavern, and yet every mode of transportation was accounted for. Could Jeremiah have had something to do with Ben's misfortune? The possibility gnawed at Roger's mind, filling him with a mix of anger and concern.

Roger shook his head, even as he embraced his grieving wife. He knew that Jeremiah had been difficult lately. He had even been belligerent. But he couldn't allow himself to believe that his uncle would ever hurt a child. He was simply looking for answers to a senseless accident, when that had to be all it was. Still, the continuing absence of Jeremiah made Roger wonder. He decided he would ask his uncle if he saw Ben wander off when he returned home.

As Clara's sobs quieted to sniffles, she looked up at him with eyes filled with fear and pain. The expression on her face broke Roger's heart, and he couldn't help kissing his wife on the forehead.

"It's gonna be all right," he said again. "Do you want me to go check on them?"

Clara nodded, wiping tears from her cheeks.

"Thank you, Roger," she said. "I just can't imagine what would make Ben wander off like that. He's never done that before. I don't understand it."

Roger nodded, thinking about how he was pondering the same thing. Ben was a good boy, and Roger didn't think he would disobey his mother or him when they told him to stay close to the house when he played alone.

"I'll go talk to the doctor," he said, rubbing her back as he moved away from her.

Quietly, so as to not disturb the doctor as he worked on Ben on the living room couch, he slipped inside the house and tiptoed over to the fallen boy. He was still unconscious, and Roger could see the doctor working carefully to tend to his wounds. He took a deep breath, unsure if he would have the answers he sought, but needing to seek them just the same.

"Doctor, do you have any idea what could have happened to Ben? Why would he wander so far from the house?" he asked, his voice low and filled with urgency.

The doctor paused for a moment, glancing up from his task. "It's hard to say, Roger," he replied, his voice laced with professional caution. "Children are curious creatures, and sometimes their curiosity leads them astray."

Roger nodded, his mind still swirling with unanswered questions. He didn't tell the doctor that both he and Clara knew Ben would never wander off. But Jeremiah's face flickered through Roger's mind again, and he had to bury another vile thought.

He went back out to Clara, who had finally managed to regain some semblance of composure. He held her once more, his arms a comforting shield against the uncertainties that surrounded them.

"How is he?" she asked, her bottom lip trembling. "Will he be all right?"

Roger wiped more moisture off her reddened cheeks.

"The doctor is fixing him up now," he said. "We'll get through this, Clara. We'll find out what happened to Ben and ensure his safety."

Clara looked up at him, her eyes filled with a mix of gratitude and hope. Together, they would uncover the truth and bring justice to whoever had caused harm to their family.

As the doctor finished tending to Ben's wounds, the room fell into a quiet stillness. The journey to healing would be long, but Roger was determined to see it through. Roger carried Ben gently to his bed, staring helpless at his still-unconscious form as he pulled the blankets over the boy. The doctor's words hadn't been significantly comforting, and Roger worried about whether Ben would ever wake up. Anger blended with his distress, and he balled his hands into fists. Jeremiah would need to explain himself when he finally dragged himself home. Although Roger didn't think there would be any explanation that would satisfy him.

The night had cast its heavy blanket over the ranch, and silence settled around the house. Ben lay asleep in his bed, his young face peaceful despite the ordeal he had endured. In the kitchen, Roger, Clara, and Hiram gathered, seeking solace and respite from the weight of the day's events.

Clara, though slightly calmer than before, still carried the burden of exhaustion and distress upon her features. Roger's heart ached for her, knowing the unimaginable fear that must have gripped her when she thought she might have lost Ben. He reached out and gently squeezed her hand, offering his silent support.

Hiram busied himself in the kitchen, preparing a modest meal. The aroma of freshly-cooked food filled the air, but the heaviness of the situation weighed upon their souls, dampening even the simplest pleasures.

They gathered around the kitchen table, attempting to engage in lighthearted conversation, but the air remained thick with tension. The words hung heavy between them, their attempts to distract themselves from the gravity of the situation falling flat. Their minds were consumed with thoughts of Ben and the danger he had faced.

When supper was ready, Hiram served the plates, sitting at the other end of the table with his own. It was clear that no one had much of an appetite, though, so they stared silently at their plates, doing little more than pushing the food around. Hiram broke the silence, the sympathy for Roger and Clara evident in his voice.

"I know y'all are worried sick," he said gently. "But y'all can't do anything for the poor boy if y'all don't keep your strength up."

Roger glanced at Clara, grimacing at the pallor of her worried face. He reached over, putting his hand over hers.

"Hiram's right," he said, using his free hand to force himself to take a bite of his own food. "You gotta eat, honey."

Clara nodded, giving his hand a weak squeeze as she also took a bite. The room fell silent again as everyone forced down as much of the food as they could bear.

An hour later, as if summoned by the darkness itself, Jeremiah stumbled into the kitchen. His bloodshot eyes and disheveled appearance were clear signs of his intoxication. Roger's gaze hardened as he watched his uncle enter the room, a mix of anger and disappointment simmering within him.

Before anyone could speak, Roger took a deep breath and began to recount the events that had transpired, sparing no detail. He explained how Ben had gotten trapped, the blood he had lost, and the danger he had faced. Jeremiah's presence only fueled the fire within Roger, intensifying his resolve to protect his family.

"That trap could have killed Ben, Jeremiah," Roger's voice was laced with a mixture of anger and concern. "I thought I'd removed all of them months ago. It's a barbaric and dangerous practice. We won't tolerate it on this ranch anymore."

Jeremiah scoffed, his words slurred with contempt.

"Those traps have been here long before you came along, boy," he retorted, his voice dripping with disdain. "We've used them to catch deer and varmints for years. Ben's just a stupid boy who should watch where he's going."

Clara's anger flared, her fists clenching at her sides. She rose from her seat, ready to confront Jeremiah, but Roger swiftly stepped between them, his protective instincts taking over. His voice was firm as he addressed his uncle. Hiram also rose, putting himself beside Jeremiah, close enough to grab him if necessary.

"Clara, why don't you go check on Ben?" he asked.

His wife looked at him, and he could see the anger and hurt in her eyes. He wondered if she might suspect Jeremiah of something nefarious, as Roger himself was starting to. But after a moment, she nodded, turning on her heel and leaving the kitchen.

Roger watched her go, her steps heavy with worry. He knew she needed to see for herself that Ben was safe, that his injuries were being tended to. But she also needed to be as far away from Jeremiah as she could get. If nothing else, Jeremiah was acting as though Ben's accident was no big deal. Truthfully, Roger wouldn't have blamed her for slapping his uncle, with him having such a terrible attitude and being so drunk right then.

As she disappeared down the hallway, his attention shifted back to Jeremiah, whose presence continued to taint the room with tension.

Jeremiah sneered, his eyes clouded with the remnants of his drunken stupor.

"You think you can just come in here and take what's rightfully mine?" he slurred bitterly.

Roger's jaw clenched, a mix of anger and frustration bubbling within him. He had tolerated Jeremiah's disrespectful behavior for far too long, and now, with Ben's safety hanging in the balance, he was unwilling to let it slide any further.

"Jeremiah, this ranch was left to me by my father," Roger said, his voice steady, his eyes locked with his uncle's. "I've worked hard to maintain it and build a future for my family. You have no right to claim what isn't rightfully yours."

Jeremiah let out a harsh laugh, the sound grating on Roger's nerves.

"Your father always favored you, didn't he?" he spat. "Well, I won't stand for it any longer. You're nothing but a greenhorn, playing cowboy."

Roger's patience wore thin, his fists clenched at his sides. In the few months he had known his uncle, Roger had always tried to find some common ground with Jeremiah, but the man's constant antagonism had worn away any hope of reconciliation.

"Jeremiah, I've had enough of your disrespect," Roger said with complete finality. "This is my house, and I won't have you poisoning it with your bitterness. At a time like this, where a young boy is fighting for his life, you would make it about a piece of property. And frankly, I wonder what you know about what happened to him. It's time for you to leave, Jeremiah."

Jeremiah's face twisted in fury, his bloodshot eyes narrowing into slits.

"You can't make me leave," he sneered, trying to fight through the alcohol haze to sound defiant.

Hiram shifted, anticipating a move from the drunken man, but remained quiet. Roger took a step closer, his voice firm and resolute.

"I won't ask again, Jeremiah," he said. This is your final warning. Get out of my house."

The room grew still, the weight of their confrontation hanging heavy in the air. Jeremiah seemed to consider his options, his face contorted with rage and resentment. Finally, with a bitter snarl, he turned on his heel and staggered toward the door.

"You think you're so high and mighty, Roger," Jeremiah hissed. "But mark my words, this won't be the end of it. You'll regret crossing me."

Roger stood his ground, his gaze unwavering.

"I'm done with your threats, Jeremiah," he replied calmly. "Leave now, and don't come back."

Jeremiah stormed out of the house, slamming the door behind him with a resounding thud. Roger let out a breath he hadn't realized he was holding, the tension dissipating in the wake of his uncle's departure. He wanted to feel relieved to have the sour, unreasonable man out of his home. And yet, he only felt like he had swallowed a boulder that sat, heavily and painfully, in the pit of his stomach. If Jeremiah was leaving, that would have to be the end of it. Wouldn't it?

Chapter Twenty-One

The air held an unspoken chill as dawn unfurled its gentle light upon the ranch. Clara, in her faded apron, moved about the kitchen, the soft rustle of her skirt playing a mournful tune against the wooden floorboards. The aroma of sizzling bacon and brewing coffee wound its tendrils around the hushed house, seeping through the crevices and cracks, an attempt to bring some semblance of normalcy after yesterday's storm.

Roger sat slumped at the head of the table, his face pale and lined with worry. His strong hands, usually so steady, nervously fidgeted with his coffee cup. His silence was thunderous, echoing in the empty spaces of their home. Clara knew him well enough by then to read the thoughts that lingered behind his steely gaze.

He was reliving the painful incident, the heart-wrenching sight of Ben, hurt and bloody after the bear trap accident. His quarrel with Jeremiah, his own blood, was clearly still fresh in his mind, too. As upset as she herself was about her son's close call, her heart ached for her husband. She wished she could do something to make him not be so hard on himself.

"Roger, you've barely touched your breakfast," Clara said, her voice soft, trying to penetrate the wall of silence. She motioned to a plate of bacon and eggs before him, the bright yellows and reds a stark contrast to his somber demeanor.

Roger shook his head, clenching his jaw tightly.

"I ain't hungry, Clara," he said, his voice barely a whisper. His gaze remained fixed outside the window, looking at the very woods that harbored the bear trap, that harbored the cause of their current predicament.

Clara sighed, caught in this turmoil of guilt and anger. She perched on the chair next to him, placing a comforting hand on his.

"Roger, you cannot blame yourself for what happened," she said. "You couldn't have known..."

His hand tightened around hers, eyes meeting hers in a silent plea for absolution.

"I should have," he said. "It's my property, my responsibility." His voice trembled, anger and guilt intermingling.

She shook her head, squeezing his hand reassuringly.

"No, it's not your fault. It's not Ben's fault, either," she said firmly, remembering the horrible accusation Jeremiah had thrown at the young boy.

Roger's jaw clenched. The old man had been reckless, irresponsible, and his words last night, suggesting that Clara's son deserved his fate, were inexcusable. His demand for Jeremiah's departure had been met with shock, but Clara had been proud that Roger would not risk his family's safety for the sake of familial bonds.

She could see the same resolution in his eyes now, the hard steel of his will forged in the fires of this adversity. His silence was not of defeat, but contemplation. He was laying the foundations of a safer future, one where they would never have to fear for their child's life again.

"It's going to be all right, Roger," Clara said softly, her voice barely above a whisper. Roger had surprised her by the concern and love he had shown after Ben got injured. She knew that no matter how awkward and rocky things had been between them since they were married, they could stand together to handle what was to come. At least, she hoped they could.

As the echoes of breakfast began to fade, and Roger went out to begin the day's work, Clara gathered herself, and with a heart full of trepidation, ascended the staircase. The second floor of their ranch house was quieter, holding its breath, it seemed. Ben's room was at the end of the hallway, the normally lively sanctuary now a quiet sickbay.

At the door, Clara paused, her hand resting on the cool brass knob. As silly as she knew it was, part of her was terrified that she would walk in and find Ben in worse condition than he had been the night before. Or, worse, she would find that he was no longer with them. Flashes of the night Thomas died overwhelmed her mind, and she shuddered. She couldn't allow herself to think such things right then. Ben needed her, and she needed to come to her senses.

Gathering her courage, she pushed it open. Ollie, the faithful old hound, was sprawled across the foot of Ben's bed. His wise, chocolate eyes met hers, and his tail thumped against the quilt in a slow, cautious rhythm. Quietly, she crossed the room, reaching out to scratch the mutt behind his ears.

He accepted the affection for a brief second. Then, he rose slowly, moving closer to the sleeping, injured boy and curling up right beside the child's knees. He didn't try to stop Clara as she moved closer to her son. But he watched her with careful regard as she made her way to the side of her son's bed.

With a soft sigh, Clara sat in the chair by the bed. Ben lay propped up against the pillows, his eyes closed and unmoving. His face was pale against the stark white of the linens, a heartbreaking reminder of the previous day's horror.

She longed for his eyes to open and show her the same spark of spirit that she loved so dearly. He was her son, her brave little soldier, and she would do anything to take away his pain.

"Morning, sweetheart," Clara said softly, her hand brushing lightly over his shaggy hair.

Ben's gray eyes, so much like Thomas's, flickered open at her touch. A small, pained smile spread across his lips.

"Morning, Ma," he rasped, wincing at the pain that speaking caused him.

Clara felt a sting at the corners of her eyes, but she blinked it away. She had to be strong, for both of them. Taking Ben's small hand in her own, she gave him a reassuring squeeze.

"How're you feeling?" she asked.

He gave a small shrug, flinching again at the movement. His gaze dropped to the blankets.

"I'm... I'm sorry, Ma. For all the trouble..." he said, trailing off as his voice cracked.

Clara's heart clenched. The words were like a physical blow, the injustice of them piercing her deeply.

"No, Ben," she said firmly, lifting his chin to meet her gaze. "None of this is your fault, honey. None of us knew that trap was out there, or we could have warned you. And anyway, all that matters is that you're all right."

It was all she could do to keep herself together as she spoke. She knew it hadn't been Ben's fault, even though Roger had told him to stay near the house. But she also knew there was more to the story than Ben simply disobeying. However, he was in no condition to tell her what had happened to make him disregard Roger's warning and wander so far into the woods. And she truly couldn't care less in that moment. As she had just told him, all that mattered to her was that her son was alive. The mystery would wait until later to be solved.

Ben shook his head, wincing once more. Clara nearly screamed at the notion that her son was suffering in ways she couldn't fix. But she bit her lip and waited for him to speak again.

"But I shouldn't have been out there..." he said, the guilt apparent in his eyes as he echoed her thoughts. "Roger told me not to, and I did it anyway..."

"You're a boy, Ben," Clara interrupted, using all her strength to keep her voice steady. "You're curious and adventurous, and there's nothing wrong with that. What happened... it was an accident. It could've happened to anyone."

Ben's expression darkened, and his eyes filled with unshed tears. The sight tore at her heart, but Clara held her own tears at bay, squeezing his hand reassuringly.

"We're going to get through this, my sweet boy," she said. "You're going to heal, and everything's going to be all right. I promise."

As Clara spoke those words, she believed them. She had to. They were a promise, a vow she made to her son and herself. They would heal, they would mend. They were a family, built not just from love, but resilience and strength. As the early morning sun streamed through the window, casting a warm glow on them, Clara believed that she would keep this promise, no matter what.

Clara sat with her son until he drifted off to sleep. Once he did, she pulled the blanket up over his clammy arms and then slipped out of the room. She closed the door so that she wouldn't disturb her wounded son as she went about her chores. But by the time midday had come, she had succeeded only in staring at the same shelf for hours, halfheartedly dusting the same spot over and over again.

With Ben seemingly stable after the horrific accident and resting comfortably, another problem plagued Clara. Roger's pain had been evident, and she couldn't sit by and let both the important men in her life suffer like they were. She needed to talk to Roger. She thought there might be a way to fix part of her husband's heartache.

The sun rode high in the sky when Clara exited the house, her shawl draped around her shoulders to guard against the midday heat. As she approached the barn, the familiar sounds of labor greeted her. Roger was hard at work, his muscular frame silhouetted against the sunlit backdrop of the open barn doors.

She paused, watching him in quiet admiration. Even in the midst of their turmoil, Roger was unyielding, a steady rock amidst the raging storm. His strength was comforting, yet it also filled her with a pang of worry. His unrelenting push to keep things normal, to protect their family, left little room for him to heal his own emotional wounds.

Clearing her throat, she announced her presence.

"Roger," she said timidly.

He paused in his work, turning to face her. His face, smeared with dust and sweat, softened as his eyes met hers.

"Clara," he said, the weary lines around his eyes deepening. "Is Ben..."

"He's resting," she replied quickly, her hands twisting the edge of her shawl. "I... I wanted to talk to you about something else."

He nodded, setting aside his tools. His hands, calloused and strong, found hers. The touch was comforting, a silent assurance of his attention. She drew a deep breath, gathering her thoughts.

"Of course, honey," he said softly. "Tell me what's on your mind."

Clara drew a deep breath. She hadn't fully formed the thoughts she had in mind. She would just have to go on her feelings.

"It's about Jeremiah," she said.

Roger held up one of his hands, his expression hardening at the mention of his uncle.

"I know that he doesn't belong here," he said. "I took care of that last night. The way he spoke about Ben was unacceptable, and I won't tolerate that here."

Clara squeezed his hand, shaking her own head as she pressed on.

"I know what he said was wrong, unforgivable even," she said. "But... he's your only family left. He was wrong for letting Ben get out of his sight, and for talking the way he did. But maybe he feels guilty for Ben getting hurt when he should have been watching out for him. And just maybe the two of you could talk about it and make amends."

Roger looked away, his grip on her hand tightening. She knew how much the incident had hurt him, how it had torn at the bonds of family. Clara wasn't Jeremiah's biggest fan either, because his reckless demeanor and sharp tongue often rubbed her the wrong way. However, she couldn't deny the fact that he was Roger's kin. And in these uncertain times, family was more precious than ever.

"You don't have to forgive him, not yet," Clara continued, her voice soft but insistent. "But maybe, just maybe, you should try and talk to him. Perhaps there's a way to mend things."

Roger was silent for a moment, his gaze distant as he absorbed her words. Clara waited, her heart pounding against her ribcage. The silence stretched between them, a tenuous thread of anticipation.

Finally, Roger turned back to her, his eyes meeting hers. There was a flicker of something in his gaze, a spark of uncertainty, perhaps even hope. He didn't speak, but his grip on her hands tightened, a silent acceptance of her words. It wasn't a promise, but it was a start, a small step toward healing the fractures in their family. It was enough, for now. Together, they would navigate these tumultuous waters, guiding their family to safer shores.

Chapter Twenty-Two

Roger stared into his wife's tired blue eyes. She had surprised him by coming out to talk to him about Jeramiah. Roger himself had thought of nothing all morning except for the fists with which he would greet his uncle if he ever showed his face around their little house again. But his feelings weren't the only ones that mattered on the subject. Frankly, he didn't care one bit if Jeremiah was his kin.

He would have kicked the man from his home if it had been his own father after the way he acted the previous night, and after leaving Ben alone so that he found himself wandering off and getting hurt so badly. Roger blamed Jeremiah for what happened just as much as he blamed himself.

But Clara's eyes pleaded with him to consider what she had said. And Roger realized that while it might be a little more peaceful without Jeremiah around, he wanted to teach Ben the value of family, and of forgiving people who wronged others. The idea that he and Jeremiah might be able to reconcile and help Ben learn something so valuable about life gave Roger the smallest bit of hope. He just prayed that Jeremiah didn't make him regret considering letting him come back to the house.

Roger finally sighed, nodding reluctantly.

"All right," he said. "I'll try to find him and talk to him. But if he pulls something like this again, he will be outta here all over again, Clara."

Clara nodded, looking relieved despite her apparent fatigue.

"I think that's more than fair, Roger," she said. "Thank you."

Roger nodded, pulling his exhausted wife close to him and embracing her. "Why don't you take a nap while Ben is napping?"

Clara shook her head, pulling away from her husband. "I need to make y'all some lunch. I was thinking about stew. Something simple that we can eat for supper, too, and something I can help Ben eat, too."

Roger smiled warmly at his wife.

"That sounds wonderful, honey," he said softly. "You worry about getting Ben fed. I'll come in when I get hungry."

Clara nodded.

"I better get back in to see about him," she said, gesturing toward the house. "And I hope it goes good with Jeremiah, when you talk to him."

Roger nodded, giving her another, tighter smile. "Me, too, darlin'."

He watched as Clara turned and headed back toward the house. She was strong, but her body told the tale of how stressed and bone-weary she was. His heart hurt for his wife. He was trying to keep things business as usual for Ben's and her sake. But his guilt made concentrating very difficult for him. And a big part of him wanted nothing more than to go back in the house and hold her close to him until Ben was recovered. *But then, would I ever wanna let her go?* he wondered to himself.

Roger was more relieved than he ever had been in his life when the sun sank too low in the sky to provide adequate light. However, it wasn't until then that he realized he had forgotten to go in for lunch. He dragged his weary bones back to the house, unsurprised when he found the kitchen empty, save for a plate full of pork roast sandwiches on the table.

He was genuinely touched that Clara had even bothered to do that for him, considering the condition her son was in. He made a mental note to thank her for being so considerate at such a difficult time for her. It also made him feel guilty for forgetting to come in for lunch, and for not being hungry enough to eat right then. He put the plate in the ice box, vowing to take the sandwiches to lunch the following day for him and Hiram.

Half an hour later, Roger found himself alone in the old armchair in the living room of his small ranch house, the scuffed floor, the well-worn furniture, and the bottle of whiskey he had pulled from the end table in the corner of the room his only companions. The dim light from the oil lamp on the table fought the encroaching darkness, casting long, stretching shadows.

His mind wandered back to the simmering resentment he held for his uncle. The drinking, the constant hatred toward Clara and Ben, the selfishness Jeremiah had shown—all seemed impossible to forget. Yet Clara asked him to give his uncle another chance, to foster their kinship, their family.

He closed his eyes, thinking about his father, and wondering what the elder Mr. Banks would have done. It was odd that his father had never mentioned a brother. But perhaps, if there had been a falling out between those two brothers, maybe it was time to bury it all and leave it in the past. But could Roger do that?

Family, Roger mused, a concept both foreign and familiar. It was a bond he yearned for but one with a past marred by both loss and grief. But Clara's plea for understanding, her hopeful words, had stirred something within him. A deep sigh escaped his lips as he steeled his resolve.

He would go seek Jeremiah out right then. No sense in waiting since Roger had already made up his mind. Maybe it would go better than Roger expected. After all, he had given Clara a chance after she had hidden Ben from him. And it had been the best decision he had ever made. Perhaps, he could find the same results in giving his uncle another chance.

Just as he was about to rise from his chair, the sound of footsteps echoing in the chilly night air reached his ears. The rhythmic crunching of boots on gravel grew louder until the front door creaked open, revealing the bulky, somber figure of Jeremiah. Roger's heart pounded in his chest, a swirl of emotions—anger, anticipation, and an inkling of hope—making his palms sweaty.

Yet he sat still, maintaining his stern demeanor as Jeremiah stepped into the room. His uncle looked older, the lines on his face deepened, his eyes holding a look that Roger couldn't quite decipher. That is, except for the redness in his eyes, indicating that he wasn't completely sober.

"I came to talk, Roger," Jeremiah began, his voice strained. He paused, swallowing hard before continuing. "I... I owe you an apology."

Roger stiffened, eyeing his uncle skeptically. Suddenly stricken with pride, he couldn't bring himself to tell his uncle that he had been just about to go to him for the same reason. Instead, he gestured to the worn sofa, giving the burly man a nod.

"Come in," he said, keeping his tone even but firm. "Have a seat."

Jeremiah nodded, but he didn't move to sit down right away. To Roger's surprise, as he stepped into the glow of the candlelight, he noticed that Jeremiah looked contrite. And, so far as Roger could tell, he wasn't completely drunk, though there was the faintest hint of alcohol that lingered around his uncle.

"I've been a fool," Jeremiah said, his words echoing in the silence of the room. "Blinded by worry and paranoid, I hurt you, and for that, I am truly sorry."

The words hung in the air, a poignant testament to months of discord. Jeremiah looked earnest, his eyes almost pleading for forgiveness, a raw honesty reflected in his words that Roger had never witnessed before.

Roger sighed. "You didn't hurt just me. You hurt Clara, too. And Ben... he coulda been killed yesterday. What were you thinkin'?"

Jeremiah nodded, looking away from his nephew.

"I know," he said. "I didn't know the boy was here, Roger, honest. I never woulda left if I had known."

Roger bit his lip. He wanted to believe his uncle. And Jeremiah's face did appear truly remorseful. Still, Roger wasn't ready to let him know that he was already on his way to forgiving him. He wanted his uncle to finish speaking. And he wanted to be sure that Jeremiah was sincere.

"What made you decide to come to apologize?" Roger asked.

Jeremiah looked at Roger again, removing his hat and twisting it in his hands.

"I want us to be a real family," Jeremiah said, the strength in his voice wavering. "I want to be a good uncle to you,

Roger. Joshua would have wanted it that way. I want to try harder, make amends. I want... I want us to move past our differences."

Roger listened, a storm of thoughts swirling in his mind. He looked at Jeremiah, the uncle he'd only known for a few months, the man he currently resented, standing before him, seeking reconciliation. It seemed to be a heartfelt plea, a confession filled with regret and a desire for change. His gaze softened, his grip on the armrest loosening. It was not an easy task to forgive, to let go of the past. Yet, Clara's words echoed in his mind once again, her pleas for understanding, for forgiveness. Maybe, just maybe, they could be a family after all.

"I suppose everyone deserves a second chance," Roger said, his words measured and hesitant.

Jeremiah blinked, surprise flickering in his gaze. But Roger held up a hand, silencing the words bubbling up in his uncle's throat.

"I ain't saying it's gonna be easy," Roger continued, his voice stronger now. "You've done wrong, Jeremiah, and that ain't something to forget. But if you're truly sorry, truly willing to make amends... Well, then... I think we can give this family thing a shot."

Relief washed over Jeremiah's face, and he let out a breath he'd been holding.

"Thank you, Roger," he said, rubbing his eyes. "I'll do whatever it takes to prove to you that I mean it."

Roger couldn't tell if his uncle was emotional or just rubbing dry, alcohol-reddened eyes. But Jeremiah seemed apologetic enough. Perhaps Clara had been right about him, after all. Eventually, however, Roger simply nodded, holding his uncle's gaze.

There was a long road ahead of them, full of challenges and potential pitfalls. But in that moment, sitting in the old armchair in his parlor, Roger felt a flicker of hope, a spark that might just kindle into the warmth of brotherhood.

Later that night, as Roger lay in his bed, the house echoed with familiar yet strange sounds. The faint rustling from Jeremiah's room, the soft, distant noises of a home that was no longer just his. Clara would normally be breathing rhythmically beside him, but she was sleeping in Ben's room since he got hurt. Yet despite her absence, the walls seemed less silent, less lonesome.

It was a comforting noise, a hopeful noise. A noise that whispered of potential reconciliation and an unfamiliar, yet deeply yearned for, sense of family. And yet, something still gnawed at Roger. What had prompted Jeremiah's sudden change of heart?

No matter the reason, Roger came to a firm realization. Clara's words had found root, and Jeremiah had come home. There was a lot to be done, much to mend, but the first step had been taken. As sleep finally claimed Roger, he felt a peace he hadn't known in years. His last thought before darkness claimed him was a simple, heartfelt realization. After all the heartache and strife he had endured, he had a family once again.

***

The next morning, the first pale rays of sunlight seeped into the ranch house, painting the world in hues of gold. Roger shot out of bed like a bullet from the barrel of a gun. He dressed quickly, tearing open the bottom drawer of his dresser. He reached in and pulled out the last gift that Willa had ever bought for him, just days before she died. It had gone unused and forgotten since her death. But now, Roger knew exactly where it belonged—with his stepson.

As Roger headed to the room at the end of the hallway, his fingers traced the smooth cover of the brand-new notebook he carried, its leather-bound cover soft and untouched. It was a simple thing, but it held a significance that made his heart race. It was a replacement for one Roger had noticed that Ben had lost—a small, comforting gesture of care for his young stepson. Even if Ben wasn't quite well enough to use it right away, Roger hoped it would give him something to look forward to when he did recover enough. It might also help stave off boredom for the young boy until he could go back outside again.

Ben was propped up against his pillows, and Roger's heart squeezed at how frail and sickly he looked. Clara was sitting in the chair by his bed, her eyelids fluttering open. When she saw Roger, she rose, giving him a tired smile.

"Morning, Roger," she said. "Do you want me to make breakfast?"

Roger patted her arm with his free hand and shook his head with a warm smile.

"No, honey," he said as quietly as he could manage. "You go on and sit back down. I brought something for Ben, but I hate to wake him."

"Mah-nin, Oger," Ben said sleepily, his own eyes wrestling their way open. "I'm 'wake."

Roger chuckled softly.

"I can see that," he teased gently. "How're you feeling, tough man?"

Ben shifted in bed, and Roger thought his heart would break into pieces when the boy winced with the movement. He rushed over to help the child. But by the time he reached the bed, Ben was sitting a little more upright, and he gave Roger a flicker of a smile.

"I'm okay," he said, still trying to fight the fatigue. Roger wondered if he shouldn't wait until later to give the child his present. But Ben reached for Roger, his small fingertips just grazing Roger's arm. "How're you, Roger? You doin' okay?"

Roger gave the child another smile, awed by his question. Despite his own terrible condition, he was worried about his stepfather.

"Got something for you, Ben," Roger said brightly.

Ben smiled again.

"That's real nice of you," he said, finally sounding a bit less groggy. "What is it?"

Roger held out the notebook, putting it close to his stepson's face so he could see it without straining to look. Ben's eyes finally flew open, and he blinked as he looked at the cover of the notebook.

He reached out slowly, his fingers brushing the cover, his expression one of disbelief. "This... this is for me?"

"It's yours," Roger confirmed, a warmth spreading through his chest at the boy's reaction. "I know you lost your old one, and... well, a boy needs his notebook."

Ben's face lit up in a bright smile, a hint of color returning to his pallid cheeks.

"Thanks, Pa," he said, sounding more like his old self than he had since his accident. The way he said 'Pa,' with such trust and affection, hit Roger like a wave. It wasn't a word he'd ever thought would be meant for him.

Beside him, Clara's hand slipped into his, her fingers interlacing with his. He glanced at her, finding her eyes misty with unshed tears. He squeezed her hand gently, his heart throbbing in his chest. The emotions in the room were overwhelming, yet beautiful in their sincerity.

"It's my pleasure, Ben," Roger said, swallowing hard to keep his own tears at bay. "I'm glad you like it."

Ben looked back down at the book, opening it with loving reverence. Roger hadn't been able to admit it until that moment. But he truly did love Ben like the boy was his own son. He couldn't wait for Ben to recover. He planned to do all the things that any father should do with his son.

Just then, a noise from the doorway drew Roger's attention. He found Jeremiah watching them, his face shadowed. There was a strange look in his eyes, a mix of emotions Roger couldn't quite comprehend. It gave Roger pause. He was reminded of the heartfelt conversation from the night before, the earnest apology and plea for forgiveness.

It seemed that Jeremiah's intentions were genuine, after all. Yet he couldn't read the expression in Jeremiah's eyes as he stared at Ben. If Roger hadn't known better, he would have thought it was jealousy. But how could a grown man be jealous of a small, injured child?

Chapter Twenty-Three

After Roger went out to the ranch for the day, Clara kissed Ben's forehead.

"Will you be all right for a few minutes?" she asked. "There's something I want to do real quick."

Ben grinned, still holding his new notebook. "I sure will. Can you bring me a pencil when you come back?"

Clara nodded, overwhelmingly relieved to see her son feeling better. "I sure can, honey."

She left the room, hurrying down the hall. She had noticed Jeremiah standing in the doorway as she and Roger sat with Ben. But he was gone before either she or Roger could say anything to him. She wanted to speak with him, as Roger clearly had, and make her amends with him, too. But he wasn't in his room, or anywhere else on the top floor of the house.

She ran downstairs, hoping to catch him looking for coffee or breakfast in the kitchen. But he wasn't anywhere to be seen, she realized with disappointment. He must have gone out to the ranch when Roger did. With a sigh, she decided that she would try to talk to him after supper.

Next, she went on the hunt for Ben's pencil. In her nervous cleaning spree after his accident, she had rearranged everything, and it took her a while to find one. She did at last, however, in the end table in the living room. She hurried back up the stairs, not wanting to keep Ben waiting any longer to use his new notebook. But when she reached his room, she found him sound asleep once again, clutching the notebook tightly to his chest.

Quietly, she tiptoed across the room, placing the pencil on the table beside her son's bed. She blew him a silent kiss, then sneaked back out of his room, closing the door behind her. With no one to make breakfast for, she decided she would go begin collecting laundry to wash that morning. She would start with Roger's and her room and get Ben's later, since he was resting again. And the task would give her something productive but tedious to do to help settle her nerves.

As she worked, she thought about the exchange between Roger and Ben earlier. It had been a wonderful gesture for Roger to give Ben such a thoughtful gift. It had made Ben happier than Clara had seen him in what was, for her, far too long. But then, Ben had called Roger 'Pa.' Her heart melted again as she recalled the fond moment. Ben had looked at Roger like he used to look at Thomas. And Roger had choked up, clearly just as touched as Clara herself had been. Clara wouldn't have believed it from the way Ben's and her relationship with Roger had started. But right then, she was sure they were well on their way to being a real, loving family.

She was so preoccupied thinking about Ben and Roger together that she bumped right into someone as she headed down the stairs. She nearly dropped the clothes and linens, looking up into a pair of faintly reddened eyes.

"Oh, Jeremiah," Clara gasped, chuckling nervously at her reaction. "I'm sorry. You scared me to death."

The burly man gave her a smile, but Clara couldn't help noticing that it didn't reach his eyes.

"Didn't mean to startle ya," he said. "Just don't forget that God gave us two eyes to see stuff like that coming."

Clara giggled again softly, and Jeremiah's smile widened. She thought he seemed to be trying to be lighthearted with his words. But what was that look in his eyes that didn't at all match his words?

"I'm glad you're here, though," she said, making her way to the sofa and putting the laundry on one of the cushions so she could look her uncle-in-law in the eyes. "I wanted to say that it's good that you and Roger made up."

Jeremiah nodded, his gaze drifting to the pile of clothes.

"I agree," he said blandly.

Clara nodded, wiping her sweaty hands on her apron. She was having trouble reading Jeremiah. But she decided to try to get out what it was she wanted to say.

"I also wanted to say that I'm sorry things have been so tense—"

"Sorry, Clara, but I think I hear Roger calling from outside," Jeremiah interrupted.

Clara nodded, confused. She hadn't heard anything, and she wondered how Jeremiah could have. But she didn't get the chance to say anything else. Jeremiah turned sharply and headed right back out the front door. Clara stood staring at the door, puzzled. It was by far the strangest, yet most pleasant interaction she had ever had with her uncle-in-law. So, why had it left her feeling so unsettled?

Trying to shake off the odd encounter, she went to the sofa and collected the washing. She took it to the small table that stood beside the wash tub, placing it there. Then, she went to ensure that she hadn't missed anything other than Ben's dirty clothes and bed coverings. If Ben didn't wake until later in the day, she would wash his things the following day. Right then, she needed to keep herself busy to try to soothe her freshly jangled nerves.

She quickly found the silence comforting as she scrubbed at the clothing in the wooden wash bucket. Her delicate hands swished through the soap-scented water, rhythmically working to remove the dust and sweat-stained evidence of ranch life from their clothes. The midday sun glared down from a clear sky, beating onto her bonnet, and casting a light, dappled shadow over her work.

A flutter of paper from the pocket of her apron startled her from her trance. A folded square slipped out and floated onto the tabletop, threatening to get soaked. Her brow furrowed in confusion as she recognized the familiar handwriting.

"Jeremiah," she breathed, her heart skipping a beat. It was the letter she had meant to return but had forgotten about in the hustle of chores and responsibilities.

"Oh, Clara," she chided herself aloud, her hand pausing mid-scrub. "How could you forget something as simple as that?" She looked at the letter, considering the proper course of action. Her sense of integrity told her to return it immediately, unopened, untouched.

But then, a nagging curiosity tugged at the corner of her mind. It wasn't her business, of course. Yet wasn't it about her family, her home, her life? The thin line of impropriety wavered, making her internal compass needle spin wildly.

Clara bit her lower lip, engaging in a silent debate with herself. She took a deep breath, smelling the sweet scent of the soap mixed with the dry, dusty air. And then she made her decision. Her heart pounded as she unfolded the letter. She took a deep breath, then looked down at the yellowed piece of paper.

She only intended to skim the words written on the page, enough to satisfy her curiosity. But she was immediately horrified as she read the first few lines. Her heart thumped against her chest as she began to read, her lips moving silently over the rough, uncouth language:

George, the letter began, the tone already ripe with bitterness and thinly-veiled resentment. *This darned ranch should've been mine to run, not that lily-livered greenhorn, Roger. He don't know the first thing about cattle, about land. He's soft, like his ma. Not built for this life.*

Clara felt a flash of anger at the disrespect toward her husband, but she forced herself to continue, to sift through the venomous words.

His pa, the letter continued, *God rest his soul, made a wrong turn leaving everything to him. That city boy can't distinguish a milk cow from a steer, let alone manage a whole ranch. Every morning, I watch him rise with the sun, his eyes wide, as if they're trying to swallow up everything, and all I can think is what a mess he's making of the legacy his father left him.*

She could almost hear Jeremiah's raspy voice, drunk on too many whiskeys, bitterly spitting out the words. The more she read, the clearer Jeremiah's cruel intentions became, as if his anger and bitterness were seeping out of the page.

When I return from this cattle drive, I plan to shake things up, the letter went on. *I'll make his life such a living hell, he'll wish he never set foot on this land. Mark my words, George, before the first frost, that boy will be begging me to take over. He'll sign the deed over faster than a snake sheds its skin, and hightail it back to Oklahoma.*

Her hands shook as she read about Jeremiah's insidious plan again. Her mind reeled from the shock. She had defended Jeremiah to Roger, convincing him that the old man deserved another chance. Yet in her hand, she held proof that

Jeremiah Banks was beyond redemption. How could he be planning something so sinister to his own flesh and blood?

Clara leaned against the table, the letter crumpling slightly in her trembling hands. She was overwhelmed, shocked at the betrayal. She thought back to her pleas to Roger to speak with his uncle and forgive him. She had let herself believe that Jeremiah was just a troubled, haunted soul who simply didn't know better than the way he behaved. She'd thought he felt threatened by her and Ben suddenly appearing in Roger's and his lives. But the letter was dated six months prior. The animosity that was evident in the letter clearly had nothing to do with her or her son.

Her heart pounded in her chest, echoing the rhythm of the swaying branches of the sycamores under the afternoon sun. The rustling leaves whispered secrets in her ears, secrets she held in her hands, in the form of the incriminating letter. She clutched Jeremiah's letter tightly, the edges of the paper digging into her palm. She looked toward the distant field, where Roger worked tirelessly under the harsh sun. He was strong, reliable, always filled with an unyielding optimism about life on the ranch.

Her gaze softened, and a lump formed in her throat as she thought about the truth she held, and how it could shatter his world. Jeremiah, Roger's only living family, was planning his downfall. It was a bitter pill to swallow, and one that Clara knew would leave a lasting scar on Roger's heart. At that idea, anger began to trump the sorrow she felt. How could anyone want to purposely hurt someone as kind and dedicated as Roger, especially his own relative?

As the wind picked up, rustling her hair and the hem of her dress, Clara looked down at the letter again. A horrifying thought came to her mind, and she nearly dropped the letter into the wind with the suddenness of her sudden worry. The cattle mysteriously disappearing, the 'accidental' fires, the spider in Jeremiah's bed... and blaming Clara and Ben for it all. It was a bit of a stretch, but it seemed that Jeremiah was not just biting the hand that fed him, he was planning to sever it completely.

Clara cradled the letter against her chest, her heart aching at the dilemma she faced. She respected Roger's bond with Jeremiah, understood the significance of that last tether to family. But the incriminating letter was proof that it was, indeed, likely Jeremiah who was behind all the strange things that had happened on the ranch. And could she let her husband walk blindly into a trap set by his own kin?

"Roger deserves to know," Clara murmured to the wind, folding the letter, and tucking it back into her apron pocket. The decision weighed heavily on her, but she felt a certain relief too. The path ahead was filled with thorns, but it was the right one.

With one last look at her hardworking husband, Clara turned back toward the house, her steps resolute. She decided she would tell him after supper, when they could sit down and talk. Tonight, under the starlit sky, she would share with him the truth about his treacherous uncle, even if it tore their world apart. They would face the storm together, as they had promised each other, in sickness and in health, for better, for worse.

Chapter Twenty-Four

The sun blazed overhead, drenching the Kansas ranch in a fierce heat that caused mirages to shimmer on the horizon. The day was almost half over, and Roger had hardly gotten anything done except for feeding the animals, fixing the latch on the pig pen, and working in the hayfield. And yet ranch work was hardly the biggest concern.

He hadn't been able to stop thinking about his interaction with Ben that morning. He had been thrilled with the notebook. Then, he had called Roger 'Pa.' And the more Roger thought about it, the more he decided that he liked the sound of it.

Poor young Ben was lying inside the ranch house, suffering in his bed. His leg was torn up from that blasted bear trap that had been erroneously left in the woods. A distant neighing of a horse rang through the air, followed by the dull thudding of a hammer on wood.

Life on the ranch went on, no matter what personal tragedies unfolded. The ever-resilient Roger frowned, pushing these reminders aside. Today, the ranch owner's task was different; he was on a mission for a boy who was more to him than just a stepson.

Roger's heart clenched as he thought about Ben's face, so pale under his freckles, his youthful energy sapped by pain and frustration. The boy's eyes, once brimming with innocent mischief, now held a kind of quiet sorrow that tugged at Roger's heartstrings. *No child should have to feel trapped,* Roger thought, *whether by a bear trap or by the four walls of his room.* An idea struck Roger, and he hurriedly put away his pitchfork, hammer, and nails in the barn, grabbing a jar from a nearby shelf and then racing back out to the shade of the nearest sycamore tree.

Before he knew it, Roger found himself on his hands and knees, dust settling on his rugged denim trousers, and his wide-brimmed hat providing a measly defense against the relentless sun. This was a position he never thought he'd find himself in—a full-grown ranch owner, sifting through the dirt and dust for insects.

And yet there he was, out in the field, searching for another special present for his stepson within the brittle shrubbery and parched earth. If the poor child couldn't come outside and study the bugs, as he so loved to do, Roger would take the bugs to him.

His work-hardened hands, accustomed to the feel of the reins, a branding iron, or the stock of a rifle, seemed ill-suited for this delicate task. He was a man used to dealing with problems that could be solved by muscle and determination. But Roger had encountered a new challenge, one that he couldn't simply wrestle into submission or shoot. It was his most important task yet, and he was determined not to fail.

Shaking his head to try to get rid of the frustration, he redoubled his efforts, scanning the parched ground for any sign of life. A movement caught his eye; a tiny, black speck crawling over the dry, cracked earth. Roger slowly reached out, hand steady as he carefully picked up the little beetle. The creature's tiny legs wiggled in the air, as if surprised by the sudden change in scenery.

A smile tugged at the corners of Roger's mouth as he gently put the bug in the jar, his eyes lighting up for the second time that day. He placed the beetle in the glass jar he'd brought along, adding it to the small collection of other insects he'd found.

His gaze wandered back toward the ranch house, standing strong against the backdrop of the western sky. He imagined Ben's reaction to this little trove of critters, his curiosity piqued, his eyes brightening, forgetting for a moment the trap, the injury, the confines of his bed.

A rush of love welled up in Roger's chest, a warmth the Kansas sun could never hope to rival. Ben might not have been his by blood, but he was his, nonetheless. He would not let a bear trap or a confinement to a bed steal the light from Ben's eyes. Not if he could help it. With renewed determination, he went back to his search, this time his purpose not just to find, but also to heal. Every insect was a promise of relief, a pledge of devotion, a testament to an unspoken bond between a rancher and his stepson.

A strange day indeed, he mused. The day a hardened ranch owner found tenderness on his hands and knees, amidst the dust and bugs of his land. For the love of a boy, for the promise of a smile, it was a task he embraced with all his heart.

As the shadows lengthened and the late afternoon sun painted the sky in hues of orange and crimson, the quiet rustle of fabric and a familiar, gentle voice broke Roger's focused silence.

"What are you doing down in the dirt, Roger?" Clara asked.

He craned his neck over his shoulder to look at the woman who'd walked into his life with a tender heart and an iron will, forever changing the rhythm of his own. She stood a few feet away, dressed in a simple, blue cotton dress, her hair escaping from a matching bonnet, the setting sun making her look like she was surrounded by a halo of gold.

Roger smiled at her, then pointed back at the jar filled with various insects. After ensuring that the beetle couldn't climb out when he wasn't looking, he shifted so that he could look straight up at her.

"I'm collectin' these critters," he said, pointing to a spot he had just cleared that was now covered with all kinds of creepies and crawlies.

Clara giggled, looking at Roger with a puzzled expression.

"I can see that," she said. "But why? I don't think I've ever seen a rancher so invested in digging for bugs and stuff as part of their daily chores."

Roger blushed, suddenly feeling self-conscious.

"For Ben," he said softly. "I feel terrible that he can't come play with them like he likes to. So, I wanted to give him something to look at when he gets bored. Maybe he can even write some notes about them in his new notebook."

He looked shyly away her as he spoke, focusing instead on a little grasshopper that had hopped onto his knee. Yet he could feel her gaze on him, a gaze that seemed to penetrate his very soul.

For a moment, there was silence between them. The only sounds were the distant calls of ranch hands wrapping up for the day and the occasional chirping of a cricket.

Finally, he chanced a look at Clara, meeting her deep blue eyes. He was unprepared for the emotion he found in them— a mixture of surprise, warmth, and a profound tenderness that tugged at his heartstrings. Her eyes shimmered with unshed tears, reflecting the vivid colors of the setting sun.

His heart stuttered, then resumed its rhythm, pounding an echo of a melody that only he and Clara knew. His strong, hardened fingers tightened involuntarily around the glass jar, and he pushed himself up from the ground.

"Roger..." Clara whispered, her voice quivering like the last leaf in fall. She moved closer, reaching out to gently touch the hand that held the jar. Their fingers met, brushing against each other in a moment of shared understanding, the glass jar standing testament to their silent vows. Vows of love for each other, and for the boy who had brought them even closer. "You've been so wonderful to Ben. I can't tell you how much I appreciate it. How much we both do."

He looked at her, seeing her in a new light, the strength of his feelings for her overwhelming. The love he felt for her was a mighty river that never stopped flowing, even when boulders of hardships stood in its way.

"I'd do just about anything to see our boy smile, Clara," Roger murmured, his voice thick with emotion as he thought again about the child calling him 'pa' earlier. Clearly, Clara was thinking about it, too, because her smile lit up her whole face and tears of happiness filled her eyes.

"I know, Roger. I know," she said.

Neither of them spoke for a couple of minutes. But the message passing between them was clear to Roger's mending heart. It was love. Love for Ben. Love for Clara. The love they were forming for one another. A simple yet profound love that had him on his knees in the dirt, searching for bugs, just for a smile. His love for Clara deepened with each beat of his heart, each tick of the clock, each grain of sand that slipped through his fingers.

Clara's hand on his still held a warmth that spread through his body, a comforting blanket of affection that stirred an urge to express the feelings he'd been wrestling with.

"Clara," he began, "there's somethin' I need to talk to you about."

A sudden flicker of apprehension crossed her face.

"Roger," she replied with an echo of his urgency. "I need to talk to you too."

His heart, still pounding from the silent exchange of love, paused for a moment, apprehensive yet hopeful.

"Well then, you go first," he said, gesturing toward her with a nod.

Clara shook her head, suddenly looking very shy and timid.

"No, you go first," she insisted, a slight blush creeping into her cheeks.

For the next half a minute, they found themselves in a classic impasse, two proud individuals locked in a 'you first' stalemate. But hearing Clara giggle as they took turns offering to wait to speak was everything to Roger in that moment. In the end, however, he relented, his curiosity growing, but there was a confession that couldn't wait anymore.

"Clara, I... I want you to know that I've got feelings for you," he said, his voice laden with sincerity. "Strong feelings."

He watched her carefully, every muscle in his body tensed in anticipation. But the words he yearned to hear in return didn't come. Instead, she looked down, her eyes shadowed, her voice caught in her throat.

Disappointment washed over him, deflating the hope that had been rising within him. Yet, he quickly gathered himself, refusing to let his feelings transform into resentment.

"Now, your turn," he encouraged, masking his disappointment with a wistful smile.

Her eyes met his, a sea of confusion and uncertainty.

"It was nothing," she finally responded, her voice barely a whisper. "Just... I'm sorry to have bothered you."

His heart sank a little as she looked away again. He was hurt, and he wondered how he could have misjudged what had been happening between him and Clara so badly. But he couldn't let his wife's lack of reciprocation get to him right then. Instead, he chose to focus on the task at hand, his love for Ben acting as an anchor. He glanced back at the jar in his hands, the bugs still wiggling inside.

"Well, would you help me catch some more of these critters for Ben?" he asked, trying to reinstate the earlier warmth.

She looked surprised, but then a spark of amusement lit in her eyes, and she gave him a small nod.

"All right, Roger," she said, giving him the smile that always melted him. "Let's catch us some bugs."

The ensuing hour was filled with laughter and shouts of triumph as they stumbled, raced, and fell in their pursuit of grasshoppers. Clara's laughter rang out across the field as she chased after a particularly elusive one, her dress hem dirtied, and strands of hair flying loose.

They worked together, a team fueled by love for a boy, their shared laughter echoing around the vast expanse of the ranch. Every now and then, their hands brushed, sending jolts of warmth shooting through him.

Her lack of confession stung him, yes, but in the wide plains of his heart, he made room for patience. He understood that he might have spoken up a little too soon after Ben's accident. And love, he knew, could be as elusive as the grasshoppers they chased. But he was ready for the chase, ready to wait, ready to hope. Because, in the end, love was worth it. Clara was worth it. And for her, he'd go on a thousand bug hunts.

SALLY M. ROSS

Chapter Twenty-Five

Clara stared at the yellowed, crumpled piece of paper, its edges rough and frayed from the tremble in her hands. The words scrawled in Jeremiah's spidery handwriting seemed to leer at her, a stark, ugly reminder of the man Roger's uncle was.

Her heart pounded in her chest like a blacksmith's hammer against the anvil, a dreadful rhythm that marked the passing of time, the echoing of each harsh word in her mind. Even with as harsh and cruel as Jeremiah could be, she couldn't believe that he would be so vindictive against his own nephew.

I have to tell Roger, she thought as the wind dried the sweat building up on her brow. *He needs to know what Jeremiah is up to before it's too late.* She knew it was true; Roger needed to prepare to protect himself and the ranch against his uncle.

She couldn't imagine what Jeremiah had planned to run Roger off. But if the unexplained events around the ranch were, in fact, Jeremiah's fault, she had a pretty good idea of what he was capable of.

But how could she tell her husband now, after he had confessed his feelings for her? She had wanted nothing more than to hear him say those words to her. But now that he had, she hadn't been able to say that she loved him, too. She had been so weighted by Jeremiah's letter that she couldn't even enjoy such a wonderful moment with her husband.

And if she told Roger now about what his uncle was plotting, it would devastate him. She felt guilty that she had been the one who suggested letting Jeremiah come back and forgiving him. What would Roger think of her if she had to tell him something so horrible?

Her gaze fell upon her husband, who was leaning against the wooden porch railing, watching the sunset paint the endless Western sky. She loved him, this kind-hearted man who had been handed a harsh life and yet managed to keep a soft heart. He had already been torn between duty toward his family and the newfound love he held for her. To bring him more pain, more worry, was something she couldn't bear to do.

In the end, Clara decided that she could never tell Roger. Not about the spiteful things Jeremiah had penned. Not now. Roger's love for her, she felt, was too new, too fragile to be tested in such a way. It was something she cherished, a budding hope amidst the cruel reality of their circumstances. Something needed to be done to protect the ranch, and her husband. But there had to be another way. There had to be something she could do without involving Roger.

She made up her mind then, tucking the offensive parchment into her dress. She would confront Jeremiah. Alone. She knew it was a bold move, and it would likely enrage the drunken, spiteful man. But for all the things he might have done, Jeremiah had never been physically violent toward Roger or her.

One thing he would never get away with was doing physical harm to her. She didn't care if he tried to frame her for something else going wrong around the ranch. So long as he remained nonviolent, she felt sure she could handle him herself.

***

The next morning, Clara woke early, before the first rays of dawn had a chance to pierce the soft veil of night. Her mind still churned with the foul words etched in Jeremiah's letter, the echoes of his malice woven into the silent tapestry of the still-sleeping house. The confrontation with Jeremiah was unavoidable, she knew, but the weight of the impending conversation lay heavy on her like a damp woolen blanket. She lay there, listening for any signs of movement downstairs or in the hallway.

Roger, she noted with a pang of guilt, was still fast asleep, a peaceful oblivion shielding him from the storm that was about to break. After planting a feather-light kiss on his brow, she slid out of their shared bed, her bare feet barely making a sound against the worn wooden floor. She got dressed, choosing to wear the dress she wore the day she married Roger.

She thought that, after she spoke with Jeremiah, she might feel light enough to speak to her husband about what he had said the day before. He deserved to know her feelings, just as she now knew his.

But as Roger sighed and turned over in bed, it occurred to her that if Jeremiah became argumentative, Roger would hear the conversation about the letter and his uncle's plans to get rid of him. That was exactly what she was trying to avoid. She couldn't speak with Jeremiah while Roger was still in the house. She would have to wait until he was out on the ranch for the day.

With a sigh, Clara slipped back into bed beside Roger. She closed her eyes, thinking to just rest them for a few minutes. But when she next opened them, the sun was beginning to shine in through the window, and Roger was no longer beside her.

Carefully, she tiptoed down the stairs, peeking out the living room window just in time to see Roger step off the porch and head for the ranch. She let out a small sigh, chewing her lip. She decided to make some coffee and wait for Jeremiah to get up. But as she reached the downstairs hallway, she heard muffled shuffling in the kitchen. *He's already awake,* she thought, acutely nervous as she realized it was time to confront him.

As she approached the kitchen, the rich, heady aroma of freshly brewed coffee laced with a harsher, more acrid scent assaulted her senses. She didn't even need to see Jeremiah to know the smell. She stopped quietly in the kitchen doorway for a moment, a cold shiver running down her spine. Sure enough, there he was, sitting at the kitchen table, a cup of coffee in one hand and a bottle of whiskey within arm's reach.

Clara's heart pounded in her chest as she walked into the room, her gaze fixed on Jeremiah. She knew there was no sense in wasting time. She needed to seize the opportunity while she had it. And before Jeremiah was too drunk.

"We need to talk," she said, her voice surprisingly steady.

Jeremiah looked up, his eyes bloodshot and bleary enough to make her think that even at such an early hour, she was too late to catch the burly man before he had had too much to drink.

"About what?" he asked, slurring his words and taking a gulp of his adulterated coffee.

"This," she said, producing the letter from her apron pocket and throwing it onto the table. "I found this when I was making your bed the other day. Do you wanna explain to me just what you're up to?"

A flicker of surprise, then annoyance, crossed Jeremiah's face as he glanced at the letter.

"How should I know?" he asked with a dry, bitter chuckle. "I ain't even looked at it yet. And what are you doing, putting your grubby paws on my belongings?"

Clara shook her head, undeterred, her anger from the previous day returning.

"I'm not the one who's done wrong, Jeremiah," she said. "And don't play stupid. You're planning to try to take this ranch from Roger. You and I both know you have no rights to it."

Jeremiah had paled at the sight of the letter. But now, his cheeks were reddening again with the burn of the liquor and anger at Clara for touching his things. Or, perhaps, anger because he had been caught making nefarious plans.

"What of it?" he asked, a hint of defiance creeping into his voice. "And who are you to say who has rights to what? You don't know nothing about this ranch. Neither does Roger, for that matter."

Clara narrowed her eyes, trying to give Jeremiah a steely gaze as she gathered her thoughts. She had expected Jeremiah to at least try to deny the accusation, even though the words were right in front of him. But he seemed almost proud of himself as he sipped his whiskey-laced coffee, wearing a smug smirk as he stared back at her.

"Your words... they're poison. You need to stop," she said. "Roger was kind enough to bring you into his home, and to forgive you for all your nonsense and hatefulness. And this is how you repay him?"

Jeremiah's laughter echoed in the quiet kitchen, a harsh, jarring sound that chilled Clara's blood.

"And why not?" he asked, wiping his watery eyes. "This ranch should belong to me. Joshua had no business leaving it to that greenhorn kid of his. And then, he messed around and got himself a wife and a kid. Now, you and that boy are the only things standing between me and this ranch."

The words hit Clara like a physical blow. She reeled for a moment, her mind whirling with disbelief, anger, and a touch of fear. She was aware of the letter, the animosity, but to have it spoken aloud, the depth of his resentment was a punch to the gut. Part of her wanted to ask Jeremiah if he was the reason Ben fell into that bear trap. But a bigger part of her knew she probably didn't want to know.

"You think that because we are here, you're entitled to less?" she asked, choosing the path of trying to reason with the man. "Roger has done nothing but work this land and care for you in your drunken stupors." Her voice had risen to a shout, her hands clenched into fists at her sides. She was angry, to be sure. But anger was beginning to give way to fear as she stared into Jeremiah's cold, dead eyes, which were starting to look black.

Jeremiah sneered at her, a grotesque twist of his lips that mirrored the ugliness of his words.

"If not for you and that brat, this would've been my ranch already," he snarled, slamming his coffee cup on the table, and sloshing the spiked coffee everywhere.

The accusation hung in the air, tainting the scent of coffee and whiskey with the bitter tang of spite. Clara felt a fierce determination welling up within her, a hot, righteous anger that washed away the last vestiges of fear.

"You're wrong, Jeremiah," she said. "This is not your land, not your life. You've done nothing to earn it. Roger is a better man than you'll ever be, and he's a fine rancher, at that."

Her words echoed through the kitchen, a challenge laid bare. The morning had begun on a bitter note, but Clara knew the day was far from over. This confrontation was only the beginning of a long, arduous battle. But for the sake of Roger, and their son, she was willing to fight.

Jeremiah rose from his chair, moving surprisingly deftly for his inebriated state. He was inches away from Clara's face in no time, and Clara took an instinctual step back. But before either of them could say anything else, the kitchen door swung open, casting a long, wavering shadow across the room.

Hiram stepped inside, his sun-weathered face looking as though it had been carved out of granite. He took in the scene before him, his gaze moving from Clara to Jeremiah, and back again.

Clara met his gaze with wide, frightened eyes. It didn't take Hiram more than a second to sense that something was terribly wrong. He crossed the room in three large bounds, gently pushing Clara behind him and facing off against the angry drunk.

"Jeremiah," he growled, his voice as rough as sandpaper. "Leave."

For a moment, Clara thought Jeremiah would refuse. The sneer still lingered on his face, the malice in his eyes undimmed. But something in Hiram's stare must have made him reconsider. With a scoff, he pushed away from the table and stumbled out of the room, muttering under his breath.

The silence that followed was deafening. Clara felt like a storm-battered ship, the tempest having suddenly dissipated, leaving her adrift on a tranquil sea. She turned to Hiram, her eyes welling up with unshed tears.

"Oh, Hiram," she said, her voice barely a whisper. "I didn't want to believe it..."

His gaze softened as he put gentle hands on her upper arms.

"What happened, Clara?" he asked, his voice now kind and warm, not cold and accusatory.

Taking a deep breath, she recounted everything. The discovery of the letter, the confrontation, and Jeremiah's bitter words. Hiram listened in silence, his eyes hardening like a pair of flint stones. When she finished speaking, she took the letter off the table, grateful that Jeremiah hadn't thought to snatch it up on his way out, and handed it to Hiram. He read it quickly, his face twisting into a horrible scowl as he read Jeremiah's toxic words.

"We need to tell Roger," he said once he finished reading. His voice held an undeniable finality, the words dropping like stones in a calm lake.

"But..." Clara began, her gaze drifting toward the kitchen window. "He'll be devastated. He loves his uncle, despite everything..."

"He needs to know, Clara," Hiram interrupted gently. "Better to hear it from us than to find out some other way."

Clara knew he was right, but the thought of breaking Roger's heart was more painful than anything Jeremiah could ever do. It was her duty to protect her husband from such pain, wasn't it? But as she looked at Hiram, his determined gaze unwavering, she understood the necessity of it. Roger might be hurt. But he stood to suffer much more if she said nothing about what she knew.

"All right," she said, her voice steady despite the whirlpool of emotions within her. "We'll tell him together."

Chapter Twenty-Six

The morning sun streamed through the slats of the barn, striping the interior with bands of gold and casting long shadows over the well-worn tools and bales of sweet-smelling hay. Roger, his broad shoulders hunched over the anvil, was lost in the rhythmic pattern of forging.

His hands, hardened and calloused from years of hard, grueling work, were the very symbol of his indomitable spirit. As each strike sang through the barn, his mind drifted to Clara, his wife of three short months.

He had purposely slipped out to the ranch while Clara still lay sleeping that morning. After the awkward encounter where he had confessed his feelings for her and she had blatantly ignored him, he wasn't yet ready to face her. He had thought she had been dressed, wearing her simple wedding dress. But he immediately dismissed the thought. Why would she put on the dress in which she married the man who she clearly didn't love?

What had she been about to tell me? he wondered as he finished at his anvil, moving on to the next of his chores. He filled two buckets with grain to feed the cows, smiling to himself as the newest calf began stamping with excitement as it watched him prepare their meal. But his smile was short-lived.

It pained him to think such a thing, but it occurred to him that she might have been coming to tell him she was unhappy there with him. He didn't want to think such a thing. But why else would she have looked so miserable when he confessed his feelings for her, and then completely changed the subject, without saying a single word about it?

Roger sighed, pausing to rub a crick in his back from leaning over the grain buckets. He scolded himself for thinking such a thing about his wife. She might not have reciprocated his feelings. But she had also been through a great deal in her short time at the ranch; not the least of which was her son's horrific injuries. It was possible that she had just been tired and surprised by his sudden confession, that he should have picked a better time to tell her such a thing. So, why couldn't he convince himself that was the only thing troubling her?

He continued with the cow feeding, thinking of the fun they had had, catching bugs for Ben together. The way she had laughed with him, smiled at him, and blushed each time their hands touched had certainly not seemed like she was unhappy with him. And when the two of them had taken Ben the bugs they had collected, and Ben had reached out to hug Roger, Clara had put her hand in his again, leaning against his arm. And yet she never said a word about how Roger felt about her. It was as maddening as it was confusing, and Roger had no idea what to do about it.

A sudden raucous hiccup broke his reverie. He looked up to see Jeremiah swaggering in, his face flushed, a whiskey bottle swinging lazily from one hand. Roger's nostrils flared at the sickly scent of the liquor that seemed to cling to his uncle like a second skin.

"Mornin', Uncle Jeremiah," Roger said, giving the drunken man a small smile. It was rare to see Jeremiah while Roger was working. And as he studied his uncle, his stomach twisted with inexplicable dread. His uncle looked angry, and he hoped that the man hadn't come searching for him to cause more trouble.

Jeremiah grunted, leaning drunkenly as he took a swig from the bottle. He wiped his mouth with the sleeve of his dingy blue jean shirt, hiccupping again and sputtering as some of the liquor dribbled from the corner of his mouth. Roger sighed, resisting the urge to shake his head. Had he made a mistake bringing Jeremiah back into his home and forgiving him?

"Rog," Jeremiah slurred, the bottle gesturing erratically in his direction. "Need to talk to ya."

Roger put down the buckets, surprised. Jeremiah had never called him 'Rog' before. It should have been an endearing moment between uncle and nephew. But for some reason, it only increased Roger's dread.

"Sure, Uncle," Roger said. "Do you wanna sit and talk?"

Jeremiah shook his head, squinting at what Roger was sure appeared to be three of him to Jeremiah.

"This's fine," he slurred, rubbing his eyes with his free hand.

Roger gave his uncle a curt nod. "All right. What's on your mind?"

Jeremiah swung the bottle back toward the entrance to the barn, its contents sloshing so that Roger feared it would spill.

"That wife a yours been sneakin' round my room," he said. "Been goin' though my things, too."

The accusation hung in the air like a dust devil, sucking the oxygen out of the barn. Clara? His Clara? Roger's heart clenched at the thought. He wiped his forehead with the back of his hand, trying to collect his thoughts.

"What are you yammerin' about, Jeremiah?" he asked, trying to keep his voice steady. "She has to clean the house, you know. I'm sure you're just mistaken."

Jeremiah stumbled a step closer, his bloodshot eyes wide.

"I seen her, Roger, in my room," he said. "She was goin' through my letters. I seen her. With my own two eyes." He punctuated his last two words by holding up three fingers on his empty hand. It would have been comical that Jeremiah was too drunk to count properly, but Roger was far from amused. His heart pounded against his ribs. Clara was a woman of integrity, of kindness, not someone who would betray their trust.

"You're drunk, Jeremiah," Roger said, his voice carrying very little conviction. "You have to be mistaken. Clara wouldn't do such a thing. She was probably just moving stuff around so she could clean properly."

Jeremiah was relentless, however. He shook his head, tightening his jaw and narrowing his eyes.

"I ain't blind, boy," he said, slamming the bottle down on a nearby shelf, causing Roger to flinch. "She was there. In my room. I seen her readin' my letters. She didn't know I was watching her, but I was."

Roger's blood ran cold. He glanced at the entrance of the barn, half-expecting, half-hoping to see Clara there, her face white with innocence and her eyes pleading for understanding. But she was nowhere in sight. Why would Clara invade Jeremiah's privacy? And what could she be searching for among his uncle's personal belongings?

Jeremiah seemed to sense Roger's reluctance to believe his story. He shook his head, giving Roger what he assumed was meant to be a sympathetic look.

"I told ya, Rog," he drawled, an ugly sneer twisting his features. "Your sweet Clara, she's just here so her boy can inherit your land."

The words felt like physical blows, each one landing heavy and painful in Roger's chest. He tried to brush them aside, attempted to assert his belief in Clara's love, even though she hadn't professed it yet.

"You're wrong, Jeremiah," he said, ignoring an icy jolt up his spine. "Clara ain't like that."

But Jeremiah just laughed, the sound harsh and devoid of mirth.

"She don't care about you, boy," he said, his voice steady despite the liquor in his veins. "It's all about the boy and this land."

Roger recoiled, his mind reeling as he tried to reconcile Jeremiah's words with the woman he thought he knew. His Clara, with her soft laughter and gentle touch, using him? It seemed inconceivable. And yet the more Jeremiah spoke, the more the boulder of dread expanded in Roger's gut.

"Drunken nonsense," he whispered, bending down to prepare to return to his work, but his hands shook as he gripped the buckets. He was trying hard to maintain his disbelief, but deep inside, a seed of doubt had been sown.

"Whass that, Roger?" Jeremiah said.

Roger nearly jumped, surprised that the drunk man could hear his soft whisper. He thought fast. He wasn't sure that he believed his uncle. But he knew he had to do something to pacify him to keep another argument from breaking out.

"I'll talk to her, Uncle," he said, trying not to sound too patronizing. "I'll get to the bottom of this and set things right."

Roger thought that would please his uncle. But for a moment, Roger thought he looked nervous. But Jeremiah took another sip from the bottle, sneering at Roger before turning abruptly on his heel and, after nearly running into the barn doorway, stepping back out into the morning sun. Roger sighed.

He wanted to completely dismiss Jeremiah's accusation as exactly what he had called it—nonsense. But as much as he loved Clara, he could never quite shake off the feeling that she was holding something back. For the first time in weeks, Roger thought about how she had hidden Ben from him. She had been true to her word about never deceiving him again after that. Hadn't she?

Jeremiah's words echoed in his head, insistent and biting. Clara had always been curious, yes, but she would never invade a man's privacy. She had never done it to him, as far as he knew. He thought back to the missing shirts, wondering again how they would have ended up under their bed. It did seem a bit convenient that she had been the one to find them, and she did so while she was cleaning. But immediately, he shook off the notion.

There was no way that Jeremiah was correct. He found it hard to reconcile the woman he knew with the picture Jeremiah was painting. He would speak to Clara as he had told his uncle he would. He was sure that Jeremiah was purely mistaken. Yet he couldn't escape the nagging sensation that there was more to this than met the eye. And as he returned to his work, even the sounds of the hungry, impatient cows couldn't drown out his inner turmoil.

He thought again about the previous day when he'd poured his heart out to her. How he'd spoken of his love, his voice trembling with vulnerability. And how she'd remained silent, her face a cryptic mask that revealed nothing of her feelings. Not only that, but she had also clammed up, even though she had asked to speak with him about something with a considerable sense of urgency.

He'd almost convinced himself that her silence was born of shyness and stress. But now, Jeremiah's words injected a new, bitter interpretation. Had she remained silent because she didn't reciprocate his feelings after all? Was she, as Jeremiah suggested, more interested in securing a future for her son than in building a life with him?

Roger clenched his jaw, abandoning the now-empty buckets and grabbing the pitchfork, gripping it tightly. He desperately wanted to dismiss Jeremiah's words, to believe in the woman he had married. He wanted to trust that Clara cared for him as he cared for her, that her silence was merely a woman's way of being coy. But Jeremiah had planted a seed of doubt that was sprouting faster than he could control.

The wind picked up, rustling the nearby trees, and bringing with it the intoxicating scent of Clara's lilacs through the slits in the barn walls. He remembered how she'd once told him that they were her favorite, that they reminded her of hope. He wondered if she saw the same hope in their marriage, in him, or if he was just a means to secure her son's future.

He felt betrayed, yet he knew not if the traitor was Clara or his own thoughts, manipulated by his drunken uncle's words. The doubt gnawed at him, casting a pall over his heart. His paradise was under threat, yet he knew not from which direction the danger came. All he knew was that he needed answers, and he needed them soon.

Chapter Twenty-Seven

As the late afternoon sun bathed the prairie in hues of scarlet and gold, Clara and Hiram had agreed to share a word with Roger while Jeremiah was wandering drunkenly around the ranch. Or, with any luck, maybe he would stumble into town and hide in the saloon for the rest of the day.

The impending conversation was of grave importance, a matter that concerned the future of the vast ranch they inhabited. Clara had always liked and trusted Hiram. He had become just as much a friend to her as he was to Roger in her short time at the ranch. But even her trust in him didn't ease her mind about the trouble she was about to have to take to her husband.

As the minutes ticked by, Clara felt a shiver of dread creep up her spine. No matter how necessary it was to warn Roger of his uncle's insidious plans, she couldn't shake the sense of foreboding that washed over her each time she thought about how her husband would react.

She had spent the last hour pacing by the kitchen window, waiting for Hiram and Roger to finish the day's work and come inside for supper. She splashed some water on her face, trying to calm her nerves. She needed to go check on Ben, who had been asleep most of the day. And she couldn't go in there a flustered mess and get him all upset.

Just when she thought the day couldn't get any worse, she saw that her son's face was damp and waxy. She touched his cheek, recoiling at the furiously hot skin beneath her fingers. Ben was burning up with a fever, she realized with horror.

She'd hoped the wounds on his leg were healing, but it seemed a cruel infection had snuck in unnoticed. She lifted the part of the blanket that covered her son's legs, gently peeling back the bandage she had put on him the night before. Her heart pounded in her chest as her fears were confirmed. The wound was seeping, angry and swollen, and horribly discolored.

"Oh heavens, sweet boy," she muttered under her breath, her hands trembling slightly as she soaked a cloth in cool water. She would have to tell Roger that he needed a doctor, which she knew would greatly distress him. How could she cope with a sick, injured child and telling her husband that his uncle was plotting to kick him off his own ranch and land at the same time?

She looked around the rustic little room, her gaze wandering toward the door. She hoped for Roger's figure to appear, silhouetted against the fading sunlight pouring in through the window. But the man she had chosen to share her life with was nowhere to be found.

A wave of disappointment washed over her, but she forced herself into action. Right now, her focus was on Ben. The house was ominously quiet, save for the eerie chorus of the cicadas outside and the raspy breathing of her fever-stricken boy.

"Ben, honey?" Clara said softly, gently patting her son's arm. "Can you sit up a little for me? I need to give you a sponge bath to get your fever down."

To her dismay, the boy didn't stir. She realized he was unconscious, as he had been the night they found him in the bear trap. Panic rose within her, and she considered going out to find Roger instead of waiting for him to come inside. But the ranch was huge, and she would likely end up missing him when he and Hiram finally did make it to the house. Besides, she couldn't bring herself to leave her son. She needed to get his fever down as quickly as possible.

Everything else, including the discussion about Jeremiah, would just have to wait.

An hour later, she heard footsteps in the hallway. Her hope rose and she looked up at the doorway. But instead of Roger, Hiram appeared. He gave her a tight smile that faded the instant he noticed Ben's condition.

"Is he all right?" he asked, concerned.

Clara shook her head, explaining the situation. Hiram nodded, his brow furrowing with worry.

"We can talk to Roger tomorrow," he said. "I'll go let Roger know the boy needs a doctor."

Clara nodded, feeling the first bit of relief since finding her son in such a state. "Thank you, Hiram."

But that was the last time she saw Hiram that evening. And as sunset turned into twilight and then full dark, there was still no sign of Roger. What could be keeping him? She needed him right then, more than she ever had. Where was he?

Throughout the night, Clara sat vigil by Ben's bedside. She sponged his heated skin, whispered soothing words, and prayed for the fever to break. The oil lamp flickered, casting long, grotesque shadows across the room, matching the fear in Clara's heart.

Each passing minute seemed longer than the last. Clara's eyes, heavy with sleep, fought to stay open as the night stretched out, a black canvas speckled with starlight. The house remained silent, and Roger was still absent. In her exhausted worry, she silently cursed him. How could he ignore her and Ben with him in desperate need of help?

The thought that something might have happened to him crossed her mind, but she forced herself to not consider it. She couldn't bear the thought that something had happened to Roger, too. Besides, Hiram would have come to tell her if that were the case. And yet, as Jeremiah's letter came to mind, she wondered if it wasn't too farfetched to think that they both might have run into trouble with the drunken man.

The first rays of dawn pierced through the window, causing Clara to stir a few hours later. She realized that she had drifted off, and she immediately reached for her son. She choked back a sob of relief when she realized that Ben's fever had broken.

His eyes were still closed, but they moved slowly behind his eyelids, indicating that he might soon come around. She exhaled an exhausted sigh as she listened to Ben's chest. His breathing had evened out, and his face no longer looked completely slack and lifeless. She couldn't hold back the tears that welled up in her eyes. She wiped them away quickly, then caressed her son's hair.

"You're gonna be okay, sweetheart," she whispered, trying to convince herself more than to reassure the sleeping child. "Everything's gonna be all right."

She was tired to the bone, her limbs heavy, but a weight had lifted from her heart. Ben was on the mend, and for now, that was all that mattered. Her husband's absence stung, a reminder of the conversation that hadn't happened, a shadow of uncertainty that hung over their future.

Her eyes drifted toward the window, looking out at new day dawning on the ranch. Clara knew that the sun would set again, and maybe then, she would find the strength to speak to Roger. But for now, she clung to the fleeting moment of peace, her son's steady breathing acting as the sweetest lullaby she had ever heard. Her eyes grew heavy again as she finally began to relax. Before she knew it, she drifted off to sleep once more.

Half an hour later, the rhythmic sound of Ben's breathing was pierced once again by the sound of footsteps, Clara turned her head. Roger stood in the doorway, his broad shoulders nearly filling the frame. The sunlight played hide and seek with the rugged lines on his face, but even the morning light could not soften the storm brewing in his eyes.

"Clara," he said, his voice holding a sternness that was rare. "I need a word."

Clara felt a knot tighten in her stomach. It wasn't like Roger to greet her with a face of such seriousness, or a voice so cool and distant. She motioned toward Ben, hoping Roger would understand.

"Roger, Ben's been ill," she said. "Hiram said he would go find you. His fever's broken, but I'd like to stay by him in case it comes back—"

"I understand, Clara," he said. "Hiram didn't find me last night because I fell asleep in the barn loft. But we need to talk. Now." His words hung heavy in the room, slicing through her protests.

The urgency in his voice sent a shiver down Clara's spine. She rose from her chair, her gaze lingering on Ben one last time. The lines of worry etched on her face deepened as she stepped out into the hallway, pulling the door closed behind her.

Her heart pounded against her chest like a wild stallion as she turned to face Roger. His stern gaze was fixed on her, a sharp contrast to his usual warmth. A knot of dread started to form in her stomach.

"What's wrong?" she whispered, fearing the worst. The ranch, their future, everything seemed to hang in the balance of that moment. But all she could do was wait, the wooden floorboards creaking under the weight of her anxiety, as she braced herself for the storm that seemed imminent.

The light of the early morning sun seeped into the hallway as Roger beckoned Clara to follow him to their bedroom. Her heart pounded a rhythm of trepidation, each footfall echoing her growing anxiety. Something was terribly wrong, she was sure of it. Why else would Roger insist that she leave her ailing son to have a serious conversation right then? And why didn't he seem concerned about Ben?

The wooden door closed behind them with a soft creak, shutting out the world and trapping them in a bubble of uneasy silence. Roger turned to face her, the stern lines of his face etched deep by shadow and doubt.

"Clara, did you read Jeremiah's letter?" His voice, usually full of warmth and strength, was now hard and cold.

She felt a stab of fear. Jeremiah had gotten to Roger before she and Hiram could. She realized instantly that he must have tried to stir trouble between Roger and Clara. And judging by the expression on her husband's face, he had clearly succeeded.

"Yes, I did... but it wasn't on purpose." Clara's voice shook as she spoke. She had been making the beds a couple of days ago when the letter slipped from the mattress seam. She tried to explain, her words stumbling over each other in her haste. "It fell on the floor when I was cleaning his room. I meant to talk to you about it, but Ben got sick, and—"

"Is it true, Clara?" he demanded, his voice rising as he interrupted her again. "Is that the reason you're really here?"

The questions hung in the room like dangling nooses. She shook her head, confused by what her husband was asking.

"I... I don't understand, Roger," she said. "What do you mean? Is what the reason I'm here?"

Roger scoffed, shaking his head. "Don't take me for a fool, Clara. Tell me what you're really doing here. Now."

Clara shook her head again, the room spinning. Why was Roger so angry with her?

"I answered an ad seeking a mail-order bride," she said. "You know that. That's why—" But she was cut off once more.

"Is that it, Clara?" he snapped. "Is that the real reason? Or are you here so that Ben can inherit my ranch one day?"

Roger's words stung like a whip. Clara felt her world shatter, the pieces piercing her heart. The accusations were harsh, unfounded, and hurtful. She could hardly believe this was the same man who had told her he was falling in love with her two days prior.

"Roger, why would you even think such a thing?" she asked, her voice trembling as fresh tears filled her eyes. "How could you say such cruel things?"

Roger chuckled dryly, his eyes filled with anger and doubt.

"You had no right to go through Uncle Jeremiah's things," he said, each word laced with venom and disbelief.

Clara shook her head again, reaching out to her husband, who immediately evaded her touch. Brokenhearted, she let her hand fall back to her side, sniffling as the tears spilled down her cheeks.

"It fell on the floor," she repeated. "I picked it up, meaning to give it back to him. Maybe I was wrong to read it, instead. But there's something you should know—"

"What I know is that you're a snoop," he growled, sounding angrier with her than he had when he learned that she had a son. "You're sneaking around, reading people's private things. And you're keeping secrets from me. Remember the other day when you suddenly decided not to tell me whatever important thing it was you had to say?"

Clara barked out a sobbing laugh. "I'm trying to tell you what that thing is now, Roger."

But her husband held up his hands. "It's too late now, Clara. I don't think I can believe another word you say. Not ever."

Every word Roger spat felt like a dagger to her heart. She was there because she had hoped for a fresh start, a chance at happiness. The thought of scheming for an inheritance was so far from her reality that it physically hurt. She wrung her hands, pleading with Roger to be reasonable with her eyes.

"Roger, please," she said. "Ben is very sick. I need to be taking care of him. He might not need a doctor anymore, but he sure needs me. Let me get him well again, and I will explain everything to you. It's not what you think, and I am certainly not out to get your ranch, for Ben or for myself."

Her husband just shook his head the whole time she was talking, ignoring every word she spoke.

"You've explained more than enough, Clara," he said. "Go take care of Ben. But this ain't over. I'll get to the truth, one way or another."

With that, Roger turned on his heel and stormed out of the room. A moment later, the front door slammed shut, causing her to flinch. She stood, paralyzed with shock at the fight that had just taken place. Roger's questions left her reeling, and the way he had accused and interrogated her made her question everything she had come to believe about their marriage.

His words echoed in her mind, a haunting melody of doubt and suspicion. She had no doubt that Jeremiah had put the ideas in his head. But Roger had wounded her terribly by just believing whatever Jeremiah told him, without question. She had no idea what to do next to fix this awful situation.

Chapter Twenty-Eight

Roger slammed the door behind him, leaving Clara in the confining heat of their tiny wooden home. His mind was ablaze, a tempest of betrayal and anger. Jeremiah, his hard-drinking, conniving uncle, had once again spun his web of deceit, and the fact that Clara had read that accursed letter was a twist of the knife he hadn't anticipated.

Huffing, Roger stormed across the yard, the sharp scent of horse and hay and the wide-open wilderness filling his nostrils. His heart pounded in rhythm with his boots thumping against the hard-packed earth. He needed to work off this fury, and the new fence line at the north end of the ranch was waiting for him.

He grabbed a hefty wooden post from the pile next to the barn and heaved it over his shoulder, his muscles straining under the weight. A sheen of sweat soon coated his skin as he started to dig, the rhythm of the shovel stabbing the ground a soothing constant.

"Hell of a time to be workin' on the fence, Roger," a familiar voice drawled from behind him. Hiram ambled over, his brown cowboy hat shading his aged eyes from the midday sun.

Roger didn't look up from his digging.

"Feels like the right time to me," he grumbled, punctuating his statement with another thrust of the shovel.

Hiram hitched up his pants and leaned against a nearby tree.

"Y'know, Roger," he said, his tone treading the line between wisdom and caution. "Your uncle, he's nothin' but trouble."

Roger's grip tightened around the handle of the shovel. Jeremiah's visage flashed across his mind, the snake-like charm that had fooled him more times than he cared to admit.

"I know," he admitted reluctantly. He wasn't ready to tell Hiram what Jeremiah had said, or the fight he had with Clara. Instead, he kept aggressively stabbing at the earth with the shovel, the morning sun already hot enough to make him pour sweat with the effort.

"Well then, why do you keep puttin' up with that rotten behavior of his?" he asked.

Silence hung in the air. Roger clenched his jaw, contemplating the right answer. Clara, his wife, his partner, had turned out to be everything Jeremiah said she would be. He had defended her to his uncle, even been prepared to kick Jeremiah out of his home permanently. And all the while, she was scheming to secure the ranch for her son.

"Clara's been snoopin' around Jeremiah's room," he finally confessed. His words were quiet but the hurt behind them was loud and clear. "Worse still, she's only here for the ranch."

Hiram blanched. He didn't say anything for a long moment, and Roger thought he was stunned into speechlessness. Eventually, Hiram cleared his throat, shifting his weight.

"Roger," he said slowly, seeming to weigh his words. "I really think you should think about what you're sayin' right now."

Roger chuckled.

"I've thought about this for two days," he said. "Clara's been keeping secrets from me. Again. She came to tell me something the other day, but she never did. She can't tell me she loves me. And it's awful coincidental, all the things that have happened around here since she and Ben arrived. There ain't never been a fire or a bear trap accident here in all my years. Yet suddenly, we have both in the same week? Don't you think that's suspicious?"

To his surprise, Hiram didn't agree with him. Instead, the man shook his head, narrowing his eyes at Roger.

"Don't you think it would be a foolish thing to try to burn down the house and ranch you plan to try to get for your son?" he asked. "And what mother in her right mind would jeopardize her son's life for the sake of him inheriting anything?"

Roger opened his mouth, then promptly closed it again. Despite his anger, he had to admit that Hiram had a point. He might question many things about Clara. But he didn't question her intelligence, or her love for her son. Still, he wasn't convinced. He continued digging at the ground. There was something going on with Clara, he was sure of that.

"She admitted to taking a letter and reading it, instead of putting it back where she found it," he insisted.

Hiram sighed, clicking his tongue. "And did she happen to tell you what the letter said?"

Roger shook his head.

"Doesn't matter what it said," he scoffed. "It wasn't hers. She was wrong for reading it."

Hiram fell eerily quiet. Roger could all but hear the gears in his old friend's mind working. He guessed that Hiram must be experiencing the same surprise and disbelief that he first had when Jeremiah told Roger what Clara was up to. The silence between them was pregnant; with what, Roger wasn't sure. But the issue weight heavily on him. He didn't want to believe terrible things about his wife. But she had confessed to doing exactly what Jeremiah had said she did with his letter. Who knew what it was that she wasn't telling him?

"Do you really believe Clara could be so calculating and manipulative?" Hiram asked at last, his words once again cautious and measured.

The shovel felt heavier now, or perhaps Roger was just feeling the weight of his emotions. He stood up straight, turning to face Hiram. He wanted to believe his old friend, to cast aside the blood tie that had brought nothing but chaos. But Jeremiah was family, and Clara... she was his world.

"I don't know what to believe, Hiram," he admitted, a flicker of desperation in his dark eyes. "Everything's muddled up."

Hiram nodded, a soft sigh escaping his lips.

"I understand, Roger," he said. "Just remember, sometimes, the ones who ain't blood are more family than those who are. And Clara, well, she loves you, boy. But you gotta follow your heart. Can't no one tell you what's right and what's wrong. But mark my words. Things ain't quite what they seem."

Roger nodded, the storm within him raging. Hiram's words were meant to be a lifeline, something solid to grasp onto in the chaos. But he still couldn't reconcile the idea that someone he cared about could be dishonest with him. Who could he trust? His own, albeit drunk and belligerent, flesh and blood? Or the woman who couldn't even say that she loved him?

Roger's mind turned to the two faces at the heart of his turmoil—Clara, his wife, beautiful and complex with a past she'd initially hidden from him, and Jeremiah, his uncle, a man who reeked of whiskey-soaked mischief. He hadn't known either of them for long. Clara, with her timid smile and son Ben, had only arrived a few months ago, while Jeremiah had shown up shortly after he'd inherited the ranch. It seemed like his life had been upended overnight.

The moment was abruptly shattered when a young ranch hand burst into the scene, his face flushed with urgency. Roger's heart sank as he realized this wasn't going to be a peaceful afternoon on the ranch.

"Roger! Hiram! We got trouble!" the young hand panted, struggling to catch his breath. "Some of the cattle escaped. We didn't know it until we spotted them wandering past the paddock. We're trying to find them, but I think we're gonna need y'all's help."

Roger and Hiram exchanged glances, their shovels abandoned in the dirt. Duty called, interrupting Roger's personal battles. The weight of the situation settled upon them as they hurriedly followed the young hand, their strides purposeful.

The scene that greeted them was chaos incarnate. A group of skittish cattle had broken free from the corral, stampeding across the open range. Dust hung in the air as hooves thundered against the earth, the panicked bellows of the livestock echoing in Roger's ears.

"Tarnation," Roger muttered under his breath, adrenaline surging through his veins. Wrangling escaped cattle was no easy task, especially when they were in such a panicked state. It would take every ounce of skill and teamwork to corral them back to safety.

Hiram's voice rang out above the tumult, his authoritative tone cutting through the chaos.

"Roger, we'll split 'em up," he said. "You head to the right, I'll go left. We'll try to steer 'em back toward the northern pasture."

Roger nodded, his focus sharp as he assessed the situation. With a grim determination etched onto his face, he veered to the right, his lasso at the ready. He needed to be quick and decisive, every movement precise, or risk losing control of the situation entirely.

The sun beat down on his back as he galloped alongside the thundering cattle, his eyes scanning for an opportunity. Sweat dripped into his eyes, stinging the corners, but he didn't falter. He swung the lasso in a wide arc above his head, the loop spinning gracefully through the air. The moment was ripe, and with a practiced flick of his wrist, he let the lasso fly.

The rope sailed through the air, landing with precision around the neck of a fleeing heifer. Roger's heart leapt with a surge of triumph as he tightened his grip on the rope. With a swift pull, he directed the panicked animal off its course, herding it toward the desired path.

This became their routine for hours, Roger and Hiram working in tandem, their lassos dancing through the air. They herded, they roped, and they steered the wayward cattle back toward the sanctuary of the ranch.

It was a grueling endeavor, muscles straining and throats parched, but the men persisted. Gradually, their efforts began to pay off. The stampede slowed, their unified presence guiding the cattle back to the safety of familiar fences.

As the last of the cattle returned to the corral, Roger wiped the sweat from his brow, his chest heaving with exertion. Hiram approached, a weary smile etched upon his face, mirroring the fatigue and satisfaction that Roger felt.

"Well, we did it," Hiram said, his voice tinged with relief. "Not a smooth ride, but we got 'em back."

Roger nodded, his gaze sweeping across the scene. The dust settled, the air finally still. It had been a challenging afternoon, but amidst the chaos, he had found solace in the shared purpose and camaraderie. He realized that even in the face of uncertainty and personal conflicts, the ranch and its community were his anchor.

"How could they have escaped?" Roger mused.

Hiram shrugged.

"We could try askin' em," he said, grinning as he wiped sweat-soaked dust from his face with his sleeve.

Despite the tumultuous thoughts from the morning, and the hard work they had just finished, Roger laughed.

"If you been talking to the cattle, you got bigger problems than me," he said.

Both men laughed, the strain of the day momentarily forgotten.

As they made their way back to where they had left off earlier, the unfinished fence post beckoned. Roger knew that the battles within his heart and home were not yet over, but with the memory of their successful endeavor still fresh, he found renewed strength to face the challenges that lay ahead.

By the time they finished the fence repair, the sun was well on its way to setting. They put away their shovels, the broken fence pieces, which would be used as firewood, and their hammers and nails. Then, they walked in unison toward the house, their footsteps echoing in the evening silence.

The door creaked open as Roger pushed it aside, his heart pounding in his chest. He stepped into the dimly lit interior, listening to see where his wife was. Silence greeted him, the emptiness of the room echoing his growing concern. He moved through the space, his eyes scanning for any sign of her presence. But Clara was nowhere to be found. Panic clenched at his heart, his mind racing with a flurry of questions.

"Clara?" Roger called, his voice carried a mix of worry and confusion. "Where are you?"

No response came, only the haunting stillness of an abandoned room. The air seemed heavy with unspoken words, leaving Roger to grapple with the uncertainty of her sudden absence. Where could she have gone? Had their conflicts driven her away? Guilt tore through him at the thought that his untampered anger that morning could have made Clara flee from him. He had to close his eyes to keep the world from tilting. He loved Clara. If he had run her off, he would never forgive himself.

Hiram joined him, concern etched into the lines of his face.

"Roger, we'll find her," he assured, his voice a gentle anchor in the tempest of uncertainty. "She can't have gone far. Probably just went for a walk or decided to pick some berries for a pie."

Roger nodded, but he wasn't convinced. She wouldn't wander too far from Ben, especially since she had said he'd had a terrible fever the night before. He called to her once more, debating on whether to check Ben's room for her. But if the boy was resting, Roger didn't want to disturb him. If she was in there, she would have come downstairs. So, instead, he and Hiram turned around and went back out the front door.

As they stepped back outside into the fading light, Roger's heart carried a heavy burden. The sun dipped below the horizon, casting long shadows across the land. The search for Clara had just begun, and with each step he took, he hoped to uncover the truth behind her absence.

Chapter Twenty-Nine

Clara was sitting by Ben's bedside, her fingertips trailing across his bandaged leg that bore wounds that matched the ones now left in her heart. The small upstairs room was thick with tension, the air heavy with a mother's worry and a wife's sadness about a fight with her husband.

Ben's soft, pain-filled moans were a stinging reminder of their precarious circumstances, and of how far they'd strayed from the life they had once known. And then, another horrific thought occurred to her, to further her heavy heart. May hadn't yet written back to her. She shuddered, struggling to force away images of the woman having fallen ill. Or worse, no longer being with them.

She scolded herself for allowing such thoughts in her mind. She also made a mental note to write to May again and see about her. She could also ask the doctor back home to call in on her. She would cover the cost of the visit, even if May was ill. She needed to tell May about what had happened to Ben, as well.

But admittedly, she didn't want to say anything to her mother-in-law until Ben was more recovered and guaranteed to pull through. If May wasn't ill yet, she would be after hearing such awful news about her grandson.

Her chaotic thoughts moved back to Roger, and the confrontation that morning. No matter how many times she went over the conversation, she couldn't make sense of why he had been so harsh and brutal with his words. There was no question in her mind that Jeremiah had something to do with it. But how could Roger take his drunken uncle more seriously than he took his own wife?

The sound of hoofbeats and the rattle of wagon wheels stirred Clara from her troubled thoughts. Squinting out the window, she spotted the outline of Jeremiah's burly frame dismounting from his wagon. The pit in her stomach deepened. Jeremiah was not a man given to casual visits.

Swiftly crossing the room after covering Ben with his blanket once more and kissing his still-cool, fever-free forehead, Clara descended the stairs just as the front door creaked open. Jeremiah's rough-hewn face was a mask of discomfort, his eyes evading hers as he stepped inside, removing his dusty hat.

Clara stared at him, unsure what she should say. She was sure he was responsible for whatever had upset Roger earlier. But as angry as she was, she didn't want to start a fight with him. It would serve no purpose other than to further anger Roger. So, she just stood on the third bottom stair, looking awkwardly at the ground.

"I've been speaking with Roger, Clara," Jeremiah finally said, his voice gruff with a severity that made her heart sink. Her hands clasped tighter around the railing.

"Is that so?" she asked, keeping her tone flat and matter of fact. "About what, exactly?"

Jeremiah looked up at her, seemingly surprised by her directness. But instead of answering her, his cold eyes flickered with something. Amusement? Smugness? She wasn't sure. He stepped further into the living room, not bothering to remove his hat or shake off his muddy boots.

"I think it's best that you pack your boy's and your things," he said.

Clara's mouth fell open. Was he trying to kick her and Ben out behind Roger's back?

"And why is that?" she snapped, her knuckles turning white on the staircase banister.

Jeremiah smirked then, confirming what she had seen in his eyes previously and making her heart bloom with rage.

"Are you trying to convince me that we're not welcome here anymore?" she asked, clipping her icy words. "I spoke with Roger this morning, too, and he said no such thing."

Jeremiah was not a man known for his tact, but his next words were a cruel knife, slicing through her fledgling hopes. She thought she had been prepared for anything the horrible man had to say. But she was quickly proven wrong.

"Roger's realized the marriage was a mistake," he said, looking up at the ceiling as he spoke. "He says he rushed into it. The pressure from Hiram, y'know, to find a wife."

Clara's anger dissolved, giving way to a renewed ache in her heart. The room spun as Clara steadied herself against the railing. A mistake? She'd thought that Roger, with his kind eyes and gentle manner, had been a godsend, a chance for Ben and her to have a real family again. She shook her head, trying to make sense of Jeremiah's words.

"But... Jeremiah," she stammered, her voice hoarse with emotion. "We are a family now. Ben and I... we love him. And I thought—I thought he loved us."

Jeremiah's gaze met hers once more, and Clara flinched at the cold hardness in his eyes.

"I'm sorry, Clara," he said, not sounding sorry at all. "But I'm here to take you and the boy to the train station. You need to pack your things immediately."

"No," Clara choked out, her fury slowly returning. "I need to speak with Roger. This is a misunderstanding. And I know you had something to do with it."

Jeremiah's features hardened further, as if he was daring her to continue to challenge him.

"Roger's not here," he said, clenching his teeth. "And he wants you two gone before he gets back."

As the words hung heavy in the air, Clara felt the world collapse around her. The safety and warmth of a family she'd dared to hope for shattered, leaving her shivering amidst the cold, biting shards of despair. The confusion and pain tore through her, but Clara knew she had to be strong, not for her sake, but for Ben's. She would fight, if not for Roger's love, then for the well-being of her son. But the question remained—where could they go now?

Refusing to give Jeremiah the satisfaction of seeing her cry, she set her jaw and turned to go back up the stairs. Jeremiah muttered something under his breath, something that sounded like she should have never messed with him.

But she didn't turn back to question him. Her heart ached too much, and her tears were already spilling over. Instead, she went to the room she shared with Roger and slammed the door behind her. Once she was safely out of sight and earshot of Jeremiah, she let her tears fall.

How had her life changed so drastically for the worst in just a couple days? She and Ben had finally found true happiness after Thomas died. And even with the kitchen fire, the missing shirts, and the spider fiasco, they had managed to grow closer as a family. Roger had been wonderful since Ben was injured, as well. That was, up until that morning.

He hadn't even batted an eye when Clara told him how sick Ben was. He had only cared about her reading Jeremiah's letter. How could her husband care more about something like that than he did about an injured, suffering child?

She did as Jeremiah had suggested, packing as quickly as she could manage. If Roger really was angry enough to want them gone when he got back, she didn't know how much time she would have. When she had finished collecting her belongings, she slipped into Ben's room, doing the same with his. Ben stirred, hearing her rummaging around in his room.

"Ma?" he asked, his voice weak and filled with pain. "What're you doing?"

Clara took a deep breath, wiping the tears from her cheeks.

"We're gonna go see Grandma," she said quickly. She didn't know if that was true. But she felt like it was the only option they had right then.

Ben murmured a weak consent, instantly falling asleep again. Clara's heart broke once more. How could Ben ever survive a trip in his current condition? How could Roger be so cruel, even if what Jeremiah had said was true?

When she had finally finished packing everything, she quietly carried the bags downstairs. She could hear shuffling and silverware clinking against metal, and she knew that Jeremiah was drinking coffee. *And probably whiskey, too,* she thought bitterly, her anger flaring momentarily once again.

She put the bags by the door, then went back upstairs to get Ben. She knew she would have to carry him, and he was getting too big to make that an easy task. But she still managed to get him out of bed and carry him down the stairs without waking him or injuring his wounded leg.

By the time she made it downstairs with Ben, Jeremiah was stepping into the living room. He threw back the metal cup in his hand, drinking its remaining contents in one gulp.

Clara winced. She knew the coffee must have still been scalding and filled with a potent dose of whiskey. But she recovered, gesturing to the front door with her head, holding close to keep him from being jolted around too much.

"We're ready when you are," she said, fighting to keep her voice hushed and not distressed.

Jeremiah smirked at her again just briefly. Then, he sauntered across the living room as slowly as molasses from a jar in winter, opening the door just as slowly, and only a crack. Fuming, Clara nudged it all the way open with her knee, carefully stepping through the doorway with Ben, and heading for the wagon that Jeremiah had pulled up in front of the house.

None to her surprise, Jeremiah boarded the wagon, leaving Ben's and her bags inside the house. She got Ben as comfortable as she could make him in the back of the wagon, then went back for their bags. Then, she returned to the wagon, climbing in the back with Ben, praying that he would be strong enough to make the trip that lay ahead of them, and that Jeremiah wasn't so drunk that he got them all injured. Or worse.

As soon as the wagon cleared the driveway and turned onto the road that would carry them away from the ranch they had come to love, Jeremiah began driving at a pace that even seasoned riders would find reckless. Her knuckles whitened as she held onto the side of the seat. The dust of the dirt road rose in a billowing cloud behind them, obscuring the home she was being forced to leave.

"Jeremiah, please, slow down," she begged as Ben began to groan because of the jostling of the buggy. "Ben is suffering."

But Jeremiah ignored her, despite her speaking loudly enough to be heard over the horse hooves and the rattle of

261

the speeding wagon wheels as they rotated at maximum ability along the bumpy road. She tried once more to appeal to him, but the only response she got was an agitated growl.

She fell silent again, her mind spinning. Her situation still didn't make any sense. She couldn't fathom why Roger wouldn't tell her himself that she and Ben needed to leave, especially when he had every chance to do so that morning. And now that she thought about it, Jeremiah seemed to be in quite a big hurry as he drove along.

She could have understood if Roger had really wanted them gone before he got back. But they were gone now. Things were rapidly not adding up, and her suspicion spiked.

"I need to talk to Roger before we do this," Clara insisted. "This is just... it's not right. He needs to hear me out."

Jeremiah grumbled, his irritation clearly rising.

"Enough, Clara! Enough," he growled.

Clara wouldn't be deterred. She narrowed her eyes, leaning as close to the driver's seat as she could to keep from disturbing Ben by yelling so close to him.

"If he still wants to leave after I talk to him, then we'll go," she said. "But I don't believe for a second that—"

Thrusting a crumpled piece of paper toward her, Jeremiah glanced over his shoulder to glower at her.

"Here," he shouted. "Roger left this for you."

She took the note with trembling hands. Unfolding the paper, she saw scribbled handwriting, the letters tight and angry. There was only one line, but it was enough to stop Clara's heart.

I cannot trust you, Clara. Go back home.

Home. The word resonated with an ache. She'd thought she'd found a new home there with Roger. But was that merely another illusion now, another shattered dream?

Tears stung at her eyes, but Clara forced them back. She had to stay strong, for Ben. She'd find a way to clear this up, to make Roger see. Her love for him was genuine, as real as the heartache she felt now. But until then, she had no choice but to endure the bumpy ride to the train station, and an uncertain future.

The rhythmic creaking of the buggy provided a cruel counterpoint to Clara's tumultuous thoughts as she cast a glance at her son, Ben. He was pale, his little body looking frail, and his face scrunching up in pain. His injuries from the bear trap had almost taken his life, and now they were being banished without even a chance to fully recover. She tightened her hold on him, her heart aching just as much as it had when she had lost Thomas.

To make matters worse, Jeremiah, with his constant drunkenness and volatile temper, seemed to revel in their misery. His insistence on their immediate departure, his refusal to let her speak to Roger, and the cold, cruel delight in his eyes. Was it possible that this was really all his doing?

But the note—Roger's note—was there in her trembling hand. The words were clear, the handwriting surely his own. It seemed an undeniable truth. Yet, she couldn't suppress the suspicion that prickled at the edges of her despair. If Roger wanted them gone, then so be it. But what if she left her husband behind when it truly was all Jeremiah pulling the strings?

Chapter Thirty

"Clara," Roger called, finally ascending the stairs. "Are you up here?"

Not a single stir of noise came from any of the rooms on the top level of the house. Even before he reached Ben's door, his heart was already sinking. He hesitated before turning the knob to Ben's room. He knew what he would find when looked inside. But he was hoping against hope that it was only worry and guilt making him fear such a thing.

With one rapid push, Roger finally opened the door. His knees went weak as he noticed the empty, unmade bed, the bare, toyless floor, and the open, empty closet. He shook his head, not believing what he saw. He turned and left the room, starting for Clara's and his bedroom. He was now more certain than before what he would discover. And a quick search of the room confirmed the suspicion. Clara and Ben's belongings were gone. And so were they.

Filled with horror, Roger raced back down the stairs and out the door, leaving it wide open and not caring. He called for his wife and stepson, searching the animal pens, the stables, and even the barn. He even went to the spot where Ben had been hurt by the bear trap, but they weren't there, either. Roger scanned the plains surrounding their homestead, his gaze lapping over every scrub and rolling hill, but Clara and Ben were nowhere in sight. His heart pounded in his chest like a stallion's hooves on the hard ground. The setting sun offered no solace to his growing anxiety, and the endless darkening sky felt like a reminder of his isolation.

"Clara, Ben, where the devil are you?" he muttered, his voice snatched by the prairie wind and carried off across the barren plains. A cloud of dust in the distance had been his only company for the past hour. His mind teetered on the edge of worst-case scenarios. His intuition, honed by years of living in the unforgiving west, was jangling like a church bell on a stormy night. There was something decidedly wrong about the afternoon's unsettling silence.

Another bolt of terror coursed through him as he remembered the first thing Clara had said to him that morning. She had mentioned that Ben had had a fever, and that she had been up with him all night. He grimaced as he recalled how little he had cared in that moment, how he had been more focused on his own anger than the condition of the young boy. What if Ben's condition had worsened and she had had to get him to the doctor in a hurry?

Roger had to force himself to take a breath and calm down. It was possible that she had taken Ben to the doctor, but it was very unlikely. There was no way she would take the time to pack up their things before rushing him into town.

Maybe there had been an emergency with Ben's grandmother. But why wouldn't she have left him a note? His mind wouldn't stop racing with the worry and all the possibilities. If he wanted answers, he would likely have to go searching for them himself.

Just as Roger was about to mount his steed and gallop off toward town, the creak of wheels and the clip-clop of hooves drew his attention. A horse and carriage, dust-ridden and weary, pulled up in front of the house. The driver, a familiar, grizzled old man with a weather-beaten face, climbed down with a parcel wrapped in brown paper.

"Delivery for you, Roger," he grunted, handing over the package.

Roger's mind was barely on the delivery as he numbly took the package in his hands.

"Did you happen to see Clara and Ben on your way here, Jed?" he asked hopefully.

Jed shook his head, his brow furrowing in thought. "Nah. But I did see your uncle, what's-his-name, barreling into town like the hounds of purgatory were on his tail."

Ice flooded Roger's veins.

"Jeremiah?" He tried to keep his voice steady, but it faltered under the weight of his concern. "Was he alone?"

Jed shook his head, switching the toothpick in his mouth from one side to the other.

"No," Jed replied, his eyes narrowing. "There was a woman and a young boy with him." He paused. "Oh, heavens. Now that I think about it, that must have been Clara and Ben."

A vise tightened around Roger's heart. Jeremiah was always drunk. Even if they had gone with him willingly, he would no doubt be driving like a madman. He could see Clara's frightened eyes and Ben's confusion as clearly as if he was looking right at them.

How could Clara have ever agreed to go anywhere with a drunken man with her injured son, no matter what her reason was? What games was Jeremiah playing now? Every interaction with the man left a bitter taste in Roger's mouth; he was a snake coiled and ready to strike. What would have made Clara trust Jeremiah enough to agree to go anywhere with him?

"Thank you, Jed," Roger finally said with a curt nod. "I think I best be getting to town myself, then."

Jed nodded, patting the empty seat beside his in his buggy. "Want me to give you a ride?"

Roger shook his head. "I can get there faster by horse. And I suspect that I need to get there as fast as I can."

Jed nodded again, tipping his hat. "Good luck to you, Roger. I hope your wife and the boy are all right."

Roger nodded, waving as he watched as the carriage rattled off into the horizon. The box slipped from his hands, the contents spilling onto the dusty ground, forgotten. His thoughts were a tempest, torn between fear and anger. Jeremiah had never been one to play fair, but involving Clara and Ben was a new low, even for him. *I sure hope they're all right, too,* he thought, cursing himself for having ever spoken so terribly to his wife.

What in the world could Jeremiah be up to? The question echoed in his mind, but the desolate plains offered no answers. There was only thing that was clear to Roger. If something happened to the two of them because of Jeremiah's recklessness and stupidity, Roger would see to it that he suffered for the rest of his life. With a grim set to his jaw, Roger ran to the stables and saddled one of his horses. He would ride to town, confront Jeremiah, and bring Clara and Ben home. He'd be darned if he let his hateful uncle manipulate his family.

On his way to the driveway, Roger found Hiram by the horse pen. He pulled the reins tightly, bringing the horse to an abrupt stop.

"Hiram," Roger said, his voice rough as sandpaper. His friend looked up, instantly reading the distress etched on Roger's face. "Clara and Ben left. And I think Jeremiah had something to do with it."

Hiram's expression distorted into a wild fury.

"I knew he was no good," he spat, shaking his head. "How did he manage to talk Clara into leaving?"

Roger ran his hands through his hair as guilt washed over him.

"Clara and I had a fight this morning, Hiram," Roger confessed, explaining everything that he had said to his wife, and why he had confronted her.

Hiram grunted, looking none too pleased.

"Roger, you're like kin to me," he said. "But I can't believe that you'd be stupid enough to believe that dastardly uncle of yours over your sweet, loving wife."

Roger looked at his friend, wanting to be insulted by what the ranch hand had said. And yet, he knew he couldn't be. He knew Hiram was right. He *had* been stupid. The things he had said to Clara had been nothing short of cruel. For the first time, he thought about the things she had been trying to tell him over the past couple of days. Was it possible that, if he had kept his mouth shut and his temper in check, he might have gotten the answers he sought?

"Maybe Jeremiah just took them to town, to try to cheer them up," Roger said, not believing the words even as he said them. "Maybe Ben was feeling better and restless, and he thought he'd go buy him a treat. Jeremiah's been good since he came back..."

Roger trailed off. Each thought sounded more ridiculous than the last as they spilled from Roger's lips. He knew better; no quick trip into town would involve Clara taking all their possessions with them. He wanted to believe that Jeremiah really had changed, that he really would try to make peace and do something nice for Clara and Ben. But could such a hard man change overnight?

Hiram let out a huff of disbelief.

"Roger, you know as well as I do that Jeremiah's idea of cheering someone up is filling them with whiskey. Besides," he added, an edge creeping into his voice, "Ben's still hurt from that bear trap incident. He shouldn't be traipsing around town. And you're a fool if you think that Jeremiah don't know that."

The realization was a blow, driving the wind from Roger's lungs. Clara wouldn't have willingly put Ben at risk. The argument they'd had, no matter how fierce, surely wouldn't have clouded her judgment that badly. Not even if Ben was asking to go somewhere. A knot of dread twisted in his stomach as he digested Hiram's words.

Hiram's face turned grim.

"You need to go, Roger," he said. "Stop giving Jeremiah credit he don't deserve. Something's not right. I guarantee you this ain't no act of contrition on his part."

His mind a whirl of confusion, pain, and fear, Roger didn't waste another moment. He spurred his horse into a gallop and tore off toward town. His heart pounded in time with the horse's hooves, each thud echoing his growing fear. The plains and trees whizzed by him in a blur as he rode as fast as the brown horse would carry him. His face stung each time a bug made impact at such a speed, but he paid it no notice. The stinging in his heart was far worse. He vowed that if Jeremiah had done anything to chase off Clara and Ben, he would make sure Jeremiah never set foot on his ranch ever again. At any cost.

As the town came into view, a plume of smoke filled the air. The train. All at once, everything made sense, and he raced toward the station even faster than he had ridden to town. He arrived just in time to see the last train car disappearing into the horizon.

His heart sank, and he stared dumbly until the smoke from the train cleared. Then, he saw Jeremiah, leaning lazily against the station wall. His uncle caught sight of him at the same moment, and Roger leapt off his horse and barreled over Jeremiah.

"Where are they?" he demanded, putting his face close enough to his uncle's to smell the pungent scent of alcohol. "What did you do?"

Jeremiah shrugged, trying to feign innocence.

"They wanted to go home, Roger," Jeremiah drawled, a smirk on his cruel face. "After your spat, Clara felt it best they returned to their own kin. I didn't do nothin', nephew. I just helped them do what Clara said was best for them."

His words were a punch to the gut, leaving Roger winded and reeling. He couldn't believe that Clara would just up and leave without telling him, even if she was hurt or angry. But what else could have made her leave? He stared at the empty tracks, the finality of the train's departure settling over him like a shroud. His heart, full of love for Clara and Ben, shattered into a thousand pieces. They were gone. And he had no idea if they would ever come back.

Chapter Thirty-One

The wooden edges of the train car arm rest felt rough under Clara's fingertips as she traced the carved initials, CR+RW, of two lovers long forgotten. Her gaze was distant and melancholy, lingering on the sun-kissed landscape rushing past.

It was an afternoon scene of scrub brush and cactus silhouettes, a spectral painting of the Kansas part of the frontier she'd come to call home. Spectral, much like the life she was being forced to leave behind, which would too soon become nothing but a ghost, a memory of a time when she and Ben had almost found happiness again.

Tucked under the cocoon of her crinoline skirt, Ben slumbered with an angelic serenity that belied the traumatic experiences of his young life. His boyish features seemed to have aged within the short span since the bear trap incident. Pain lines traced around his dark-circled eyes, prematurely etching into his too-youthful, too-pale skin.

For a moment, her sadness was smothered by anger. The idea that a grown man could see fit for a small boy in Ben's condition to have to leave the safety of shelter boiled her blood. Any man who would jeopardize a child that way was a man Clara didn't think she could ever forgive. So, why was she only angry and hurt, rather than enraged and unforgiving?

Jeremiah's words from earlier in the day echoed in Clara's mind, his weathered face grim as he told her that Roger wanted her and Ben gone. That Roger was angry with her. A knot of bitterness twisted in her stomach at the memory, knotting tighter with each clack of the train wheels.

She knew he had been angry with her that morning. But no matter how much she thought about it, she still couldn't understand why Roger hadn't told her himself to leave before storming outside.

"No," Clara said softly to the whispering wind coming through the open window, a futile protest swallowed by the night. "No, something's not right."

She remembered the fight, the words, the accusations, like a hurricane that had upturned her entire world. The worn letter of Uncle Jeremiah in her hands, the misunderstood secrecy... It had caused Roger to explode in rage, his anger finding an unjust target in her. She had tried to tell Roger what had happened, to explain how she came upon the letter, and how the contents of the letter were more important than he realized. She knew Roger had been upset and that when he was upset, he was hard to talk to. Perhaps, she should have tried harder to get him to listen. Maybe if she had just raised her voice, just a little, or let her tears fall when they first began to sting her eyes as she pleaded for him to hear what she had to say...

Clara had always been the type of woman who faced her problems head-on. Marrying a rancher and adapting to life on the frontier had tested her strength and determination, and she had not shied away from the challenge. That part of her—the woman in her who braved storms, wrangled cattle, and bore the harsh desert sun—should have stayed. Should have waited for Roger to cool off.

"I should've insisted..." Clara murmured, her fingers lightly brushing Ben's sweaty hair.

Her heart ached for the son who was being dragged away from the stepfather he had grown to love, to call 'pa', due to... to what? Misunderstandings? Arguments? It also ached for the husband, who, she was certain, loved her despite the heated words and anger.

Thomas was the only experience she had ever had with love before Roger, but she knew one thing for sure—when you loved someone, you always talked things out, no matter how big or small. Anger never equaled hatred, and tempers could always be cooled.

She knew she should have confronted Roger, explained everything, sorted out the twisted thread of miscommunications. Leaving without a word, based solely on the say-so of an embittered uncle, felt wrong. And the more she thought about it, the more she wondered if Jeremiah hadn't had something to do with it all.

The letter was written in Roger's handwriting. Perhaps Jeremiah had forced Roger's hand in the matter. She should have insisted that she wouldn't leave until she spoke to Roger. After all, Jeremiah couldn't physically have forced her to leave, right?

Yet, here they were, aboard a train traveling farther away from home with each passing second. Clara closed her eyes, feeling the steady rhythm of the train beneath her, the comforting warmth of Ben's slumbering form. The bitter regret of unspoken words and missed opportunities gnawed at her, but she held her son tighter, her resolve strengthening. All at once, she knew what she needed to do.

"Your mama has made a lot of mistakes, Ben," she whispered, her voice barely louder than the clacking of the train on the track. "But I promise you, I'll make this right."

The sound of the train whistle echoed across the open desert as the ghost of her promise was carried away on the wind. Far behind them, the ranch grew further into the distance, a beacon of a life she vowed to reclaim. She wouldn't let love and a happy life be lost to her and Ben. Not a second time.

The train came to a grinding halt at a station, a small outpost that barely qualified as a town. It was little more than a scattering of wooden buildings standing at the crossroads of two trails worn into the prairie by wagon wheels and hoofprints. Clara felt the breath she'd been holding whoosh out of her. She knew this was her chance, her only chance, to rectify her mistake.

The carriage shuddered to a halt, waking Ben. He blinked up at her, his eyes cloudy with sleep. "Mama? Where are we?" he asked, wincing as his voice croaked out the painful words.

Clara gave her son a reassuring smile, swallowing the guilt she felt at having complied with Roger's insane demand that she subject Ben to a trip he was not ready to take.

"We're at a stop, sweetheart," she said, her voice steady despite the tumult within her. "We're going to get off here."

The decision felt monumental, heavy, as she gathered Ben into her arms and disembarked onto the wooden platform. She was about to do something reckless, and she knew it. Yet she also knew she could not live with the consequences of her earlier flight from the ranch. She had no idea how she would get them back to Cattle Creek. But they weren't staying on that train. And she wouldn't give up until she had found a way.

A few yards away from the train platform, a man was standing by a dust-covered carriage, lazily swatting at a fly with his hat. His horse, a grizzled mare, flicked her ears lazily, seemingly unbothered by the desert heat. Clara approached him, carefully cradling Ben to her, the words rolling off her tongue before she could second-guess them.

"Sir, I need your help," she said, her eyes pleading. "Can you drive us to a ranch about twenty miles west of here? It's in Cattle Creek."

The man looked at her skeptically, his gaze flickering from her face to the sleeping boy in her arms and the large bandage on his leg. After a moment, he shrugged, dusting off his hat and putting it back on.

"Well, ma'am, I s'pose I can," he said. "Ain't got much else to do this fine evening."

Clara sighed in relief, her heart pounding in her chest as she helped Ben into the carriage.

"Thank you, sir," she said sincerely, her gaze steady on the man's weathered face. "You can't imagine how much this means to me."

The man shrugged again, a shadow of a smile playing on his lips as he looked at Ben again.

"Just doin' my part, ma'am," he said.

Clara started into the passenger's seat, wobbling as she tried to step up with Ben in her arms. The man, who had started around the wagon to the driver's side, stopped and came back to help her. When she was in the seat, the man once more went around the wagon, climbing into the driver's seat. He looked at Ben again, his eyes filling with sympathy and curiosity.

"Are you needin' to get the boy some medical attention?" he asked. "I can take y'all to the doctor here in Ridge River."

Clara shook her head, smiling softly at the man.

"No, thank you," she said. "We just need to get home."

The man looked at her cautiously. Eventually, he nodded.

"Sure thing, ma'am," he said, picking up the reins and urging the mare into a trot.

The first few minutes of the ride were silent, and Clara noticed that it was edging close to evening. The shadows of the plants and flowers were beginning to stretch along the ground and the sun was beginning its slow descent on the western side of the sky. The brutal heat of the day was beginning to cool down, thanks to a soft breeze coming in from the north. The dry earth created constant clouds of dust with each step of the horse's hooves and every turn of the wagon's wheels. It was a much different view of the scenery than she'd had as the train sped down the tracks.

As the train station faded behind them, the man turned to Clara.

"I don't believe I introduced myself," the man said. "Name's Clyde. I'm the wagon-for-hire in River Ridge, as well as all-around handyman."

Clara smiled, grateful for the man's friendliness. "I'm Clara. And this is my son, Ben."

Clyde looked at Ben again and nodded once. "Looks like he's been through a rough time."

Clara bit back tears and nodded. "He got badly hurt the other day. A doctor's already tended to him, but it's a slow recovery."

Clyde grunted as the horse pulled them along the dusty road.

"Looks like," he said. "I was wondering how a boy in such shape could handle a train ride."

Clara understood that the man was curious, not judging. But she also didn't feel like telling him her whole life story. She just gave him a small, polite smile.

"That's why we're going home," she said. "Back where we belong."

Clyde looked as though he wanted to ask more questions. But he eventually decided against it. The rest of the trip passed in similar silence, with only the occasional remark about a dip in the road or a bird that flew close to the wagon.

That gave Clara a lot of time alone with her thoughts, which all revolved around Roger. A quote she'd read in one of her old novels came to mind: "It's never too late to correct our mistakes." And as she looked out over the arid landscape, Clara realized she was living that quote, in every sense. She was doing what needed to be done, for her son, for her husband, and for herself.

It was almost dark by the time they arrived at the ranch, and the sight of their homestead filled Clara's heart with an unspoken sense of relief. The wooden ranch house, half-shadowed by twilight, stood as a symbol of the life she had chosen, and refused to abandon.

Clyde helped her and Ben out of the seat, and Clara clumsily fished around in her dress pocket until she found the handful of coins she had put there before she and Ben had left the ranch. She held them out to Clyde, not even bothering to count them. But Clyde just looked down at her hand and shook his head.

"That ain't necessary, ma'am," he said. "It was no trouble helpin' a mother and her child."

Clara smiled gratefully at the man. "Thank you, Clyde. We sure do appreciate it."

Clyde tipped his hat, coated in fresh dust from the trip. Then, he hopped back up into the wagon and headed away from the ranch.

With Ben in her arms, she quietly unlatched the front door. As she treaded up the familiar wooden staircase to Ben's room, every creak felt amplified, echoing her tension. She gingerly set Ben down in his bed, tucking the blanket around his injured leg with motherly gentleness.

"Rest, my little cowboy," she whispered, planting a soft kiss on his forehead. Ben mumbled a sleepy acknowledgment, his little hand grasping hers in trust. With a last glance at her son, Clara descended the stairs. She would speak to Roger, she decided. Explain everything. Perhaps he wouldn't forgive her immediately, but at least she would have tried.

Turning the corner, her thoughts churning like a whirlwind, she collided with a hard figure. She stumbled, barely catching herself on the banister. Jeremiah stood in front of her, his features twisted in surprise and anger.

"Clara?" His voice was a low growl, echoing in the quiet ranch house. "What in the devil's name are you doing back here?"

"I live here, Jeremiah," Clara retorted, her heart pounding with confrontation. "Or did you forget?"

"You've got a nerve coming back," he seethed. "After Roger—"

"I didn't come here to argue with you," Clara cut him off, her tone laced with determination. "I came to talk to Roger. Now, if you'll excuse me."

She stepped to the side, preparing to step around Jeremiah's intimidating frame. But before she could move past him, he grabbed her arm, his grip firm. Clara recoiled, trying to pull free. The commotion seemed to echo through the silent house, and her heart pounded with a mix of fear and adrenaline.

"Let me go, Jeremiah," she said shrilly.

Jeremiah sneered at her, his lips parting in a hideous grin.

"No," he said, drawing out the word in a way that gave Clara chills. "I don't believe I will."

Clara tried to pull free from him, but his grip was firm and unrelenting.

"What do you think Roger will do if he comes in and sees you putting your hands on me?" she asked.

Jeremiah snarled at her, pushing his face close to hers.

"What do you think he's gonna do if he comes in and sees that you're here?" he retorted.

Clara put distance between her face and Jeremiah's, swallowing waves of nausea at the acrid odor of sour coffee and liquor on his breath.

"I'm willing to take that chance," she said, praying she sounded braver than she felt. "Why don't I ask him now?"

For an instant, Clara saw fear in Jeremiah's face. Then, the hateful sneer returned, and he grabbed the vase from the small round table at the base of the stairs. He smashed it on the ground, causing Clara to flinch and cry out.

"You ain't doin' no such thing," he growled. "You and that kid are gonna get outta here right now, if I have to drag you myself."

Faster than Clara would have anticipated for a big drunk man, Jeremiah reached out and grabbed her other arm. She really believed that Jeremiah meant to drag her from the house. And she wasn't sure in what condition she would be if he did so. She struggled against him, suddenly thinking of nothing but Ben. If Jeremiah incapacitated her, what might he do to Ben?

A door creaked open, and Roger stepped into the hallway. His eyes widened at the sight of Clara struggling in his uncle's grip.

"Jeremiah, get your hands off her!" Roger bellowed, his voice like a whip crack in the quiet. He quickly crossed the room, pulling his uncle's hand away from Clara. His gaze fell on Clara, a mix of shock, anger, and something else she couldn't quite decipher. "Clara? What are you doing here? I thought you were gone?"

Clara fumbled, trying to speak through the lump in her throat. But the emotions flying were too much for her to find her voice. This was the confrontation she had wanted with Roger. Would he want her to stay? Or would he tell her from his own mouth to get out, once and for all?

Chapter Thirty-Two

Roger's heart clenched in his chest. He had been too late to catch the train that was carrying Clara and Ben from his life. And yet, there she stood, looking hurt and angry, but also filled with a certain determination. He blinked hard, as if the action could erase the illusion before him.

But no, she was there, even prettier than she had been that morning. Jeremiah remained, for the moment, forgotten. Though Roger had every intention of having words with him again, as well. No man would ever put his hands on Clara so long as Roger drew breath. Not without walking away without a scratch or two. Jeremiah, least of all.

"Roger," she said, her voice laced with uncertainty and yet an underlying resolute tone that was distinctly Clara.

He found his voice after a moment that stretched out like the vast prairies.

"Clara," he choked, floundering for words. He wanted to say a hundred things to her. But right then, not one of those things would dislodge itself from his mind and move past his lips. There was another long moment of silence.

The air around them seemed ready to burst with tension, questions and, perhaps, even tears. Roger wanted to take Clara in his arms and yell at her for leaving all at once. And yet, he could do nothing except watch his wife and see what she was going to do.

Her gaze held his as she stepped closer. Her hand trembled slightly as she extended it, revealing a crumpled piece of paper.

"I got your note," she said, finally breaking the suffocating silence.

His brow creased, his heart imprinting an abrasion against his ribs with each drum like beat.

"Note?" he asked dumbly. "My note? What do you mean?"

She nodded, her lips a thin line.

"This one," she said curtly. She thrust the paper into his hands, her gaze never leaving his. "It said you wanted Ben and me gone."

It took him a minute to understand what she had just said. He blinked, shaking his head in disbelief as he tore his gaze from hers and looked down at the paper. He didn't realize his hands were trembling until he had to steady them to bring the words on the page into focus. His mind whirled as he read the short note, his heart pounded in his ears. A sick feeling of dread washed over him as he reached out to take the note, his roughened fingers grazing against her softer ones. The note was written in a hand uncannily similar to his own, the message harsh and unyielding. He shook his head, trying to make sense of what he was seeing.

"I never wrote this," he said, his voice hoarse with emotion and his mind reeling with confusion. "I didn't want you gone, Clara. I thought... I thought you left on your own."

The wind picked up outside, causing the living room windows to utter a mournful groan. She brushed a stray strand of her strawberry hair aside, her blue eyes filled with confusion and hurt.

"Why would I leave, Roger?" she asked, stepping away from the staircase and putting her hands on her hips. "This ranch... you... were our home. I would never have just left, unless I believed you wanted us to go. Especially with Ben in the shape he's in."

Roger shook his head, his mind not piecing together yet just what had happened. The only important thing to him was keeping Clara there, now that she had come back.

"I thought that after our argument this morning, you..." he trailed off as the lump in his throat choked him. He tried to clear it, but he didn't trust himself to speak for the moment.

Clara spoke for him, though her words were as sharp as daggers.

"It looks like you were the one who got ideas after our argument," she said. "Argument or not, I would have told you if we were leaving. I never wanted us to leave, Roger." She paused, her expression changing from anger to hurt as tears filled her eyes. "I still don't."

Roger swallowed a sob of relief. If Clara didn't want to leave, they could figure out everything else later.

"I'm glad to hear it," he said. "But I didn't write that note. I swear. Clara, you have to believe me."

Clara took it back from him, glancing down at it and frowning.

"It looks an awful lot like your handwriting," she said, turning the note around and holding it up to his face. "I want to believe you, Roger. But... well, just look for yourself."

Roger sighed in defeat. He realized that it did look a lot like his penmanship. But he knew he had never written any such note. Could he convince Clara of that?

"Clara, if I wanted you and Ben gone, I would have told you myself," he said. "I promise you, I would never write such a note and then just disappear. I'm not a perfect man, but I would never do something so cruel."

Clara's eyes softened slightly. He could see that she really did want to believe him. The handwriting must be difficult for her to reconcile as not his own, he realized.

"I don't understand," Clara said, her voice just above a whisper. "If you didn't write this, then who did?"

Roger narrowed his eyes, glaring at Jeremiah, who immediately shifted his gaze down to his scuffed boots.

"I don't know," he said, even though the culprit was becoming very clear to Roger. "I promise you, Clara, I never wanted you or Ben gone. This ranch, it's as much your home as it is mine." He felt stupid not being able to offer her anything other than the same phrases repeated over and over. But it was the most important thing he felt he could say. He did not want Clara and Ben gone. And he would keep saying it until Clara did believe him.

A fragile silence hung in the room, punctuated by his own heart pounding. But Clara remained quiet, her gaze steady, searching his. Then, slowly, a hint of relief softened the edges of her worried eyes.

"Do you mean that, Roger?" she asked. There was reluctance in her voice, but there was a little bit of something else—hope.

Roger reached out, gently tugging her closer. His hands rested on her waist, her warmth seeping into his cold, clammy fingers.

"I mean it, Clara. With all my heart," he said, smiling at her with all the love and affection he held in his heart for her. "This is our home. It's where we belong. I will get to the bottom of that letter. Right now, all that matters is that you and Ben are back." He paused, realizing he hadn't seen Ben. "Where is he?"

Clara pointed to the second-floor landing.

"I put him back in bed," she said. "That trip, short as it was, was real hard on him. He was asleep before I even got him into bed."

Roger, despite worrying about the boy's condition, smiled softly. Clara putting Ben in his own bed meant that she really had to come back to stay.

"I can imagine," he said.

Clara looked up at him, her blue eyes glistening in the light of the candles that burned in the living room. Slowly, she nodded.

"I believe you," she said, the tears that had been in her eyes beginning to fall.

Roger reached out and wiped them from her cheeks. He ached at the idea that she had been so hurt, especially since the reason wasn't true. But he would have the rest of his life to make up for the pain she felt, thinking he wanted her gone. And he would use every spare second from right then until forever doing exactly that. As Roger pulled her into another comforting embrace, he felt a weight lift from his shoulders. They were in this together, and he was determined to right every wrong for their family's sake. The note, like Jeremiah had previously, went temporarily forgotten.

"Clara," he began, his voice thick with unspoken emotions. "I owe you an apology."

Clara looked up at him again, surprise etched on her face. "What do you mean?"

He paused, feeling the weight of his words hanging heavy in the quiet night.

"This morning, I was a fool," he admitted, "I thought... I feared you had ill intentions. But I was wrong. I was terrible to you this morning, and all because I believed some nonsense. I'm terribly sorry, Clara."

Clara's blue eyes softened, confusion slowly giving way to understanding.

"Roger..." she began, but he put a gentle finger to her lips to silence her.

"No, honey," he continued. "Let me finish." He took a moment, gathering his thoughts before he looked her straight in the eye. "I've come to realize something important. Ben... your Ben... he's become like a son to me. Like a real, true son. Far as I'm concerned, he is mine."

The words hung in the air between them, as though carried on the wind. Clara's breath hitched, her hands clasped together tightly around Roger's waist. She smiled up at him through fresh tears, which Roger bent down to kiss as they fell.

"And this ranch, it's as much his as it is mine," he continued, his heart pounding in his chest. "I want him to inherit it one day. To continue what we've built here."

Jeremiah scoffed loudly, stomping his foot and vibrating the floor of the living room.

"I'll be dead in the cold ground before someone else takes the ranch from me," he said, sounding sullen and pouty.

Roger shot another glance at his uncle, shaking his head. "You need to be quiet. I'm gonna deal with you later."

Jeremiah snorted, glowering at Roger before storming up the stairs. Roger turned back to Clara, giving her a warm smile.

"I meant what I said, honey," he said. "My father gave me this ranch. And nothing would make me prouder than to give it to Ben someday."

Tears glistened in Clara's eyes, reflecting the soft moonlight that had just begun to peek in through the living room windows.

"Roger..." she whispered, resting her forehead against his as he gazed down at her lovingly.

Roger looked out the window at the land spread out before them, the land he wanted to pass on to Ben. His heart was full, fear and uncertainty replaced with hope and longing.

"I don't want you to leave, Clara," he said once again, even though he knew she believed that to be true. "Because I can't imagine a life without you and Ben, now that I have you two."

The moon beams filtering in through the window gleamed in her wide eyes, shining with a mixture of shock and relief. She blinked, her lips parting to respond. It took her a minute, but she finally seemed to collect her thoughts.

"That letter," she said. "Do you think it was..."

Roger didn't need her to finish her thought. He had already had the same one. He knew there were two people on the ranch who could have forged his handwriting. But he knew just as well that there was only one who would. But before he could finish her sentence, the chilling click of a gun cocking sliced through the warm silence.

Roger's heart skipped a beat, his earlier heartfelt confession evaporating as instinct took over. He was on high alert in an instant, his hand instinctively reaching for the revolver at his side.

SALLY M. ROSS

"Clara, get upstairs with Ben," he commanded. Their warm heart-to-heart had been brutally interrupted, replaced by the cold dread of impending danger.

Chapter Thirty-Three

Clara's heart transformed into a furious, insistent drum inside her chest the moment she registered the cold, metallic sound of a gun clicking. The room, which seconds ago was a sanctuary filled with love and forgiveness and hope for the future, suddenly felt as oppressive and dangerous as a snake pit.

It felt like time slowed to a near stop, and she realized that Roger was saying something to her. She could see his mouth moving, the worry lines in his forehead more pronounced than usual. But his words were lost in the thunderous beat of her heart echoing in her ears.

She locked eyes with him and her blood ran cold at the fear mirrored in his normally confident gaze. Her breath hitched and she could taste the terror, thick and metallic in the back of her throat. A shiver raced down her spine as she and Roger simultaneously turned toward the source of their dread.

Clara was hardly surprised to see that it was Jeremiah. After he stormed off, they hadn't expected him to go retrieve his weapon of choice. Now, the pistol glinted malevolently in his shaking hand, reflecting the flickering candlelight in a way that was both mesmerizing and horrifying.

Roger pulled away from Clara just enough to put his hands on her shoulders. Only then did any of the world begin to feel real to Clara again. She blinked, looking at Roger as though seeing him for the first time.

"Clara, honey, get yourself upstairs with Ben, like I told you," he said. His voice was calm, but urgency ran in an underlying current beneath his words.

Clara looked at Roger, briefly confused. Then, she thought of what Roger had tried to say to her earlier and realized that he must have been trying to get her to go upstairs. She thought of Ben, alone and injured. If Jeremiah started shooting, Ben would be scared. Or worse, if Jeremiah started shooting wildly and aimed the gun toward the second floor, a stray bullet could strike her son.

That was enough to break the rest of Clara's trance. She nodded, stepping back to comply with Roger. But the gun clicked again, and Jeremiah took another big step toward them with a nimbleness that Clara hadn't expected.

"She ain't goin' anywhere," he slurred, pointing the gun right at Clara. "If she moves, I'll shoot you both before you can take another breath."

Clara froze, the paralyzing fear returning. Ben lay unprotected upstairs, and now she couldn't get to him. But she didn't want to do anything to remind Jeremiah about the wounded child. The tension thickened, hanging in the room like a dense fog as Roger straightened, his jaw setting and his eyes glittering with defiance.

"What are you planning, Jeremiah?" he demanded, his voice a deadly calm that was in stark contrast to the terror clawing its way up Clara's throat.

Jeremiah barked out a laugh, the sound as grating and harsh as the desert winds, while his lips pulled back in a leering, sadistic smile.

"Oh, Roggie," he drawled, slurring his words again. His drunkenness seemed to have reached a new level. He swayed, yet the aim of his gun never faltered. "Didn't you always wonder what I'd do for this ranch?" Jeremiah paused to belch, laughing at the sour cloud of alcohol breath that permeated from his lips as he did so. "Ah, well. I'm sure that little wife of yours already told you all about that letter she had no business readin'."

Clara's breath hitched, a knot of dread unfurling in her belly. She glanced at Roger, her heart twisting at the helpless fury etched on his handsome face. She had never seen him so powerless, so unable to protect them. She realized with horror that she had never gotten the chance to tell Roger about Jeremiah's unsent letter to his friend.

Roger looked at her questioningly, and Clara fought to gather her wits to explain as quickly as she could.

"That's what I was trying to tell you this morning," she began. But she didn't get the chance to finish. Jeremiah was either too drunk to keep up with the conversation, or he was enjoying taking center stage and having control over the situation.

"I wrote a letter to my friend, tellin' him all about how I was gonna take over this ranch when I came back from that cattle drive," he said, a drunken smirk creeping onto his face. "I told him that I would do whatever it took to get this place from you and take it for my own. Meant every word of it, too. Then, this woman had to come draggin' her son here and talk you into marryin' her. Got in my way. Messed up everything..." he trailed off as he started leaning too far to one side and nearly fell face-first on the ground. Clara prayed he would fall, but he caught himself, the barrel of the gun never moving. Such a steady aim from someone so inebriated would have been a marvel to behold, were Clara not terrified witless.

Roger's eyes widened, first in surprise, then in realization. He glanced at Clara, understanding combining with the horror in his expression.

"Oh, Clara," he murmured.

Clara shook her head, doing her best to smile at her husband.

"It's okay," she whispered.

Jeremiah didn't notice the interaction. He was too lost in his reverie of his plans to take the ranch from Roger. Which, it seemed, now included killing Clara and Roger. *And Ben,* Clara thought as ice filled her veins.

"Think about it," Jeremiah continued, the cruel gleam in his eyes flickering with some sick sense of glee. "A lovely double murder-suicide tale. What a tragedy." He hiccupped, throwing his head back in ugly laughter. "Losing my nephew, my niece-in-law, and their young boy. Ain't nobody alive who would contest me takin' the ranch then. After all, it's only right I inherit what's mine."

The horrifying implication of his words sank into Clara, her heart leaping into her throat with its impossibly fast pounding. She could hardly breathe, each intake of air a struggle. Jeremiah's drunken rant was no less than a death sentence. The room spun around her as the reality of their situation crashed down on her. She gripped Roger's arm, her anchor in this tempest, and prayed for strength to face the oncoming storm.

Clara held her breath as Roger squared his shoulders. He had been such a calming presence in her life, a gentle, sturdy rock against the world's hardships. Now, she prayed that his strength and confidence could penetrate the fog of Jeremiah's drunkenness.

"Jeremiah," Roger began, his deep voice resonating in the small cabin. "Calm down, you don't need to do this."

His eyes, as warm as the earth after a summer rain, were glued on his uncle. Clara watched him, felt the sturdy pulse of his hand intertwined with hers. She admired his determination, his courage, though the sight of his knuckles whitened with tension made her own fear spike.

"The ranch," he continued, voice steady as a lullaby, "if it means that much to you, take it. It's yours."

The room felt as if it held its breath with Clara. But Jeremiah's irrationality tore through the silence. His wild, bloodshot eyes flitted between the two of them as a mocking sneer curled his lips and he began brandishing the gun wildly above his head.

His raspy voice echoed, the words slurred and venomous, bouncing off the walls of their humble abode.

"Your father," he bellowed. "Your blasted father never trusted me, Roggie! His own brother! Said I fed the animals too much and wasted grain and corn. He always blamed me every time the horses got outta the stables.

That busybody Hiram once told him that I was responsible for the deaths of two calves when their mamas were birthin' em because I was drunk, and he believed it, without even askin' me. He even said that I was gonna bankrupt the ranch not long after Pa died. But I wasn't even drinkin' that much back then. Not as much as I drink now."

Clara tightened her grip on Roger's hand, her heart aching at the fresh pain flickering across his face. His father had been his hero, and these drunken rants were a cruel insult to his memory. She desperately wanted to say something, to defend and protect her husband as he was trying to defend and protect her. But she couldn't take the risk. Jeremiah had said he would shoot them both, and she knew that he meant it.

"I know that must have made you angry," Roger said, his voice bordering on patronizing. "I don't know why Pa left me the ranch instead of you. But I'm willing to hand it all over to you, if you just stop this right now."

Jeremiah was no longer listening. He stared up at the ceiling as though speaking to an unseen entity somewhere above him.

"Handin' the ranch to you, over me," he spat, his words coated in years of resentment and bitterness. His anger was as palpable as the dread Clara was trying to keep at bay. "There was no reason for him not to trust me. No reason, Roggie!"

His shouts filled the house, his hatred reverberating around them. Clara could taste the bitterness in his words, feel the venom they carried. She swallowed hard, fear constricting her throat.

"It's too late to just hand it over, Roger," Jeremiah hissed, leveling the gun at Roger. "I gave you plenty of time to do the right thing on your own when I came back here. You acted like it never even occurred to you that I might want or deserve the ranch. So now, I'm gonna make sure you never lay your hands on this ranch again, boy. I swear it."

His declaration hung in the air, a dark promise made darker by the glint of the pistol in his hand. A wave of sorrow washed over Clara, swallowing the remnants of her hope. She looked up at Roger, his face a mask of resolute determination. She knew then, as surely as she knew the sun would rise again, that they were standing at the edge of a precipice from which there was no return. She tightened her grip on his hand once more, a silent vow to face whatever was to come, together.

The tense standoff seemed to stretch on indefinitely, each second ticking by like a lifetime. Clara's heart pounded in her chest like a wild stallion, and she could barely hear anything over the roar of blood in her ears. Jeremiah's malicious sneer seemed frozen in time, a cruel tableau etched in the candlelight.

Even in his drunken state, he seemed to understand that he had the upper hand. And as he pulled back the hammer of the gun, Clara understood that he meant to use it. She closed her eyes, praying that after she was gone, Ben would remain forgotten by Jeremiah, and that he would be found by the ranch hands when neither she nor Roger were seen the next day.

And then, as if the heavens themselves had decided to intervene, there was a blur of movement in the corner of her eye. She dared to glance at the doorway from the living room that led into the hallway and her stuttering heart was all that kept her from crying out.

Hiram. His towering silhouette filled the doorway, his face a grim mask. He moved with the stealth and purpose of a predator, a large saucepan clutched in his massive, calloused hands.

In his drunken, angry rant, Jeremiah was oblivious to the approaching danger. Clara's breath hitched in her throat, the lingering metallic taste of fear mixed with a sudden glimmer of hope. She dared not make a sound, dared not even blink, as the distance between Hiram and Jeremiah closed inch by inch. And then, with a swift, resolute swing that echoed with the promise of salvation, Hiram brought the saucepan down on Jeremiah's head.

The thud was sickening, a sound Clara was sure she'd never forget. Jeremiah's eyes rolled back in his head before he crumpled to the floor, the pistol slipping from his lifeless grip. The menacing silence that had hung in the room shattered like glass, replaced by the harsh, ragged breaths escaping Clara's lips. She was sure she would swoon. But then, she felt Roger's strong arm around her waist, grabbing her just before she fell to the ground.

In the wake of Jeremiah's sudden fall, relief flooded through Clara. It was a sweet balm, washing over the terror that had gripped her, leaving in its wake a trembling exhaustion. She leaned heavily into Roger, her strength all but spent, as they watched Hiram drop the saucepan, its once-shiny surface now marred by the night's events.

"Thank God, Hiram," she heard Roger breathe out, his voice shaking with emotion. "Thank God for you."

Clara, her body and voice paralyzed, nodded in agreement. Thank God for Hiram, indeed. He had saved her family's life. And she would forever be grateful.

Chapter Thirty-Four

The moon cast long shadows over the ranch as Roger found himself staring at the fallen man with Hiram, the savior of his family. They were standing over Jeremiah, who was unmoving. Roger might have thought he was dead, but for the rattling snore coming from the man.

Roger suspected that the sound came from a broken nose because Jeremiah had fallen flat on his face when Hiram hit him. Hiram had a look of cold satisfaction etched deep into his weather-beaten face.

"Darn fool's lucky he didn't get himself shot," Hiram grumbled, nodding toward Jeremiah as he fondled the pistol on his hip.

Roger sighed heavily.

"We both know that's not a solution, Hiram." His gaze lingered on his unconscious uncle.

Hiram snorted.

"Bet you wouldn't have felt the same if he'd shot you," he retorted, his eyes narrowing. "Or Clara. Or God forbid, Ben."

At the thought of Jeremiah shooting Ben, Roger visibly shuddered. Only then did it occur to him what would likely have happened, had Hiram not intervened. Jeremiah had maintained a steady aim, despite the alcohol in his blood.

He would have kept his word, shooting Clara and Roger. And then, Ben would have been left all alone, unprotected, and too weak and injured to have any hope of escaping. One glance at Clara told him that she had had the thought herself. She was trembling, staring numbly at where Jeremiah had fallen.

"No," Roger said with another sigh. "I s'pose I wouldn't have felt the same way at all, in that case. Still, I appreciate you doin' what you did, instead of shooting him."

Hiram nodded, but his expression softened.

"I did it mostly for Ben," he said. "Wouldn't have done him no good to hear or see any of that mess. 'Sides, I didn't wanna have to help you clean up all that blood."

Roger gave his friend a weak smile.

"Thanks for saving us that trouble, too," he said. Then, he glanced back at Clara before dropping his voice. "Let me see about Clara. Then, we'll figure out what to do about him."

Hiram looked past Roger at Clara, his eyes filling with sympathy.

"Poor thing," he said. "She's been through it, hadn't she? But she's a tough one. I don't know many other women who could handle so much in her lifetime and not be in an asylum someplace."

Roger smiled, bigger that time, and much more fondly as he took a moment to admire his wife's strength.

"You're right about that," he said.

Hiram chuckled. Then, he pointed at Jeremiah, raising an eyebrow at Roger. "Well, what do we do with him?"

Roger thought for a minute, considering his options. At last, he realized there was only one thing he could do.

"Let's get him to bed," he said.

Hiram's mouth fell open. "Are you kiddin'? We should be fetchin' the sheriff. Or at the very least, pitchin' him out in the yard and lockin' him outta the house."

Roger nodded slowly.

"Maybe," he said. "But the sheriff ain't gonna do nothing. He didn't hurt anyone. And he's drunk as a skunk. Probably won't even remember any of this once he sobers up." Roger paused, snickering. "Especially after that bash you gave him upside his head."

Hiram puffed out his chest proudly.

"I'd be glad to help him forget anything else in the future, too," he said. Then, his expression grew serious again. "Roger, are you sure? I'd be happy to at least try the sheriff for ya. I don't think it's a good idea to keep the man who tried to shoot you here in the same house as you and your family."

Roger nodded once again.

"You might be right," he said. "But Jeremiah ain't gettin' outta that bed for at least two days. Not with the hangover he's got comin', and probably a concussion. I wanna have a talk with him before I just throw him out." He paused, patting his own gun. "But believe me, there will not be a repeat of tonight. I will be watching him very closely from now on."

Hiram pressed the tongue against the inside of his cheek for a minute, his eyes conveying a world of skepticism. But eventually, he nodded.

"All right," he said. "I don't know why you care so much about a whiskey-addled troublemaker, though."

Roger gave his friend a wan smile.

"There's more to him than the whiskey-riddled troublemaker we've come to know," he said. "He's my father's brother. The last kin I have left, the last piece of my father. I gotta try to get things right with him."

Hiram chortled, but his eyes finally lost their cool edge.

"Maybe so," he said.

Together, Roger and Hiram heaved Jeremiah's inert form up the stairs and into his bed, grunting with the effort of Jeremiah's heavyset frame. Roger hastily threw Jeremiah's blanket over his rising and falling belly. As he and Hiram stood catching their breath, Roger used the silence as a chance to say a silent prayer of gratitude that the night hadn't ended any worse than it did.

After a moment, he turned to Hiram.

"Thanks again, Hiram," he said, rubbing the back of his neck, his face flushed. "For... you know... saving me and Clara and Ben."

Hiram grunted, a small nod acknowledging his part. Hiram wasn't one for mushy moments. But Roger thought he saw a tear in the older man's eye.

"I'll go check on Clara," he said. "You sit with him."

Roger nodded.

"Thank you," he said again.

Hiram waved to him as he was walking out the door. Roger knew that Hiram's earlier irritation at wanting to keep Jeremiah in the house came from a place of care and concern. He knew Hiram wasn't really mad at him.

Or, if he was, it wasn't mad enough to sock him a hit or two, as well. Hiram had good points; any other man would have hauled Jeremiah straight to jail. But Roger had meant what he had said. His father would have hated to see his brother go to jail over a drunken stunt. Roger could give him one last chance. But one was all he would get.

Hours seemed to pass, the ticking of the old wall clock a metronome in the quiet. In reality, it was only just over an hour before Jeremiah stirred, groaning as he awoke with a start.

"Roger?" he croaked, squinting at his nephew through the dim light.

"I'm here," Roger replied, his voice soft but firm.

Jeremiah winced, one hand moving to the side of his head. "Feels like I been kicked by a mule."

"You were hit by a saucepan, not a mule," Roger told him. His tone was stern, matching his words. "And you deserved it. You're lucky that was all that happened, after what you did."

Jeremiah grumbled but didn't argue.

Roger leaned forward, looking his uncle in the eye. "We need to talk, Jeremiah. About you, about what's been goin' on around here, about the ranch... about everything."

Jeremiah just grunted in response, still trying to gather his senses. Roger had no intention of giving the man his rest just yet. He had spared him from jail. But he would not spare him the lecture he had coming.

"You coulda gone to jail tonight," he said. "You probably should have. But I wanna handle this like civilized men before I resort to that. Pa would have wanted it that way. But you're gonna listen. You're gonna answer my questions. And then, I'm gonna give you a choice. Understood?"

At this, Jeremiah's disgruntled expression wilted. He looked almost sheepish, and he refused to look at Roger. But finally, he spoke.

"All right," he muttered, all his former hatred and malice gone from his voice, leaving him sounding more like a petulant child than a man who was brandishing a gun just over an hour before.

Roger nodded. "Good. Now, I want the truth. Was it you who set fire to the kitchen?"

Jeremiah looked at Roger like he wanted to protest. But eventually, he just lowered his head, wincing as he grabbed at the lump forming where the saucepan had connected with his skull, and nodded.

Roger nodded again.

"The spider?" he asked.

Jeremiah groaned. Roger waited, still staring at him with a firm gaze. His uncle sighed heavily, shaking his head.

"Ben didn't do nothin'," he mumbled. "I took the spider from his room and put it in my own bed. Then, I blamed it on him."

Roger murmured noncommittally. He had suspected Jeremiah of all the things that had happened at the ranch for a few days. But it was good to finally hear his uncle admit to his wrongdoings.

"The shirts?" he asked.

Jeremiah nodded, his face reddening with each question.

"What about the note Clara brought back with her?" he asked.

Jeremiah moaned, leaning back against his pillows, and closing his eyes. But Roger would not be moved. He repeated the question, watching as Jeremiah's eyes flew open.

"Yes, I wrote it," he growled. "Happy now?"

Roger shook his head.

"Not yet," he said. "Did you put that bear trap out in the woods on purpose to hurt Ben?"

For the first time, Jeremiah looked directly at Roger. His eyes were wide, and Roger saw genuine hurt and guilt bursting through the remaining haze of the liquor.

"No," he said, sharply enough to make Roger twitch. Jeremiah took a ragged breath, letting out what sounded almost like a sob. "I... I didn't do nothin' to hurt that boy. Not on purpose. Yeah, I put that trap out there, but it was to try to catch the coyotes that keep eatin' the chickens. I had no idea Ben would go all the way out there on his own. I only lured Ollie away from the house with a raw steak. I... I wanted Ben to get caught playin' outside, like y'all told him not to while y'all were gone. I was gonna use that to try to prove to you that he was a troublemaker, that he was gonna cause you nothin' but problems if you didn't make them leave."

Roger couldn't suppress the shiver of relief that racked him. Jeremiah's sincere, unbridled reaction told him that his uncle was telling the truth. He took a minute to compose himself before he continued.

"Then why did you leave him here alone?" he asked.

Jeremiah sniffled, and Roger thought the burly man was crying.

"I was gonna pretend that I went to the store to get him a treat for behavin' like y'all told him to," he said. "I didn't mean to get as drunk as I did that night. And I sure never wanted Ben to get hurt so bad. I just wanted him to get in trouble. I swear, Roger, I never meant..." he trailed off, sobbing hard for the first time since Roger had known his uncle.

Roger waited for Jeremiah to compose himself. He thanked the heavens that Jeremiah wasn't so evil that he would intentionally harm a child. But he had one last question.

"Why did you decide that killing all of us was the only way to get the ranch?" he asked.

Jeremiah uttered a heavy, defeated sigh.

"Because I was too proud to ask," he said. "I didn't feel I should have to. Joshua shoulda left it to me. Not to you. You ain't never run a ranch a day in your life before your pa died. I know this place inside and out. I worked with Pa every day, just like Joshua did, when we was kids.

And I worked just as hard as he did when we got grown, 'til he kicked me outta here over all the nonsense about the calves and allegedly bankrupting the ranch, when you was a baby. I just..." he paused, sniffing again. "I just wanted a chance to carry on the way Joshua would have wanted. The way our grandpa intended when he left the ranch to our pa."

Roger nodded slowly. That was the most that his uncle had ever spoken about his past, his trouble with Roger's father, and his attachment to the ranch. Despite everything that had happened, Roger couldn't help feeling a little sorry for his uncle. And Jeremiah wasn't wrong. Roger hadn't known the first thing about running a ranch when he first arrived.

He had grown up there, but he had never taken an interest in running a ranch. He had wanted to work with metal and make tools and weapons since he was a young boy. He had even spent a couple summers as an apprentice to Cattle Creek's own blacksmith before he met Willa.

Jeremiah likely *did* know everything there was to know about the place. Roger himself had moved to Oklahoma after he and Willa married to take a good blacksmithing job there.

He realized that it must have been devastating to be overlooked when it came to figuring out who inherited it after Joshua Banks died, especially in favor of a son who had done everything he could to get away from the ranching life. But in the time he had been there, Roger had grown to love it every bit as much as Jeremiah did. Suddenly, an idea formed in Roger's mind.

"You've got a chance here," he said, his hard gaze unwavering. "A chance to be a real uncle, and a decent human being. But you've got to stop drinking. You've got to prove you're more than just an old drunk."

Jeremiah blinked slowly, trying to focus on Roger.

"If you can show me you can be a good person, if you pull your weight, work hard..." Roger hesitated, unsure how his next words would be received. "Then I'll put the ranch in both our names. We'll share it, fifty-fifty."

Jeremiah stared at Roger for a long, silent moment. The moonlight filtering in from the window illuminated his old, weary face. The offer hung in the air between them like a promise, or a challenge. The journey of redemption, Roger knew, would be a long one. But maybe, just maybe, Jeremiah would finally be willing to take the first step.

Leaving Jeremiah upstairs to think about what he had said, Roger descended the staircase, his worn boots heavy on the wooden steps. He was unsure of what awaited him in the kitchen. Clara had been through so much these last few days, their disagreements, the unsettling situation with Jeremiah, it was more than he had ever wished for her to bear.

He found her at the kitchen table, her beautiful face illuminated by the dim light of a single lantern. She looked up from a cup of tea as he entered, her eyes welling with emotion.

"Clara," Roger began, his voice thick with regret. "I'm sorry, darlin'. For all that's happened. Our fight, Jeremiah making you think I wanted you and Ben gone... and what he tried to do."

He swallowed hard, the weight of his guilt sitting heavy in his chest. Clara remained silent, her gaze steady on his.

"I want us all to be a family," he continued, hesitating before plunging into his plan. "I talked to Jeremiah. Offered him a chance to be a real part of this ranch, this family, if he can prove he's worth it. And sober up." He quickly summed up everything Jeremiah had told him, his confessions, and the truth about what had happened to Ben that night. Clara looked as relieved as Roger had felt when she learned that Jeremiah hadn't purposely set out to hurt Ben. She absorbed his words, her eyes searching his.

After a moment, she nodded.

"I see," she said. "Well, I am glad that he told you the truth. And I am happy that he wouldn't hurt Ben. Though I'm still not happy that he left Ben alone here to go drinking."

Roger nodded. "His number one rule if he's to stay here is that the drinking has to stop."

She was quiet for a moment before speaking, her voice barely above a whisper.

"Roger, I'm sorry too," she said. "For not telling you... that I love you. After you told me how you felt... I was scared."

Her confession hit him like a wave, raw and powerful. His heart pounded in his chest, echoing his love for her.

"I understand, Clara," he said, stepping closer to her. His hand reached out to gently cup her face, his thumb lightly brushing a tear from her cheek. "You lost your husband, and it must have been hard to think about loving someone again." He paused, looking deep into her eyes. "But maybe... maybe God's givin' us a second chance. After all this... maybe this is our storybook ending."

Clara's eyes glistened, the corners of her mouth twitching into a small smile.

"Maybe it is," she said.

As if drawn by a magnetic force, their faces moved closer. His lips met hers in a slow, tender kiss, their shared love and forgiveness mingling in that sweet connection. In that moment, Roger felt hopeful for their future—a future as a family.

***

The next morning came with the sun dancing on the horizon, casting long, golden tendrils of light across the ranch. Roger stirred, his body heavy with the blissful exhaustion that came with a well-earned sleep. He frowned, noticing the unusual emptiness on the other side of the bed. Clara was gone. And so was the dull ache in his heart, replaced by a soft, warm glow.

He pushed himself out of bed and dressed quickly, striding down the stairs to the kitchen. He wasn't surprised to find it empty. He was, however, shocked, and a little concerned, when he went back upstairs and found that neither Clara nor Ben was in the boy's room.

His heart began to race as he thought about the day before. He ran to Jeremiah's room, finding that he was gone, as well. Where could they be?

Roger raced back down the stairs, flying out the back door. He was preparing to call for the three of them when he heard weak laughter coming from around the side of the house. He found two of the three missing people in the garden. Clara, in a simple blue dress that caught the morning light, was sitting on the ground next to young Ben, who was nestled comfortably in a chair that usually belonged in the kitchen. Ben's pale face was touched by the faintest hue of pink, a sign of life returning to his frail body. His eyes, though still tired, were trying to regain their sparkle.

"What's going on here?" Roger asked, a curious rumble masking his previous worry as he approached them.

Clara looked up at him, her eyes glowing in the morning light.

"Ben here begged me to come sit outside for a bit," she said. "So, I carried him out here and put him in this chair."

Roger turned his gaze to Ben, who was squinting at the front of the garden.

"What are you watching, son?" he asked.

Ben's lips curved into a small, weary smile.

"The ants," he replied, his voice soft but clear. "They're building a hill."

Roger chuckled, shaking his head at the boy's imagination. He was about to reply when a figure caught his eye. Jeremiah, looking somewhat sober and quite humble, was approaching them. He was moving slowly and rubbing the back of his head. But for the very first time, his eyes were soft and filled with emotion, not cold and dead.

He stopped in front of Clara and Ben, his face etched with remorse.

"Clara, Ben," he began, his voice unusually soft. "I want to apologize for everything."

Clara met his gaze, her face guarded but open.

"Thank you, Jeremiah," she said warmly. "Roger told me what you said, about... everything. And all things considered, I believe I can find it in my heart to forgive you."

Ben turned his head slowly, no doubt still stiff from days of lying in bed. But he gave Jeremiah the biggest smile his tired body would allow.

"Me, too, Uncle Jeremiah," he said. "Everyone deserves a second chance."

Roger's heart swelled with pride. Ben was just as strong and kind as his mother. Roger understood exactly how lucky he was to have the both of them in his life.

Jeremiah then turned to Roger. "I want to be a better man, Roger," he said. "I'll work day and night to prove it to you all."

Roger met his gaze, seeing the promise in his uncle's eyes. He nodded slowly, giving Jeremiah a silent approval. This was the start of something new, a new chapter in their lives. And for the first time in a long time, Roger was optimistic about the future of his ranch, and his family.

"I'll hold ya to it, Uncle," he said.

Chapter Thirty-Five

Fear and uncertainty lingered in the back of Clara's mind like a specter, haunting her thoughts despite the weeks that had passed since the gun incident. Jeremiah's drunken rage that night, his bitter accusations, and wild threats, had left a scar that Clara couldn't seem to forget.

It didn't help that he was Roger's uncle, a man who once held a place of esteem in her husband's eyes, only to fall from grace so spectacularly.

She didn't dare voice her concerns to Roger. She wanted to share his optimism, his belief in Jeremiah's redemption, but the protective mother in her was far from convinced. Ben, her heart and soul, had been caught in the crossfire of Jeremiah's wrath. The fact that he hadn't intentionally harmed her son didn't erase the fear he had instilled in their lives.

She wondered if Jeremiah would try to drive her and Ben away again. More troubling was the lingering doubt that he could truly leave his alcoholic past behind. Despite Roger's reassurances, Clara found it hard to place faith in a man who had shattered their peace so brutally.

Yet, with each passing week, Jeremiah made an effort to show that he was changing. As it turned out, when he wasn't drunk or intentionally trying to be difficult, he was actually quite sweet. He was courteous at mealtimes, even engaging in lighthearted banter with Ben.

He worked diligently on the ranch, shouldering tasks that eased the burden on the others, even acting as Hiram's assistant most days. And, to Clara's astonishment, he abstained from drinking, as if determined to prove that he could overcome his addiction.

One sunny afternoon, as Clara was engrossed in washing clothes, Jeremiah ambled over with an armful of fresh wildflowers. She stared at him in surprise as he handed them to her with a gentle smile.

"For the vases," he offered, his voice rough with uncharacteristic shyness, and his breath without the slightest hint of alcohol.

Clara took them, noticing their strong, sweet fragrance before she even lifted them to her nose. Jeremiah had gathered some from all over the property, clearly putting thought into the gesture. She gave him a warm smile, reaching out tentatively and patting his arm.

"That's very kind of you, Uncle Jeremiah," she said. "Thank you. I'll go put these in water right away."

Jeremiah nodded, removing his hat and giving her a sweet, gentlemanly bow.

"Glad you like 'em, Clara," he said. "It's my pleasure."

Clara smiled again, waving to the burly man as he put his hat back on and headed back out toward the ranch. She did as she said, going immediately to fill the vases with water and arranging the flowers carefully, with more than enough to put in every room.

After dinner that night, he presented Ben with a collection of jars, his gruff exterior melting away as he spoke to the boy with an unexpected warmth.

"These are for your bug specimens," he told Ben, a twinkle in his eyes that made Clara's heart soften a little. "I been collecting these for a while now. Thought I was gonna find a use for 'em. But I think you could use 'em more than I can."

Ben's face lit up, and he threw his arms around the big man.

"Thank you so much, Uncle Jeremiah," he gushed, smiling brightly at the man.

Jeremiah blushed, and he looked uncertain as to what to do. But he gradually put his arm around Ben, giving him a firm squeeze around the shoulders.

"Sure thing, kid," he said, ruffling Ben's hair.

Ben giggled, staring in fascination at the jars.

"Can we take them to my room now?" he asked.

Jeremiah nodded, giving Ben a smile with more affection than Clara would have ever guessed the man was capable of.

"We sure can," he said, handing Ben some of the jars. "You take those, and I'll carry these."

Clara watched as her son bounded out of the room, marveling at Jeremiah's transformation. Despite her reservations, Clara had to acknowledge that Jeremiah was making an effort. She watched him and Ben chatter excitedly about bugs, and her heart ached with hope. Perhaps people really could change. Perhaps Jeremiah truly regretted his actions and was determined to make amends.

She remained cautious, her protective instincts refusing to let her let down her guard entirely. But she also allowed herself a glimmer of hope. If Jeremiah was willing to change one day at a time, then she could learn to trust him again, one day at a time. For Roger, for Ben, and for the peace of their family, she was willing to try.

***

One warm afternoon, three months after the chilling gun incident, Clara found herself approaching the house, arms laden with the earthy yield from the garden.

Clara cradled the bundle of fresh vegetables from the garden in her arms, the earthy aroma of potatoes and onions mingling with the crisp scent of carrots. Tucked beneath the produce was a slab of fresh beef that would make for a hearty roast for dinner. As she neared the house, her brow furrowed at the sound of laughter echoing through the open back door.

She cautiously peered inside, her eyes widening at the sight of Jeremiah and Hiram seated at the table, their heads thrown back in laughter. Cups of steaming coffee were clutched in their hands as they toasted each other, their camaraderie as surprising as it was heartening. Both men had once held such bitter animosity toward each other, their feud a long-standing fixture in their lives.

As if sensing her presence, both men looked up, their mirth-filled faces softening at her sight. They quickly rose from their seats, removing their hats in a gesture of respect as they rushed over to help her.

"Brought us a feast, have you, Clara?" Hiram asked with a wide grin, relieving her of the hefty slab of beef.

Clara smiled brightly, nodding as the men took the burden from her tired arms. She rubbed her shoulder, looking at the men with bemusement.

"I'm making a big beef roast tonight," she said, her eyes bouncing between the two men. "So, I hope y'all bring your appetites. What's all the laughter about?"

The men started laughing, Hiram wiping at the corners of his eyes.

"Roger asked Jeremiah to break one of the young stallions today," he said, gasping for breath. "And it nearly broke him, instead."

Clara giggled, already liking the sound of a story that brought the former enemies so much shared amusement.

"Oh, my," she said, looking Jeremiah over. "I hope you weren't hurt."

Jeremiah shook his head, his face red and wearing an ear-to-ear grin. Another fit of laughter later, and Hiram continued his story.

"Everything looked like it was gonna be all right at first," he said. "But just as I was about to get to working on the new pig trough, that stallion took off at top speed across the paddock..." He had to pause to lean over, wheezing laughter racking his entire body. "And by the time I got to Jeremiah, he was already slowly sliding down the side of that horse, saddle and all."

Jeremiah erupted into peals of laughter with Hiram, slapping the ranch hand on the back.

"I can just imagine how that looked to you," he said, using a rag to wipe the tears and sweat from his face.

Hiram shook his head, still laughing.

"No, you can't," he said, guffawing loudly.

Jeremiah nodded, trying for several seconds to speak. He waved his hand in front of him, trying to fan air into his face.

"If it hadn't been for Ben, I'd probably still be goin' in circles with that darn animal," he said, coughing out more laughter.

Clara laughed as she imagined Jeremiah's bulky frame hanging onto a wild horse by nothing but his legs.

"Oh?" she asked, giggling.

Jeremiah nodded, finally catching his breath.

"He brought out a handful of puny carrots and dangled them over the side of the paddock fence," he said. "When that horse saw them, I thought he was gonna crash straight through the fence to get to 'em.

But he stopped right in front of Ben and started munching the life outta those carrots. Gave me just enough time to slither outta the saddle straps and onto the ground. And I think I ran faster than that stallion gettin' myself outta there."

The men dissolved into laughter again, Clara joining them that time. The images she conjured were funny, indeed, and she relished the atmosphere between the two men. Her heart was also filled with pride with her sweet child. He had been both clever and safe in helping his uncle get out of what could have been a deadly situation for Jeremiah.

"Well, thank goodness Ben was nearby," she said, still giggling.

Hiram nodded, wiping his eyes again. "I tried to get back to 'em. But every time that darned horse saw me, it took off in the other direction, faster than it was running before."

Jeremiah nodded, gasping for air.

"That boy of yours is smart as a whip," he said. "All my years on this ranch, and I'da never thought of that."

Hiram nodded, clearing his throat. The men were trying to regain their composure, but it was clear they would be laughing about that story for a very long time. Together. And Clara didn't mind that one bit.

"Then we thought we'd better give that beast a break before we try getting the saddle off him again," Hiram added with a grin.

Just then, Ben appeared in the doorway, his youthful face beaming with mischief.

"You should have seen Uncle Jeremiah, Ma," he said. "He was hanging on for dear life." He threw back his head and laughed, a sound that filled Clara's heart with a joy she hadn't realized she was missing. And when Jeremiah patted the young boy on his back and chuckled along with him, her heart melted into a pool of bliss.

Laughter, light, and a sense of normalcy filled the room. Clara found herself joining in, the tension that had tightened her shoulders for the last few months finally easing. Watching Jeremiah laugh along with Ben, Hiram, and her, Clara felt a soft sigh escape her. Maybe Roger was right about his uncle. Maybe things could change.

A slow, hopeful smile spread across her face as she looked around at the family in front of her. Yes, things just might be all right. They had a long road ahead, but for the first time, Clara felt a certainty that they could face whatever came their way, together. After all, they were a family, and that was the strongest bond of all.

At dinner that evening, Clara listened again as Jeremiah, Hiram, and Ben told their tale again, this time to Roger, laughing even harder than they had that afternoon. By the time they finished telling the story, all three of the horse-taming companions were nearly in the floor, gasping for breath yet again.

Roger grinned at the men, his eyes twinkling with mischief as he gave Ben a barely perceptible wink.

"Well, when do you think he'll be ready for ridin'?" Roger asked, snorting as though he was fighting hard to resist the urge to burst into laughter.

Jeremiah pulled himself back into a sitting position at the kitchen table, struggling to stop laughing as he looked at Roger, bewildered.

"At this rate, I'd say about ten years from now," he said, coughing through another laughing fit.

Roger, snickered again, shaking his head.

"No, Uncle, I was talkin' to Hiram," he said, his face turning red and his voice choking up with the laughter he was trying to swallow. "I was wondering when the stallion would have you ready to ride."

At that, everyone, including Clara, nearly fell onto the floor laughing. From the corner of her eye, Clara watched as Ollie took the opportunity to poke his nose over the edge of the table and sneak her last piece of roast off her plate. She didn't mind. He was enjoying the merriment of his family, too, and she wasn't about to steal his hard-earned prize.

When bedtime came that night, both Clara and Roger were still chuckling about the horse story. They dressed and climbed into bed together, Clara snuggling closely with her beloved husband. As she rested her head on his chest, Roger sighed happily.

"Well, I'll be," he said. "I had hoped that Jeremiah would come around and change his ways. But I never dreamed it would ever go this well, and in such a short time."

Clara nodded, tracing the buttons of his night shirt with her finger.

"You should have seen him and Hiram this afternoon," she said, giggling at the memory. "It was as though those two have been friends all their lives."

Roger nodded.

"I never told them," he said. "But I overheard Jeremiah's apology to Hiram a few weeks ago. I was in the hay loft when they came into the barn to get some supplies. At first, Hiram wasn't having none of it. He told Jeremiah it would be a cold day in purgatory before he believed that Jeremiah would ever be anything but a drunken layabout. I was impressed that Jeremiah didn't blow his stack right then. But he kept pleading with Hiram to give him a chance to make amends. And Hiram, being the kind soul he is, eventually grudgingly consented. A week later, those two were always working together. A month later, they were darn near inseparable."

Clara looked up at Roger, giving him a warm smile.

"Your secret is safe with me, darlin'," she said.

Roger smiled, staring up at the ceiling.

"He reminded me so much of my father that day," he said. "Pa would bend over backwards to apologize to someone if he even thought he had unjustly wronged them. Course, Jeremiah really had done wrong. But I saw a bit of my pa in him that day. Saw it again tonight when him and Hiram were tellin' that story. Pa used to laugh like that when a young calf would get away from him, or when a horse that wasn't yet broken would get outta hand with them in the paddock. It made me feel like Pa is really watching over us here. And it helps me know we did the right thing, giving Uncle Jeremiah another chance."

Clara gave her own happy sigh. Roger used to speak about his father with such pain in his voice. Now, he was smiling as he spoke of his father, remembering him with pleasant fondness.

"I know he'd be proud of you, Roger," she said softly. "Of Jeremiah, too."

Roger nodded, turning to look at her again.

"I believe Willa and Thomas would, too," he said. "I believe those two brought us together for a reason. This reason right here. To find love again, and to share that love with people like Uncle Jeremiah, who needed it more than any of us. To patch up two broken families and make them one whole, happy, loving family."

Clara nodded, tears prickling her eyes at the mention of Thomas. However, they were no longer tears of sadness. They were tears of fond remembrance, and of joy at the second chance she and Roger had gotten at a happy life.

"It's a beautiful thing, isn't it?" she asked. "Watching Jeremiah go from an angry, bitter drunk to a hardworking man, a terrific uncle and a wonderful friend, I mean."

Roger nodded, tilting Clara's face up to meet his own.

"It sure is, honey," he said, giving her a sweet kiss. "But not as beautiful as you."

Epilogue

1881

Clara leaned on the wooden railing of the porch, her eyes drifting over the vast expanse of land that she now called home. The setting sun spread vibrant hues of orange and purple across the vast prairie, the silhouette of the ranch standing tall and proud against the painted sky. It was hard to believe that a whole year had gone by since she and Roger had married, a year since Jeremiah changed his ways and became the man that Roger had had faith he could be.

An entire year, she thought, shaking her head. Time had a funny way of healing wounds, of sweeping away the debris of conflict, and paving a path for redemption. She'd seen it all happen on this ranch. Her heart, which had once pounded like a wild drum in her chest at the memory, now held a softer rhythm, and the memory felt more like a dream.

The memory of that dreadful night, when the scorch of alcohol on Jeremiah's breath had sent icy tendrils of fear curling down her spine, felt like a memory borrowed from someone else's life. She remembered the moonlight glinting off the barrel of the gun, the dread that seeped into her soul, the real possibility that she might never see another dawn. It was a nightmare that had invaded their paradise.

But the ranch had found its equilibrium, as nature often did after a storm. A balance had been struck, between the past and the present, the hurt and the healing. Jeremiah, the storm's very eye, had found his redemption too. He'd continued with his sobriety in the year since that awful night, and he had apologized many times over, not just with his words, but through actions that spoke volumes more. He'd mended fences, literally and figuratively, a testament to his newfound peace.

She felt Roger's presence before she saw him. His hands, roughened by ranch work but always gentle, came to rest on her shoulders. His reflection in the glass door behind her, a mirror image of strength and resilience, brought a gentle smile to her lips.

"A year ago, I never would have believed that things would be the way they are now," he said dreamily.

Clara nodded, her smile widening.

"Neither could I," she said. "To think that a widow and a widower could just happen upon each other and find the kind of happiness that we've found."

Roger grinned, glancing up at the sky.

"As if our departed spouses made it so," he said with a happy sigh.

Clara nodded again, leaning her head against him.

"And Jeremiah turned out to be one of the best men I have ever known, apart from you and Thomas," she said. "It feels like all the bad stuff that happened with him a year ago was nothing but a bad dream."

Roger kissed the top of her head and nodded.

"We've come a long way, haven't we?" he asked, his voice holding a note of quiet introspection.

"We have," she answered, tilting her head to meet his gaze in the reflection. "And we did it together."

He nodded, pressing a soft kiss to the top of her head. "We faced the storm, Clara. And look at us now."

Her hand came to rest atop his, their wedding rings glinting in the fading sunlight. She thought about Jeremiah, about the trials they'd weathered, about the strange, beautiful path that had led them here. It was a story of resilience, of love conquering fear and jealousy. It was their story.

She turned in Roger's embrace, reaching up to touch his cheek, her fingers tracing the lines time and life had etched on his face. His eyes, those soft blue pools she'd fallen for a year ago, were filled with a quiet strength and love that mirrored her own.

"We did it, Roger," she said, her voice barely above a whisper. "We brought our family together with love and patience, and we made it through some rough times. And we'll continue to do that, no matter what storms may come."

She knew this was their life now, their reality. It wasn't without challenges, but it was filled with a love and unity that had been tested and proven true. And in the end, that was all that really mattered.

The next afternoon, Clara settled herself in the worn leather chair in Roger's small office, her hand instinctively cradling the small bump beneath her dress. The room was filled with an odd tension, a mix of nervous anticipation and the buzz of another new beginning. Roger stood next to Jeremiah, while Hiram looked on. Her gaze softened as she looked at Ben, engrossed in a game of checkers with Ollie, who was, as always, sitting loyally at his side.

Across the room, the lawyer was hunched over a desk, the nib of his fountain pen gliding over a sheet of cream-colored paper. The scratching sound it made was oddly soothing, a cadence of permanence that echoed in the quiet room. This was it—the new deed, the future of their family and the ranch, being etched onto paper.

As the lawyer finally set down his pen, butterflies filled Clara's stomach. Jeremiah had more than proven himself to Roger and Clara, and she was thrilled that he had earned his right to officially own half of the ranch. She tightened her grip on the arms of the chair, the worn leather cool against her fingers.

The room fell silent as the lawyer cleared his throat, turning the deed toward Roger and Jeremiah.

"Gentlemen," he said, his voice clear and steady. "It's time to sign."

Roger picked up the pen, his strong, steady hand showing no sign of the nerves Clara knew he must be feeling. He signed with a flourish, his name flowing across the page like a river carving its path. Clara felt a swell of pride for her husband; he had navigated the tumultuous waters of family and legacy with grace and humility. She was proud of Roger for what he had done for Jeremiah by giving him one last chance, and for what he was about to do for him right then.

Jeremiah was next. The man who'd once been a tempest was now the picture of tranquility. He signed his name, his hand steady and resolute. The old feud over the ranch seemed more like a long-forgotten nightmare with each stroke of his pen, the past grievances fading away into the folds of history. That day, they were making a new chapter in the Banks family history: the chapter where uncle and nephew worked side by side as partners, with equal say in the property and equal shares of the profits it brought in.

Roger extended his hand to his uncle, which Jeremiah accepted without hesitation.

"Congratulations, partner," Roger said warmly. "It will be an honor to share the ranch with you."

Jeremiah wiped at the corner of his eye, grinning at Roger.

"Thank you, Nephew," he said. "I promise you that I will keep workin' hard and provin' that I won't mess this up."

Roger nodded, glancing over at Clara with a doting wink.

"We believe that you will," he said. "We love you, Uncle Jeremiah."

They embraced, their past differences forgotten, their shared bond of family and love for the ranch healing old wounds. Clara sighed happily. The new deed was a testament to the resilience of their family, a beacon of hope for their future. She felt a flutter in her belly, a tiny affirmation from the new life growing inside her. It was a promise, a reassurance. Their family was growing, their love strengthening. In that moment, everything felt perfect. The room was filled with their shared triumph, their love for each other, and the promise of their blossoming future. Clara looked around at their makeshift family, her heart full of hope and gratitude. This was their beginning, their forever.

After the lawyer left, all the men, including Ben, went outside together. They disappeared out of sight as she stood in the kitchen, making the preparations for supper. She smiled as she thought about the past year of her life. She would have never believed that she could find such happiness after Thomas had died. And yet, she found that her happiness grew exponentially with each passing day. Best of all, her family seemed happier, as well.

Ben came rushing in a few minutes later, waving an envelope in his hand.

"Here, Ma," he said, clearly out of breath from running. "Delivery man just dropped this off for you."

Clara put down the pots she had just pulled from the cabinet, taking the letter from him. When she saw who it was from, she tore it open, eager to read the contents. She sat at the still-new kitchen table as Ben rushed back outside to play and began to read:

My dearest Clara,

How are you and Roger faring in your first year of wedded bliss? How are things going with Roger's uncle? I hope that you have found the joy you so richly deserve, my sweet girl. Not a day goes by that I don't pray for your happiness and safety.

And how is our Ben? I can hardly believe it's been a year since his ordeal. I trust he is fully recovered and back to his lively, curious self? I remember you saying something about him taking up an interest in studying bugs. Has he found any new ones to keep as pets? And how is his sweet companion, Mr. Ollie?

Oh, Clara, I have so much to tell you. I had to get me some spectacles, and I can see much better now. I managed to get some work, baking my special recipe oatmeal and cocoa cookies for the little café here in town. I bake as many as I can manage throughout the week and keep them wrapped tightly in the icebox. Then, Josephine has someone come to pick them up, and she pays me two dollars a week. She also sends me ingredients from the café when I'm running low, and she has extra. And she still pays me the same amount, even when she gives me the stuff I need to make them!

The man who comes to pick up the cookies is a real nice, very handsome man. His name is Jim Kooley, and we've actually been courting for a few months now. He makes me feel young again, like I did when Thomas's father was still alive. He comes and checks in on me, even when he's not picking up cookies, and he takes me to eat at the café once a month. We have a wonderful time together, darling. I wish you could meet him.

I miss you and Ben dearly, Clara. My heart aches at the thought of missing out on watching Ben grow up. But I am comforted, knowing that the two of you are happy and well and cared for. I hope to visit you for Christmas if that's all right with y'all. To meet Roger, to see your smiles, to hug my grandson again. Maybe I can even talk Jim into coming with me. I sure would love to have everyone together for the holidays.

I love you and Ben with my whole heart, and I look forward to hearing from both of you soon.

All my love,

May

Clara closed the letter, her eyes welling up with emotion. May's words were a reminder of love and connection that spanned distance and time. She looked forward to penning her reply, of sharing their life and their growth. They were a family, bound by love and a shared past. And for Clara, that was everything. And to think that she might get to see her mother-in-law at Christmas proved to her that there was always room in one's heart for more happiness.

She lovingly tucked the letter into her apron pocket, humming a sweet tune as she got back to work on the dinner preparations. She was making chicken-fried steak, beans, mashed potatoes, and cornbread, with peach and apple pies for dessert.

That was a night for celebrating, after all, with the new deed signed and all the arrangements settled for Roger and Jeremiah to share the ranch evenly. And when Ben was old enough, he would join them as their third partner, until he was ready to take it over from them.

But even as she worked on the meal in front of her, she began planning the holiday meal she would make if May and her gentleman friend were to visit. She giggled, her excitement and delight overflowing so much that she couldn't keep it in. She would ask Roger if it was all right for May and her special friend to come for Christmas. But she already knew he would say yes.

As the sun went down, Clara called the men in from their intensive game of horseshoes for supper. They barreled inside, all of them, including Hiram, reminding her of vibrant, excited children no older than Ben. Clara smiled as she watched the cheerful banter around the dinner table, her heart filled with an overwhelming sense of contentment. The soft glow of the kerosene lamps cast a warm, golden hue over the familiar faces of her family. Even Ollie was part of the tableau, his tail wagging excitedly under the table, ever ready for a scrap of food or a game.

Laughter echoed in the room as plates were passed around, loaded with hearty helpings of the meal. Clara's eyes danced between her son and her husband, a silent prayer of gratitude shaping in her heart for the love that knit their lives together. Had she been paying closer attention, she would have noticed the conspiratorial wink shared between Roger, Hiram, and Ben. But she had been busy making the last of the plates and putting them on the table.

Jeremiah was the last to finish washing up for supper, and the other three men at the table were already shoveling food into their mouths. Jeremiah didn't seem bothered, however. He just gave Clara a soft kiss on her cheek, surveying the food on the table with grand approval.

"You must be the best cook in this whole country," he said as he made his way to his chair.

Clara blushed, making her way to her own chair and plate.

"You're very kind, Uncle Jeremiah," she said. "This is a special day, so I made a really special meal."

She thought she heard Roger snicker, but he was putting more food in his mouth before she could be sure. But then suddenly, the clatter of cutlery was broken by an outburst from Jeremiah.

"Heaven almighty!" he exclaimed, jumping up from his seat as if it were on fire. Clara stifled a laugh, her eyes sparkling with mirth as she saw the reason for Jeremiah's surprise. There, in his chair, sat a sizable toy spider, the handiwork of her impish son, no doubt.

Ben's giggles filled the room, as infectious as a summer song. Even Roger chuckled, his eyes twinkling with amusement, while Hiram snorted into his napkin. Ollie, perhaps feeling left out of the festivities, let out a series of joyous barks, his tail thumping against the wooden floor.

Jeremiah, although taken aback, quickly regained his composure. To Clara's surprise, a hearty laugh erupted from him. She watched as he ruffled Ben's hair fondly, a broad grin plastered on his face.

"You little rascal," he said, his voice warm with affection. Clara couldn't help but marvel at the change in the man, from a bitter, resentful drunk to a loving, doting figure in Ben's life.

Her gaze shifted to Roger, his eyes meeting hers across the table. The silent exchange was filled with profound love and understanding. They had weathered the storms, faced the darkest hours, and emerged stronger, their love deepened, and their family knit closer together.

Clara felt a gentle squeeze on her hand, drawing her attention to her son.

"Did you see, Ma?" Ben asked, his eyes wide with excitement. "I got Uncle Jeremiah good!"

"I saw, sweetheart," Clara responded, pulling him into a hug. "But remember, it's all in good fun."

As the evening wore on, filled with laughter, storytelling, and playful pranks, Clara couldn't help but marvel at the peace and harmony that had descended upon their lives. They were a testament to resilience, love, and the healing power of family.

Yes, Clara thought as she watched her family around the table, *everything is well*. Their past, once marred by strife and pain, was now just a memory, replaced by a present filled with love and laughter, and the promise of a bright, joyous future.

THE END

Also by Sally M. Ross

Thank you for reading **"The Cowboy's Promise of Forever in Kansas"**!

I hope you enjoyed it! If you did, here are some of my other books!

Also, if you liked this book, you can also check out **my full Amazon Book Catalogue at:**
https://go.sallymross.com/bc-authorpage

Thank you for allowing me to keep doing what I love! ❤